THE

BUCHMANS

A Western Story

THE

BUCHMANS

A Western Story

JOHN HENLEY

Five Star
Unity, Maine

Five Star First Edition Western Series.
Published in 2001 in conjunction with Golden West Literary
Agency.

Set in 11 pt. Plantin by Christina S. Huff.

Printed in the United States on permanent paper.

Library of Congress Cataloging-in-Publication Data

Henley, John, 1951–
    The Buchmans: a novel / by John Henley.—1st ed.
       p. cm.
    ISBN 0-7862-2385-5 (hc : alk. paper)
    1. German American families—Fiction. 2. Publishers and
    publishing—Fiction. 3. Afro-American families— Fiction.
    4. Freedmen—Fiction. I. Title.
  PS3558.E49625 B84 2001
  813´.6—dc21   00-057803

PART ONE:

THE PROMISE
1849–1868

Croydon Libraries

You are welcome to borrow this book for up to 28 days.
If you do not return or renew it by the latest date stamped
below you will be asked to pay overdue charges. You may
renew books in person, by phone or via the Council's website
www.croydon.gov.uk

CROYDON
COUNCIL
Cleaner, Safer & Greener

Chapter One

1849

Herman Buchman looked out at the calm waters of San Francisco Bay. He could only see a few hundred feet because of the thick, cold fog. The infant boy in his arms slept soundly. The mist covered Buchman's face and blended with his tears. Suddenly he felt as though he were being burned alive and started to shiver. He took one last look at the Bay that was but a small part of the greater waters of the ocean, now the eternal resting place of Anna. The fever that had taken her during the voyage had come to him.

He went toward the firelights on the hills and came to a street. The hotels were under construction, and their owners didn't like the looks of the burning sweat on Herman's brow. One of the managers pulled out a shotgun and marched Herman out into the street.

Herman began to heave and collapsed into the mud. With all of his strength, he moved the infant off to the side of the road and covered him with his coat. He cried out for help. Nobody seemed to hear him. He wondered if the English word for help was somehow different from his own German word, so he added one word of English he had learned during the voyage.

"*Hilf!* Please!"

Seven miners in filthy trousers and torn coats paused in the mud.

"What's wrong?" one of them asked.

"Sick. Sick."

They hurried away. Herman's vision blurred from the fever and the fog. A black and ominous hooded figure approached him, stopped short to pick up the infant.

Solomon opened his eyes in the terrible darkness. He could hear his children whining and his wife whispering comforting words to them.

"Now, Columbia, you hold on tight to your daddy's fiddle," she said softly.

"Harriet?"

He started to move his arms. There was the rattle and clanking of chains. He could only move them about a little. His feet were tied together.

"Harriet!"

"Solomon."

"Honey. What's going on?"

"They's taken us for slaves, Solomon!"

Solomon yanked his chains. The dark room began to sway gently.

"Hey!" he cried. "Hey!"

"No use hollerin'," said Harriet. "We've been out to sea for a day now. Maybe longer. Can't tell in here."

"What happened?"

"They gave you somethin' in that champagne. Some kind of poison. You fell over. I thought you was dead. They took us all up and run us out to this boat on the river. They say we're runaways."

"Where's Mister Glubb? Tell 'em to get Jack Glubb. He'll tell 'em. We ain't runaways. We're free."

"No, he won't, Solomon. It was Glubb. He gave you that poison . . . don't you remember, Solomon? He asked you to play your fiddle at the governor's ball. After you was done, he's the one that gave you that glass of champagne stuff."

8

Solomon felt sick to his stomach.

Herman opened his eyes and saw the specter leering at him. Father Death had a kind smile and gentle touch. Herman laughed a little at himself. This was not Father Death at all. The monk tucked the blanket in snugly around Herman.

"Mein Kind?" murmured Herman.

The monk looked perplexed and then lit up as he suddenly understood. He went off to another room and returned with the cheerful and healthy baby.

Solomon's wrists and ankles itched. He wrestled them against the iron and could feel the scabs tear away. A small door opened, and the ghostly, half-lit face of Mr. Glubb seemed to float suspended in the door frame.

The torch moved away from the face and hovered over Solomon's family. They were in the corner. Harriet shivered, her dress covered with her own vomit, and her face gaunt and expressionless.

"It stinks in here," said another voice in the darkness.

The torch hovered over Solomon's children. The little boy was lifeless. The little girl's eyes were wide. She had her arms wrapped tightly around Solomon's fiddle.

"Damn," said Glubb.

"Won't be gettin' much for that one," said the other voice, muffled by cloth over the nose and mouth.

"Gotta get 'em out of this hole 'fore they all rot to death," said Glubb.

"The captain ain't gonna like knowin' he's got slaves aboard," said the muffled voice. "I think he's one of them damn' Abolitionists."

"I'll deal with the captain. You . . . you move 'em into some better quarters 'fore they all die."

Solomon tried to shout. There wasn't enough clean air in his lungs or muscle in his sick throat to form even a word, much less a boisterous protest. A low, wavering, groaning noise came from Harriet's throat.

Glubb held the torch over her face as her eyes rolled back and her body went into convulsions.

"So, you would be a Lutheran, then . . . being from Germany," said the old priest.

Herman thought for a moment and formed the words into a tongue that was foreign to him. "I am a Communist," he said, pulling a pamphlet out of his coat pocket. He laid the pamphlet by the bread in the middle of the table. The monk picked it up, and the priest looked disapprovingly at the monk.

"A good printing job," said the monk, looking quickly over the pamphlet before putting it back down by the bread. "We have an old mission press. But nobody uses it."

"Danke," said Herman. "I *helfe* write. I do de printing myself."

"I'm not familiar with that sect . . . the Communists," said the priest. "What brings you to California? The gold?"

"De revolution. De miners . . . ah . . . are de vorking class and vill join de revolution. De gold will make . . . ah . . . build de state of the vorking masses."

The priest smiled sadly. "Well, if you're about revolution, you best learn to speak the language of those you would be setting free. Even Bonaparte understood that. I saw his revolution. In Spain. And as a novice, in Mexico. Father Hildalgo. I like how they begin. The intelligent and lovely people all come out and speak of rights and the wonderful things to come. But I hate how they end. Having to bury the dead in mass graves. I can't seem to escape it."

Herman looked down at the bread and soup, and then at

the priest. The priest picked up the pamphlet and smiled.

"This is in German, but printed in London. I can read a little German. Let me see. THE MANIFESTO OF THE COMMUNIST PARTY . . . yes?"

Buchman proudly nodded.

"May I read it?"

"Ja."

The old priest read a little, smiled, and sighed. "I must confess . . . I would enjoy the company of an intellectual after all these Americans! Come, walk with me and tell me of recent events in France and Germany."

"A good strong back. Turn around. Good arms. Good legs," said the auctioneer.

Solomon glared out into the crowd of white faces. He looked over to the other slaves to be auctioned. One of the women to be sold held his daughter's hand. Columbia held his violin like a doll, next to her chest.

"Where my mama?" asked the girl, looking around.

"Do I hear one thousand dollars?"

"One thousand."

"Mama?"

"One thousand, one hundred."

"Mama?"

"One thousand, one hundred. Do I hear one thousand, two hundred? Not a whip mark on 'im."

"One thousand, two hundred."

"One thousand, four hundred."

"Mama?"

"One thousand, four hundred fifty."

"Mama?"

Solomon saw Jack Glubb rub his fat belly and exchange pleasantries with white women at the back of the crowd. If he only had that musket his daddy had carried in General Washington's army.

"One thousand, five hundred!"

"Mama!"

Solomon broke down and began to sob.

Chapter Two

1850

"Gentlemen! I haff come here to tell you about de revolution!" shouted Herman Buchman. The two miners sitting under the mariposa continued mending their trousers. Three miners, carrying cut boards down to the stream, stopped and looked at Buchman for a moment, and then continued on their way.

"De time has come for the vorking class to rise up and take control of the factories and mills."

An old man passed a brown jug to another old man. "You don't say," he said.

The other old man took his drink and said: "How much dust d'ya think it'll take to shut 'im up."

"Why waste the gold?" said the first, taking out a Navy Colt revolver from under his jacket. He pulled the trigger, but the gun simply clicked. He pulled the trigger again, and a pathetic puff of smoke rose from the chamber.

"Damn. Powder's wet."

Buchman's eyes were wide with terror. He threw down his pamphlets and ran along the muddy trail going back to Marysville.

"They say you can play the fiddle," said Master Tibbetts.

Solomon didn't say a word. He lifted the tote bag of cotton and slung it over his back. Tibbetts leaned over the side of his horse and struck Solomon's face with the riding whip. Solomon dropped the bag.

"You best answer me when I talk to you, boy," said Tibbetts. "You play the fiddle or not?"

"Don't have heart to, no more."

"Jack Glubb says you were the finest fiddle player in New York. Says you played for the governor's ball."

"S'pose I did. That's what got me into this mess."

"Then you can play the fiddle for me."

"S'pose it's better than howin' rows and pullin' the cotton."

"S'pose it is," said Tibbetts. "But I won't be a-needin' fiddle playin' during the day. No, sir. Too much work to be done. Just nights is all, when you all are doin' nothin' but eatin' and sleepin' anyways. Glubb says you play 'Camptown Races.' Says you told the gov'ner of New York it was your family's most favorite song."

Solomon hung his head.

"Well then, Solomon, I'll let you play it for me come Sunday night."

Buchman nervously brushed back his hair and hurried onto the plank stage. With the help of the old priest, he'd come to understand the English language and had been working on his accent. He was confident because the miners were in a good mood. But he wondered why they'd been especially excited by the sight of a horse being taken backstage. The band leader spat and put up a sign that read:

Act One
Salute to America

A large family with seven sons and eight daughters got onto the stage. The youngest ones pulled a cannon behind them and aimed the barrel over the heads of the miners. The father sang a song about America, and then the whole family broke into "Hail, Columbia." The homesick miners clapped wildly and sang along, rising to their feet and wiping the tears from their eyes. At the end of the song, the father yanked at the cord that would set off the cannon, but the cannon didn't go off, and the barrel dropped an inch lower. The miners were cheering. The children sang the ending refrain once more, and the father tugged at the cord again. The cannon went off. The miners shot their pistols into the air and were cheering so loudly that they didn't notice the explosion in the very back row. The father nervously bowed and led his family from the stage. As they passed Herman Buchman, the oldest brother scolded a younger brother: "I told you not to use real shells. You're gonna get it."

The band leader changed the sign to read:

Act Two
Fine Oratory

The miners saw Herman Buchman and began to laugh.

"Workers of the world . . . unite!" cried Buchman.

The miners roared like a stormy ocean. A wave of garbage flew from the audience onto the stage and covered Buchman from head to toe. The tuba player pulled a cabbage out of his horn, and the other band members brushed the rotten fruit and vegetables off their instruments. They began to play.

The band leader changed the sign:

Act Three
The Mazeppa

"But I'm not finished!" protested Herman.

15

A woman clad only in a white body suit was strapped to the back of the horse. The horse sauntered onto the stage, and the woman began to warble a sad song, but not in time to the music. The miners cheered the woman and continued to throw garbage at Buchman. A brick struck the horse, and it began to bolt around the stage. The woman strapped on top slipped off to the side and began to scream for help. The band members dropped their instruments and fled as two hundred miners rushed the stage.

Solomon was tied over an oak barrel. The other slaves stood in the doorways to their shanties and watched. Tibbetts took a step back and whirled a bullwhip in the air. The whip came down on Solomon's back, tearing the skin like a razor.

Solomon bit his lower lip until the blood flowed into his mouth and down his neck.

Tibbetts cracked the whip four more times on Solomon's back. He then stood over Solomon and folded his arms.

"I'm lettin' you off easy this time, Solomon, 'cause we caught you 'fore you got too far North. Next time you try this, it's gonna hurt. And if any of your talkin' 'bout freedom ever loses me one, you'll wish you was dead. You understand?"

Solomon gazed up with a defiant smile. Tibbetts shook his head and untied the knots confining Solomon's hands.

"Now you get yourself all cleaned up. You're gonna play for my family tonight, you hear? And you're gonna play nice and sweet, not like last Sunday."

"It's really for the best, Herman," said the old priest.

Buchman wiped the tears from his eyes with the hand that wasn't in a cast. The schooner's sail caught the stiff breeze and passed Alcatraz Island on its way out to sea.

"They're a good Christian family," continued the priest.

"Even if they are Protestants. This is no place to raise a boy. He'll be better off in Massachusetts."

They stood and watched the schooner become a white speck bouncing on the horizon. The priest looked at Buchman.

"Your nose is bleeding. Again."

Buchman wiped his nose with his sleeve. He pushed his hip forward to move the leg that was bound in a cast of wood and flannel sheets.

"You're lucky," said the priest.

"Lucky?"

"Yes, lucky to be alive, being the only thing standing between two hundred drunken men and an almost nude woman crying for help. Oh, but I forgot. Those miners are the vanguard of your revolution, no?"

Buchman growled, and the old priest smiled when he noted the promise of revenge in Buchman's eyes.

Chapter Three

1851

"Five dollars?" asked the greenhorn. "Why it's got no more than fifty pages to it."

"Guess we'd better get one," said his partner. "Here's ten bucks," he said to Buchman, "for two of them GUIDE TO CALIFORNIA GOLD FIELDS of yours."

Buchman put the money in a cigar box and handed the miners his publication. Two other miners entered Buchman's little shop and purchased five more copies.

"You buyin' books today?" asked a despondent man. It was one of Buchman's regulars, an educated man who had come to California for gold and had instead become a gambler. When luck was good, he bought. When luck was bad, he sold.

"Yes."

"How much you pay for these?"

"Hmm. For the Bible, nothing. But for this book of Scott's poetry, five cents."

"Five cents! I paid you two dollars for it last month! Look, give me at least a quarter so I can get a bottle of whisky."

"Five cents."

"All right. Five cents, then. Damn you anyway."

Buchman waited for the man to leave and then priced the book five dollars and put it alongside the growing collection of books in his bookstore. The gambler had bought and sold that book before, and it was Buchman's policy to raise the price asked and lower the offer given each time the book passed through his hands.

At the end of the day and when the shop was empty, Buchman took out an old map of central Europe, placed a thin piece of paper over it, and began to trace the mountains and rivers. He did not copy the names of the towns. Instead he wrote down names like Sacramento, San Francisco, and Los Angeles. He held up the tracing to the window and smiled.

"Vell, *padre*. Time for the Old Mission Press to start the new, revised and improved second edition."

Solomon put down the fiddle. The slaves clapped and shouted: "More!"

The Tibbetts allowed their slaves to rest on Christmas Day, and as was customary for the county they were allowed to visit neighborhood plantations. Solomon didn't mind playing for this audience.

Old James belonged to the folks at Broken Oaks and was no longer able to work the fields. Even so, he was expected to catch the river fish and do some amount of work for the kitchen help.

"Solomon!" said James. "Over here."

Solomon sat down beside James who looked around with a sly smile.

"Here, have some of this," he said, putting a large sugar bowl in front of Solomon. Solomon lifted off the lid and put the bowl up to his nose.

"Gin? Where'd you get gin?"

"Stole it from the kitchen," said James. "Got plenty more, so help yourself."

Solomon at first sipped and then took gulps. "Thanks," he said, passing the empty bowl back to James.

"Listen up, Solomon. I heard 'bout your daughter. Co-lumbia."

Solomon froze.

"That's right. Your daughter," continued James. "The Mahones traded her off to a family in Texas. In Austin, Texas. I guess she's on her way there by now."

"Texas," said Solomon thoughtfully.

"You know, out West."

"I know," said Solomon. "Big place, Texas. Big as the whole United States, they say. You know the family that's got her?"

"No, sir," said James sadly. "But it's in Austin."

"Austin," said Solomon, looking through James and beyond.

The old priest and Buchman hurried out of the bookstore.

"Take this," said Buchman, handing his old friend the cigar box.

"What would I do with all that money?" asked the priest.

"But I owe you so much."

"Go with God, Herman Buchman." The priest flipped a hood over his head and fled down the street. Buchman looked nervously down the street to the bay. A ragged and hungry man sadly looked down at the old horse slowly pulling his caravan up the steep and narrow street. On the side of the caravan were two words: **SHARPENING** and **GRINDING**.

"Say, you there?" shouted Buchman.

The grinder sitting on the driver's seat of his caravan pointed to himself.

"That's right."

"What can I do for you, mister?"

"I've got a business proposal that I'm sure will be of interest."

The grinder pulled back on the reins, and the horse seemed happy to come to a dead stop.

"Come here!" said Buchman.

The grinder jumped off his caravan.

Buchman led the grinder from his caravan into his bookstore.

"I wish to make a trade with you."

"Me, sir?"

"Yes, sir. You, sir."

"Trade what, sir?"

"I'm prepared to trade you this profitable little bookstore, as it is, right before you, for that caravan and horse."

"This bookstore and all its books for that caravan and that horse?"

"Correct."

"But there must be a thousand books in here."

"One thousand, seven hundred, and forty to be exact."

"I don't know. Can I think about it?"

"I'm afraid not, sir. I need an immediate decision. Before I come to my senses and change my mind."

"How much the books worth?"

"Most are worth between two to five dollars. Each. But even if you sold them for a dollar a piece, you'd have. . . ."

"One thousand, seven hundred, and forty dollars."

"Exactly."

"Can I keep my grinder, and whetstones?"

"Absolutely. Is it a deal?"

Buchman offered the grinder his hand, and they shook.

"Now," said Buchman, "we haven't a moment to lose. Let's get your grinder and stones out and be done with it."

While the grinder pulled his tools out the back of the caravan, Buchman put his German to English dictionary and cigar box into the front. Buchman took the reins of the old horse and looked down at the grinder.

"Oh, and by the way. If anyone should ask you if you own the bookstore today, I would suggest you emphatically answer, no."

The grinder scratched his head, watched his caravan roll down the street, and wondered what *emphatically* meant. He looked around at his bookstore and grinned. He'd come West on the promise of opportunities and found it to be so. True, his grinding and sharpening business hadn't panned out, but now he'd just swapped a worthless horse and old caravan for a real business. The opportunity was so rich and sudden that he'd forgotten that he could neither read nor write. But he could learn. He pulled proudly on his braces and admired the bookstore from the street.

A group of men were shouting and hollering at the top of their lungs at the far end of the street, coming up from the Bay. The grinder stepped into the doorway of his new business and watched their approach. It was only natural that he should wonder what all the commotion was about and why they brandished flaming torches in the light of day. He would soon learn that the angry mob was being led by the sole survivor of an ill-fated mining expedition into the High Sierras, an expedition that had used the folding map in BUCHMAN'S UNIVERSAL GUIDE TO CALIFORNIA GOLD FIELDS, 2ND REVISED EDITION.

Chapter Four

February 2, 1859

The white, wet substance moved slowly toward the slab of ham. The waiter had called the stuff grits, but Herman was sure that it wasn't anything more than warmed up lice. Its slow migration across his plate convinced him that, whatever it was, it was still alive. He quickly ate the ham before the grits crossed the plate. He had hoped to read the Monday morning edition of the *New Orleans Picayune* over a cup of coffee but was afraid that the grits might crawl into his pants pocket. He left some money on the table, tucked the paper under his arm, and took a walk down the busy, cobbled street.

A crowd of well-dressed men stood in a circle. Herman curiously stood at the back of the crowd. A man in a white suit stood on a platform.

"Oh, my God," muttered Herman. He'd heard about slavery and had seen slaves from afar while driving his caravan down the dirty old river roads. The man in the white suit cried out numbers, and the men in the crowd shouted out their bids. Herman was just about to turn away when the auctioneers brought up the last man to be sold.

"I won't lie to you!" shouted the auctioneer. "This one's a heap of trouble. Turn around."

Herman watched the slave slowly take off his shirt and turn around so the crowd could see his back. Herman's heart leaped to his throat. The black man's back was little more than scar tissue.

"And they had to crop his right foot!" shouted the auctioneer. "He was plenty fast, but as stupid as they come. Caught him runnin' deep into Texas."

The bidders began to check their pocket watches and talk with one another, wandering away from the platform.

"Do I hear five hundred?"

The winning bidders went over to the side of the stand to finish their transactions.

"Do I hear four hundred?"

The slave glared angrily out at the dispersing crowd.

"Do I hear a hundred?"

The bidders began to swarm around Buchman, making their way to the day's other business. Buchman stepped aside, moved ahead, moved over, and suddenly found himself in front of the platform.

"Well, Tibbetts," said the auctioneer, stepping down from the platform, "ain't no buyers. Not today, anyway."

Tibbetts growled. "I swore if I couldn't sell 'im, I was gonna put 'im down."

"And no one will blame you, sir," said the auctioneer pleasantly. "But as a kindness, sir. Please do it somewhere else."

"I'll buy him," said Herman.

Tibbetts and the auctioneer looked at Buchman.

"How much?" asked Tibbetts.

"The last bid was a hundred dollars, was it not?"

"It was," said the auctioneer.

Buchman pulled at a small chain that was attached to his vest. At the other end of the chain was a pouch. Buchman fumbled through the pouch and counted out a hundred dollars in gold to the auctioneer.

The auctioneer led the slave off the platform. The slave hobbled along, and Buchman saw that half of his right foot was gone.

"There you go," said the auctioneer. "Now, about my commission for this sale."

"Here's your damn' receipt," said Tibbetts, signing a scrap of paper and thrusting it at Herman. Herman stuffed the paper into his pouch, and then looked at the slave.

"Let's get out of here!"

Buchman walked slowly back to his hotel so that the slave, his slave, could keep up with him.

"What am I doing?" asked Buchman, looking up to the blue sky and gently slapping his forehead.

Buchman held the door open for the slave, who stopped some feet before the threshold.

"Come on," urged Buchman.

"Hey!" shouted the concierge. "He can't come in here. Take him 'round back."

Buchman frowned. "Wait here. Let me get my things. Oh. Forgive me, sir. I didn't even bother to learn your name?"

"Solomon. Solomon Freeman."

"You can call me Herman."

"Can't do that, sir. To me, you just another massa. Massa Herman."

"I see," said Buchman. "I think it best we get as far from here as possible. I'll get the caravan from the alley and bring it around front. It'll take about half an hour."

"I'se supposed to do that for you," said Solomon.

"I wouldn't hear of it," said Buchman, rushing into the hotel. "Wait here."

Before long, Solomon saw a dusty old caravan drive up in front of the hotel. Buchman patted the caravan's wooden driver's seat. As soon as Solomon was beside him, Buchman took a long stick and poked the horse's behind.

"Move along, Hegel," he said. The old horse began to

25

pull, and the caravan clattered as it went down the street.

"You hungry?" asked Herman. Solomon just stared at the old horse in front of him. Herman waited a moment and repeated the question. Solomon looked at him.

" 'Course, I'se hungry. Been hungry for a long time."

"Well, there's two baguettes and some cold meats in that box behind you. Help yourself."

Solomon took one of the loaves and bit off the end. He then took a handful of meat and stuffed it into his mouth.

"You can make a sandwich if you like," said Buchman. Solomon swallowed. "Sandwich?"

"Yes, sandwich. They make them in all the bars in San Francisco. Here, take the knife in the jockey box there, cut the bread in half, and put the meat in the middle."

Solomon opened the jockey box. Instead of the little pebbles usually used by teamsters to throw at the team, there were baby pins, pencils, a wadded-up piece of paper, and a hunting knife. Solomon picked up the knife and looked around. They were still in the city.

"You're not from around here, are you?" the slave asked.

"No," said Buchman. "Germany. Germany was where I was born. Then I moved to France. Then England. Then California. Then Santa Fé, and now, wherever I am, that's my home."

"I met me some Germans once. You don't talk like them."

Buchman considered reciting a passage from FAUST but didn't. He smiled and poked Hegel's hindquarter with the stick again. Hegel snorted and moved imperceptibly faster.

Solomon cut the bread in half and slipped the meat inside. He took a bite and nodded approvingly. Buchman smiled and studied the people on the avenue. Solomon then put the knife back into the jockey box so that the handle was closest to him.

February 15, 1859

Buchman came back to the caravan with a fistful of dollars.

"The Patterson family now has a set of Talleyrand's memoirs, and I have twenty dollars. Here you are, Solomon," he said, handing the money to Solomon.

"You want me to put this somewhere?"

"No, no, dear fellow. It's your wages."

Solomon looked down at the money in his hand, and then up at Herman. "I don't know about Germany, but here slavery don't pay all that well."

Herman looked perplexed, and then smiled. "I'm sorry, Solomon, but I see now I haven't made myself clear."

"What do you mean?"

"I mean, Solomon, that as far as I am concerned, you are free."

"Then where's my papers?"

"Papers? The only paper I have is for printing."

"If I'm free, I got to have papers of manumission."

"Manumission," said Buchman slowly to himself. "I've never seen papers of manumission." He thought for a moment. "I suppose that the wording in them has to be just so, and that being the case, when we get to Saint Louis, I'll talk to a fee lawyer and get some of these papers of manumission for you."

They got into the caravan and drove along the road that followed the eastern bank of the Mississippi.

"Why?" asked Solomon.

"Why, what?"

"Why did you buy me? Why you payin' me? Why you settin' me free?"

"Don't know. I guess I just felt sorry for you."

"I don't need you feelin' sorry for me."

"No, I guess you don't."

March 1, 1859

"Here's your paper of manumission," said Buchman.

Solomon looked down at the letter that Herman was offering him.

"I'm free?"

"As a bird."

"I can go?"

"If you like. But you have a job with me. If you like."

"What kind of job?"

"I'll teach you the mysteries of the hand press and printing. Then bookselling. You can read, can't you?"

"Not much."

"All it takes to be a publisher is to be able to read the author's name and title of a book. And a burning desire to lose money. To be a bookseller, it takes even less reading and an even stronger desire to invest poorly. All you have to do is convince the buyer you have what they want."

"What about printing?"

"Ah," laughed Buchman. "All you really have to know is the alphabet and how to arrange type on the printing forme."

"Do the folks who buy books know this?"

"Most of them don't. No. Most folks buy books because they think they should own them. People who want to read, read, whether they own the book or not."

"You don't make it sound all that nice."

"Solomon, most creatures hunt or gather or even farm for their living. Many creatures display as high a learning as humanity. Is the beehive any less of an architectural wonder than a five story building in the city? The only trade unique to our species is the book trade. No other species writes about it-self, publishes that writing, sells that writing, and then reads that writing so it can get into fights over that writing. The book trade in all of its aspects is uniquely human."

"Well, Mister Buchman, I can think of another thing, a uniquely human thing."

"Yes?"

"Slavery."

Buchman sadly smiled and nodded in agreement. He climbed onto the caravan and looked down at Solomon. "Well? You want the job?"

"Depends."

"Depends on what?"

"There's two things I want. I want to find my daughter. I want to kill the man who did this to me and my family." Solomon pointed down to his cropped foot, and then to his back.

Herman thought for a moment. "I have made only three promises in my life," he said. "I have made a pledge to the pro-letariat and the revolution. I have yet to keep that. I made a vow in marriage, and I kept that until death did we part. And then I vowed to get even with some men in California. That one I did too well, and I won't make that kind of promise again. I shall make this pledge to you. I will help you find your daughter. But we need to raise some capital to finance that ex-pedition, which means we've got books to make and books to sell."

Solomon smiled softly and climbed up onto the caravan.

"You think there's any money in printing up papers of manumission?" asked Buchman.

"It'd be a real good thing, to give some out, I reckon. To any runaways we come across. But the folks that needs 'em ain't got money to buy them."

Buchman smiled. His new apprentice was already thinking like a bookseller.

March 20, 1859

Fort Laramie wasn't what Herman or Solomon had expected. This may have been because Herman had been having Solomon carefully read Pope's translation of *The Iliad* aloud to improve both of their language skills, and, while this exercise increased their vocabularies, it also filled their imaginations with expectations. There were no marble temples or lofty walls lined with women in Fort Laramie, just plank houses, shoddy barracks, and teepees surrounding a blockhouse. All of this miraculously stood on top of mud that sucked the caravan down to its hubs and had undoubtedly pulled down toddlers and small animals into an instant murky grave.

They came upon a party in preparation for an overland journey to Oregon that made Buchman stop and set up camp outside the fort. Buchman went through all the books and papers piled around inside the caravan until he found an immigrant's guide to California. He read through the text and, with his pencil, crossed out some words and in the margins wrote in the words he wished to have in their place.

Herman then showed Solomon how to assemble the pieces of an old hand press he'd purchased the year before in Texas and explained that, according to the old Mexican bookseller he'd bought it from, this had been the very press that the Texans had used to print their Declaration of Independence from Mexico, and that was why he was willing to pay the extra dollar fifty. There wasn't enough room in the caravan to keep it in its assembled state, but the caravan had all sorts of nooks and crannies, enough to hold all its various pieces and hundreds of books, besides. It went together in about as much time as it took Herman to elaborate upon the fact that the Texan revolution had started out as a class struggle, as evidenced by the fact that the Declaration had been printed in two languages, three hundred copies in English and three hundred in Spanish, and that the working class Texicans had ultimately been betrayed by the owners of the means of production who just happened to be Americans. Solomon politely listened, but paid more attention to the details of the press assembly than to the lesson in historical materialism.

Herman then showed Solomon how to set the type, ink the letters, and the subtle mechanics of the actual printing: that is, pulling and pushing a press bar and removing and inserting paper.

By the end of the day, they had a clothesline stretched between the cottonwood trees and the caravan and on these lines had pinned the freshly printed sheets to dry in the sun. By the end of the week, Herman showed Solomon the basics of compositing the text and how to gather and fold the sheets for a simple stitch binding.

Solomon proudly held up the very first copy of his work, AN IMMIGRANT'S GUIDE TO OREGON. He then thoughtfully looked through the pamphlet. "You know," he said, "the folks who you're gonna sell this to might actually use it."

"Perhaps," said Buchman.

"What if they get lost?"

"So they end up in California. It's close to Oregon."

When they drove the caravan into the fort to sell their masterpiece to the party going West, it was no longer there.

"Where's those folks going to Oregon?" asked Solomon of a passing soldier.

"The Catley party? They left yesterday," said the soldier.

31

"If we hurry," said Buchman to Solomon, "we can catch up to them."

The soldier laughed and said before going on his way: "I would strongly advise against that. There'll be another group leaving in two weeks."

"What if we don't catch up to them?" asked Solomon.

"Then we'll set up along the trail and sell to the next group going West."

Solomon sadly shook his head and poked poor Hegel in the hindquarters. Hegel went no faster.

April 3, 1859

The dusty road had become little more than wheel ruts in the wet grass. The rolling hills had become flat grasslands. At sundown, Herman and Solomon could see a little smoke in the west, suggesting that the immigrants were no more than ten miles ahead.

It was a moonless night. Solomon finished reading *The Iliad* to Herman and began the first lines of *The Odyssey*. But wood was scarce and the reading ceased when the campfire had become little more than glowing coals.

"What's that?" asked Solomon.

Herman looked around, and Solomon pointed to his ears. Herman cocked his head as if that would increase his ability to hear.

"Thunder, I think."

"But there's no clouds. Look, just stars." Solomon's eyes began to water and his skin to itch.

Hegel snorted and slowly walked away from camp.

"He ain't ever left camp before," said Solomon, scratching his arms.

Herman didn't have to cock his head any more as the

thunder grew louder. "Oh, oh," he said. He pulled his blanket off the grass and threw it into the caravan.

"What d'you mean oh, oh?" asked Solomon, leaving his blanket and climbing into the caravan right behind Herman.

"Buffalo!" screamed Buchman.

"Buffalo?"

The ground trembled. A large, massive body crashed into the caravan, and then another. The caravan creaked and popped. The thunder was around them. The caravan was hit again and again. The boards snapped and thrust inside, knocking down the press and books. The caravan tilted to the side, being crushed. As suddenly as the thunder had come, it left. The caravan groaned and fell over on its side.

The next morning, Herman and Solomon looked at the demolished caravan.

"Buffalo," said Buchman.

"Buffalo," said Solomon.

Hegel lazily strolled back into camp as if nothing had happened.

"Hegel," said Buchman.

"Hegel," said Solomon.

Buchman looked around and rubbed his chin. "Good a place as any for a bookstore, don't you think?"

"I suppose. But there ain't gonna be much of that walk-in traffic you've been talking about. Exceptin' for buffalo." Solomon's stomach growled and, seeing that the boxes of food were smashed, added: "I sure hope they taste better than they smell."

They got on their hands and knees, looking for the dried beans, canned goods, and missing type. A sack of flour had miraculously survived the stampede, and, while the keg of lard was broken, the lard was mostly there. They did well finding their scattered supplies, but didn't have much luck with the missing type. While they found most of the consonants, they came up short on vowels.

"Think we can print much with only one e?" asked Solomon.

"Don't worry. We have plenty of the e in capitals."

"Pages gonna look pretty funny."

"No worse than the King James Bible, with all of its italicized words."

"Italicized. Oh, yeah. Words printed at an angle. So you're supposed to read 'em extra hard. They put plenty of them in the Bible."

"No, Solomon. It was supposed to show that the men who translated the Bible from the Greek and Latin versions weren't really sure about the word's meaning."

Solomon began to laugh and sat.

"What's so funny."

"I'll tell you what. That old white minister, the one who introduced me to Glubb. He used to read extra into them italicized words. He's the one who told me that words were italicized 'cause you were supposed to read 'em louder than the other words."

Buchman got off his knees and sat as well.

"And so," said Solomon in an oratorical fashion, "Jesus said unto them . . . 'Saddle me an ass.' . . . and so they saddled *him!*"

They laughed until they cried.

April 4, 1859

Solomon couldn't run. He threw down the wood he'd gathered and turned toward camp. He kept his right leg stiff, threw it out ahead with his hip, and hobbled as quickly as he could. The camp was just over the hill, and so he stopped to look back. The seven figures on horses were close enough to make them out.

"Indians!" he shouted before hobbling over the hill.

Buchman was reading a book and looked up as Solomon hurried into camp.

"Indians!" cried Solomon, annoyed that Buchman continued to read.

"Good."

"Good? Good? You crazy? They gonna cook us and eat us!"

"Goodness, Solomon."

The Indians slowed their ponies on top of the small hill and looked down at the camp.

"Where's that knife?" shouted Solomon.

Herman waved to the Indians and beckoned them to come down.

"What are you doing?"

"Inviting them into our shop."

"You're what?"

The Indians slowly rode down to the caravan, looked it over, and then rode over to Buchman.

"Please, join us," said Herman, pointing to the blankets on the grass. "Solomon, I think we have enough left to make up a fresh pot of coffee."

"You're gonna give 'em coffee with their meal . . . that bein' us?"

"Blackfoot don't eat people, you fool," said one of the Indians. Solomon froze and looked at the Indian who'd said that. The Indian pulled at his headdress and flung it over the back of his horse. He was a very old man with black skin.

"Indians? Colored. Indians are colored folk?" asked Solomon.

"Why don't you make up that coffee, like your master told you to?"

The old man waited for the other Blackfoot warriors to slide off their mounts and come over to him to help him

35

down. Solomon was frozen with fear and confusion. The other Indians didn't have black skin. Buchman put the coffee pot on coals at the side of the small campfire.

The old man looked over the caravan. "Buffalo?"

"Yes, buffalo," said Buchman.

"A lot of them?"

Buchman nodded.

"Good. You hunters?"

"No, sir. Booksellers," said Buchman.

"Booksellers! Maybe your boy here is right, 'bout you bein' crazy an' all. Ain't nobody out here gonna buy your books. This ain't Boston."

"We're waiting for the next immigrant train to pass this way."

The old man frowned, and then spat. "I suppose they will. This time a year, they's about as many of them as not going West. I seen one to the west comin' here."

"Please, have a seat," said Buchman.

The old man slowly sat down on the blanket and looked at Solomon.

"Had to cut off his foot, did ye?"

"I don't think you quite understand," said Buchman. "Solomon here isn't my slave. That is, I bought him so I could set him free."

"So, you'd be one of them Abolitionists?"

"No, I am a Communist."

"Communist? Is that some kind of Abolitionist?"

"Well, in that we don't believe in private property, and that including slaves, I guess so."

"Communist. Say, that coffee ready?"

Buchman got up and went over to the pot. "It's coming along."

"You . . . come here!" said the old man.

36

Solomon slowly moved from the caravan to the old man.

"So, you a Communist, too?"

"No. I don't think so."

"Good. Best not to get all that involved with them white folks things. If you want, you can come on along with us."

"But I don't want to eat people."

"For God's sake, where'd you get that fool notion?"

"Folks always told me that if I went West, the Indians would kill me and eat me. Those of us that got away and went West we never heard about ever again."

"Well, it just ain't so. So get that out of your head. Probably somethin' some white man told you just to keep you totin' bags for 'im."

"Here's your coffee," said Buchman, bringing the old man a large mug of scalding hot coffee. The old man began to gulp it down as if it were cool spring water. He wiped his lips and grinned.

"So, you's free," said the old man.

"I am," said Solomon.

"But it ain't been all that long, has it?"

"Not long, no."

"Then it won't be long till you know that while you is free, you really ain't welcome nowheres."

"I was free. A long time ago. Had me a wife and children," said Solomon.

"Then you knows what I mean."

"I do. But it wasn't all that bad. We all had our place. Some of the white folks were more important than others. Some of the black folks had respectable jobs. But you're right. We couldn't vote or nothin'."

"Suppose I told you I know a place where the color of a man's skin don't make no difference at all. I know that place. Two weeks ride northwest of here there's big mountains, bigger than any anywhere. The people there call themselves the Black-foot. A man is just a man. No more. No less. You can be black, you can be white, you can be the color of sunset, don't make no difference. There's places up there in them mountains where the waters boil and the mud can burn ye. But, by God, it's more beautiful than anything. You can come on along if you like. After we get us enough buffalo for the winter."

Solomon looked over to Herman. Herman lifted up a Bible and offered it to one of the Blackfoot warriors. He jumped away with an expression of revulsion.

The old man laughed. "Them black-robed priests showed 'em that book before. They don't trust no man in black, and they sure as hell don't trust a book with a black cover. 'Specially since the priests was tryin' to give it away. Now, if they had hid 'em away, my friends here'd have stolen one 'cause it'd probably have some big medicine. Say, what kind of books you got, anyway?"

"Well, let's see here. I've got some fiction. A novel by Nathaniel Hawthorne. Another by Washington Irving. And a set by Edgar Allan Poe."

"Fiction!" spat the old man. "Iffen my eyes were good enough to read, I sure as hell wouldn't want a book about somethin' that's all made up. Get me a book about some-thin'."

"Well, let me see," said Buchman. "In non-fiction, I have several hundred copies of a guide to going West, which I don't believe would interest you much. Oh, here's the memoirs of Napoléon. Volumes One and Four only, though. Cæsar's COMMENTARIES. Interlinear. Ah, and here's a complete set. Two volumes. THE EXPEDITIONS OF CAPTAINS LEWIS AND CLARK."

"Lewis and Clark?"

"That's right."

"They say anything about Captain Clark's slave?"

"I don't know. I haven't had a chance to read it myself."

"Hmm. I guess I'd better get it. Kinda of an interest of mine, the Corps of Discovery."

Buchman handed the old man the set of books.

The old man squinted as he slowly turned the pages. "I don't read so well, and the print. Couldn't make it any smaller, could they? Still, I'se got plenty of time on my hands come winter. I'll get through it. How much?"

"Well, ordinarily, I'd ask two dollars, but for you. . . ."

"I ain't got two dollars," said the old man. "But I'll give you my pony and the ridin' blanket for it."

"But that's worth more than two dollars," objected Buchman. "I couldn't possibly accept. . . ."

"I sees only one horse. You should both have a horse."

The old man spoke to the warriors. They helped the old man up and over to his pony. He slowly tied the horse to the back of the caravan and was helped onto another pony. Two of the warriors climbed on the largest horse. Buchman wrapped the set of books in some printing paper and gave it to the old man.

"We'll be half a day's ride to the south and west," said the old man, looking down at Solomon. "Like I said, you's welcome to join us. Never got your name."

"Solomon. Solomon Freeman."

"Well, Solomon. You and this Communist fellah best get a move on, one way or the other. The Oglalla and Brulé are coming down for the hunt, and, from what I hear, they ain't real friendly with the white man right now. And that includes anybody's with them. And, no, sir. They ain't gonna eat you. But they sure as hell don't want no books."

The old man gently kicked the pony's side, and it began to trot away.

"Hey!" shouted Solomon. "What's your name?"

"York!" shouted the old man, not looking back.

April 15, 1859

"What happened to your foot? Did it hurt?"

Solomon looked down at the little girl, looking up at him. "Yeah, it hurt. Got it cut off for running away."

"Auntie Clara . . . she lives in Ohio . . . she lets runaways stay in the barn."

"She does, does she?"

"Yes. She told me and my brother Billy all about Uncle Tom and Little Eva and Topsy. You know Uncle Tom and Little Eva and Topsy?"

"Can't say that I do, child."

Solomon took the borrowed hammer and began to pound. He looked around at the camp. He hadn't been in the company of so many white folks since he'd played his fiddle at the governor's ball. It had been so long ago, it was hard to remember.

"Abigail!" shouted one of the women. "Abigail! You come over here right now. Don't you be botherin' Mister Solomon none!"

"She's no trouble!" shouted Solomon.

"My name's Abigail."

"Pleased to make your acquaintance, Miss Abigail," said Solomon, bowing.

"When I grow up, I'm gonna help runaways, too. Aunt Clara says that once she helps all the slaves get free, she's gonna get women to vote."

Solomon smiled. "That's nice, dear."

"And then Aunt Clara's gonna take away all the whisky. Do you drink whisky? You shouldn't, you know. It's bad for you."

"No. I don't drink whisky. Haven't for a long time. But I had gin sometimes."

"Gin? What's that?"

"It's like whisky, but different."

"Oh." The little girl suddenly saw six of the men lift the caravan while four others placed props beneath to hold it up. The new axles were set in place, followed by the sound of hammers pounding wood and nails. She ran off to watch.

Solomon took the door back to the caravan and screwed it in place. Solomon shook his head, ashamed in the knowledge that he and Herman had proposed a trade of their entire run of the guidebook in return for getting the caravan road worthy. He looked over at Buchman who was looking a little ashamed himself.

Solomon waited for a while until he could talk to Herman alone.

"These nice folks want to go to Oregon, not California. We shouldn't ought to be . . . ," began Solomon.

"I know, I know," said Buchman. "But you wanted to get the caravan fixed as much as I did. We'd have had to leave the press behind. And, besides, they accepted the offer."

"Yeah, but we shouldn't have made it in the first place. I just don't feel right."

That evening, Solomon and Herman enjoyed a good meal and listened as each family sang a favorite song. The happier the emigrants became at each song, the more melancholy Buchman became, and Solomon could only eat a quarter of the piece of berry pie he'd been given.

"Wished I had my fiddle and could play for 'em," said Solomon.

"I didn't know you played the violin."

"Ain't got the heart to, really. Besides, last time I saw it, my daughter had it. Probably took it along to the folks that bought her. And then my massa made me play, and beat on me when I didn't. I just don't have the heart to play any fiddle. Still, it'd be nice to do something for these folks after selling them those books that's gonna get 'em good and lost."

Herman could stand the guilt no longer. He ran off to the caravan and began to give each and every member of the expedition a book.

After the families had gone to bed, Herman and Solomon sat by the glowing embers of the campfire, poking the coals with sticks.

"You gave away all your books," said Solomon.

"I know."

"You don't feel any better, do you?"

"Not really. No."

"If anything happens to these nice folks. . . ."

Buchman covered his ears, got up, and rushed into the caravan.

"Hey there," said a man's voice. The wagon master sat down beside Solomon.

" 'Evening."

"You know," said the wagon master, "I was looking over that guidebook you were givin' out earlier."

Solomon felt every muscle in his body grow tight. His mouth was dry, and he tightened his lips.

"I don't know where you got them, but if I was you, I'd go back to that publisher fellah and get my money back."

"Yeah?"

"Yeah, I would. Since you all are going back to Saint Louis, and bein' booksellers and all, you could do that. Not only did the guy who wrote it tell you it was the trail goin' to Oregon, which it ain't 'cause it's one goin' to California, but it's a copy, word for word, of the guidebook used by them poor Donner folks."

"Donner?"

"The very same."

"What happened to them?"

"Got caught up in the hills, in the snow. Ended up eatin' one another. Real bad business."

"Oh, my God!"

"I wasn't gonna let anyone use it, anyway," said the wagon master. "Ain't seen a guidebook yet that knows what's what. I think the men who write 'em never left their hometowns, to tell you the truth. Still, you ought to go get your money back. I'll tell the folks in the mornin'."

"But how we gonna pay you for all the work you done on the old caravan?"

"Hell," said the wagon master. "They'd have done it for you, anyways. Just your friend started into talkin' before any of us could get a word in otherwise, so we figured it'd make him feel better if we took him up on the offer."

Solomon began to relax.

"You're Solomon . . . right?"

Solomon nodded.

"I didn't get your partner's name."

"You got that guide handy?" asked Solomon quickly.

"Sure. Why?"

The wagon master pulled the pamphlet out of his pocket. Solomon snatched it out of his hands and held it closer to the fire.

"Just want to see who wrote this," said Solomon. "I forgot. Hmm. By some fellah named H. Buchman, eh?"

"That's right."

"My friend's name is . . . er . . . Benjamin Franklin."

"Like the inventor? Signer on the Declaration of Independence?"

"Yeah. That's right. Benjamin Franklin."

"Thought I heard folks call him Herman."

"That his nickname."

"Oh, well, I reckon you can tell Mister Franklin all this in the morning."

"Hell. I'm gonna tell Herman . . . I mean Mister Franklin . . . right now."

"But he's gone to bed."

"I'm pretty sure he ain't sleepin'. Not so good, anyway. 'Sides, I want to tell him about something I learned tonight."

"Yeah?"

"Yeah. Ain't Indians that'll kill and eat ya. It's white folks."

The wagon master laughed and wondered what Solomon meant by that.

Chapter Five

April, 1861

Solomon treated himself to a pinch of tobacco in his new pipe. As he smoked, he admired the drying sheets of paper in the old warehouse. By the way Buchman was frowning and mindlessly pulling on the press bar, Solomon could see that the letters he'd received in the mail had bothered him.

"I'm glad we're out of the guidebook business," said Solomon.

"So am I," said Herman, lifting up the printed page and laying it on a table.

"Just one thing."

"Yes."

"That bookseller on Main Street . . . you know, Mister Roeslin . . . was telling me about royalties. Seems you're supposed to pay the fellah who writes the book. You going to pay this Mister Dickens for this book of his."

"Well," groaned Buchman, pulling the bar, "Mister Dickens lives in England somewhere. I wouldn't know where to send the money. He won't mind much, us making a little money off his book."

"Well, what if he does mind?"

"Solomon, my dear fellow, we need the money more than he does."

"I suppose. But you think this book A CHRISTMAS CAROL is going to sell?"

"Well, old Roeslin says he can't keep a copy of it in stock.

And since he's the only bookseller in Saint Louis, he knows what he's talking about. We did all right with those sets of WAVERLY NOVELS . . . which we did at his suggestion."

"Took us all year to do, too. Still, we ought to set some money aside. You know, in case this Dickens fellow ever wants his due. Good thing that Scott fellow's gone home, 'cause you'd have to put a whole gob of money aside for him."

Solomon waited for Buchman to continue the argument, but Buchman remained silent.

"What's in them letters you got yesterday?"

"Oh, nothing." Buchman then sighed.

"They were mighty full envelopes. Letters must have been long ones. Got to be something in 'em."

Buchman stopped pulling the press bar. "One was from my son, Hugh."

"You got a son? You ain't ever told me about a son?"

"He's eleven. I haven't seen him since he was nine months old." Buchman looked away and brushed at his eyes.

Solomon watched the smoke rise from his pipe. "He's well?"

"*Ja*. I mean, yes. He's well."

"You miss 'im."

Buchman looked down at the floor. Solomon looked at the drying sheets and fingered one.

"They're ready," said Solomon.

Buchman finally looked up.

"Ready to fold and stitch," added Solomon. "I'm glad you got a fine boy, Herman. But if he's fine and all, you're still not actin' right. I mean, not like you usually do, tryin' to make one of them special deals of yours. Must have been that other letter. The real thick one."

Buchman sat down on a stool and rubbed his forehead. "I've been censured. By the party."

46

"I been kicked out of parties myself. When I was too young to handle my liquor."

"It's not that kind of party. The revolutionary party. The Communist Party."

"So you ain't allowed to talk about that revolution no more? How come?"

"Karl said that I can't be a capitalist and a Communist simultaneously, that this was a contradiction, and that it hurt the revolution. I wrote him and told him I was selling books to raise money for the revolution. Instead, I have been denounced as a traitor to the working class."

"So. Have your own revolution, if you want. You don't need his."

"But we went to university together. I thought we were friends."

"Guess not."

Buchman let out a sob and covered his eyes.

Solomon felt uncomfortable and began to tap the bowl of his pipe nervously. "I got an idea," he said. "Maybe we ought to go see that son of yours. After we finish selling all these Dickens. Then, after that, maybe we can sneak down to Texas and look around for my Columbia."

Buchman wiped his eyes with his sleeve and looked into Solomon's eyes. "Maybe we should."

There was shouting outside the warehouse, and both Solomon and Herman rushed to the door to see what it was all about. Groups of men ran down the street, going toward the great river or toward the governor's office. Women were pulling their children off the street and looking nervously behind as they slammed the doors of their homes.

"What's goin' on?" shouted Solomon.

An old fur trapper stopped running and turned around.

"Why, it's war, old son. The President . . . President Lincoln . . . has called for volunteers. He's drummin' up an army to take on all them states that want out of the Union!"

"States? Out of the Union?" asked Buchman.

"Ain't you been payin' attention? The whole damn' South done left the Union. You ain't heard 'bout that?" The old trapper turned away, running toward the river.

"Well, Herman. You want a revolution, you got one," said Solomon thoughtfully.

Chapter Six

May, 1863

The streets of New York were busy, and it had taken some time for the caravan to make its way up Fifth Avenue. This gave Solomon plenty of time to read the front page of the *Tribune* to Herman.

" 'The band of Confederate sympathizers were arrested on Sunday night,' " read Solomon. " 'But not before setting fire to several warehouses down by the Hudson River. The recent inclement weather extinguished the flames before they could spread to the federal arsenal nearby. There is no apparent affiliation with the Knights of the Copper Circle. The defiant ringleader of this treasonous band has been recognized as one Jack Glubb, of Washington City.' " Solomon put down the paper.

"Go on," said Herman.

"I know him."

"Really!"

"He's the one who took me and my family."

"Well, he's finally got his, eh, Solomon."

"Only if they crops his foot and whip him till he ain't got no backside." Then Solomon read quietly to himself for a moment.

"What else does it say?" asked Herman.

"It goes on and on about the Army lookin' for troublemakers. You best hold off on that revolution talk for a while."

"Well, here we are!"

49

Hegel stopped in front of the shop with the sign: **Joseph Sabin, Bookseller**. Herman jumped down to the pavement. He rubbed his hands and smiled up at Solomon. Solomon went into the caravan and grabbed a quart-size box. He pushed it out the back door, and then carefully climbed down to the street.

By the time Solomon had the box to the front door, Herman was already filling out an invoice at the counter while Sabin was drawing up a check. Solomon saw that the shop was busy and that most of the browsers were soldiers.

"There you go," said Buchman as Solomon placed the box on the counter. "Twenty copies of HISTORY OF THE REBELLION, as ordered."

Sabin opened the box, and a federal colonel reached in and pulled out a copy.

"Might have to order some more," said Sabin.

"We'll be back with some more next week," said Buchman. "Say, Joseph. Is there any possibility I could get some of that in cash?"

The colonel flipped open the book, placed his finger on the table of contents, and read aloud: "The Battle of Antietam." He smiled at Sabin. "I was there, you know."

"Let me see," said Sabin to Buchman. "Might have some of those new greenback dollars. You don't mind if I save the coin for myself, do you?"

"Not at all," said Buchman.

Solomon watched the colonel's expression grow grim. He anxiously waved to get Buchman's attention, but Buchman was watching Sabin count banknotes.

"Say, who wrote this?" asked the colonel.

"Why, I did," said Buchman.

Solomon winced and said: "Oh, oh!"

"It says here that Jefferson Davis did a forced march and

met up with the federal, Russian, Austrian, and Prussian armies at Austerlitz!"

"My fault! My fault!" shouted Solomon, waving his arms up. "Got the book messed up when I did the compositing. Mixed it up with a history of Napoléon, I did."

"Then why does it say Jefferson Davis? If it was a matter of composition, it'd read Napoléon."

"Hey, what is this?" demanded Sabin, gathering back all of his money.

"And it says Jeff Davis, and I quote . . . 'with brilliant use of artillery and swift maneuvers carried the promises of equality, liberty, and fraternity to the peoples of Austria and Prussia.' Mister Buchman, you are under arrest for treason!"

The colonel placed the book under his arm and put his gloved hand on Buchman's shoulder. Two of the colonel's men emerged from the aisles of books. As the colonel escorted Buchman out the door, Buchman smiled at Solomon.

"You were right, Solomon. Somebody did read it. Just a mite sooner than I'd expected."

Solomon stood outside Sabin's bookstore and watched the soldiers take Buchman, Hegel, and the caravan down Fifth Avenue.

May, 1864

Solomon sat on a boulder, his hands over his face. He spread open his hands and blinked. The fire had burned itself out. A few of the charred bodies, lying in heaps around the rock, still moaned in their last moments of life. He looked himself over. His brand new blue uniform was black and torn. The skin on his legs and arms had blistered from the fire. Solomon's heart was filled to the brim with every emotion, although the two predominant feelings were mean and sick.

His hands shook so he couldn't hold his pipe.

A man in a long gray coat and Confederate officer's uniform rode a white horse out of a thicket not affected by the fire. A hundred yards away, across from the rider, several hundred federal soldiers cautiously stepped over smoldering bodies and smoking tree limbs. The rider approached Solomon. His eyes were looking beyond Solomon, beyond the men in blue uniforms ahead of him.

"Ain't you a sight," said Solomon to the rider.

The rider stopped and gazed at Solomon.

"Yeah, I'm talking to you," continued Solomon. "You look like you're on your way to a Sunday dinner. Yeah, I'm talking to you, Mister Pretty Old Man On A Pretty White Horse. If you came to see the fightin', you missed it. Maybe you wanted to miss the fightin'. Don't want to get your fancy white horse and pretty gray suit all dirty. Yes, sir, I can tell you're one of them who's got it easy. You don't take orders. Hell, you looks like one of them old men that sits around and thinks up ways for men to die. Yeah, you ridin' around in those woods while all the while everybody else goes off and kills each other. Yep, just like the old man who tells me what to do. Only difference between him and you is his coat's blue. I told him I can do no fighting on account of my foot. It's safe back here, Solomon. Ain't no fightin' back here, Solomon. Just put the horses on the caissons, Solomon. He rides off to the woods just like you. Yeah, I bet you two got together and played cards the whole time. Yeah, somethin' like that, while all hell breaks loose. Yes, sir, Mister Confederate, sir. You missed it. You missed it when your boys just come runnin' out them bushes at me . . . scarin' the Jesus out of me with that yell of theirs. All your boys against little old me. And me, I don't even have a gun. Pretty brave order, Mister Pretty Old Man. But you didn't 'spect our boys come a runnin' out of nowhere at your boys, did you? No, sir. Never 'curred to you that we was lookin' all over the place for you. Well, sir, you come too late, and you missed it. But I saw it. Everybody shootin' and stabbin' everybody else. Half the time probably killin' their own. Then some fool sets my caisson on fire. Didn't bother to tell your boys not to set fire to a caisson, did you? No, you didn't. Well, you know what happens a caisson sets fire, all the powder in it goes *ka-blooey*. That's what set the whole damn' place on fire. And now here you are, lookin' it over like there ain't a thing wrong in the world, like you're riding on a Sunday afternoon on the way home to some fine ham dinner with two kinds of gravy, sweet potatoes, apples and melons mixed together. Yeah, I knows you. You sit around sipping fine liquor, talking big ideas, and in between them big words you think of things and tell us what to do. Damn you anyways. Why, if I was ten years younger, I'd jump right off this old rock and slap your behind. Yep. You white folks. You somethin' else. You probably joined the Rebs 'cause that gray old beard you're sportin' goes good with the uniform. Boy, you are a sight. Must think you're somethin' real special, huh? Probably think I belong in the field, cuttin' my fingers on your grubby old cotton plants. But it don't matter. If you were wearin' a blue suit, you wouldn't want me around, livin' and workin' in your big Northern cities, neither. Prob'ly suit you fine I was in some cotton field, totin' two hundred pound sacks. Free the slaves! Send 'em back to Africa. But I'll tell you this, Mister Old Man. I don't want to be your slave, an' I don't want to go to Africa. All I want is a good job, none this bein' a hostler in the artillery for thirteen bucks a month. No, sir, don't make no difference what uniform you got. You white folks is all the same. Pure trouble. And the only white man worth a damn . . . you know what you did? . . . you thrown him in jail. I'm sick of lookin' at you. Get

out of here. You heard me. Just turn that pretty white horse
around and get your old white hide out of here. Men's dyin'
here. It's too holy a place for an old goat like you. Now, git!"

The rider seemed to look through Solomon, oblivious to
his words.

"What's the matter with you? Ain't you heard a word I
said? You touched in the head or somethin'?"

Solomon looked around to see more federals tiptoe out
through the bodies and smoldering fires. Suddenly, a thousand men in gray and butternut coats rushed out of the woods
and up to the rider.

"Here you go again," continued Solomon. "Just don't
know when to stop, do you? Bad enough as it is, and you got
to make a bigger mess."

"You, there! Shut up!" shouted one of the men in gray at
Solomon.

"Go back, General! Go back!" said another one of the men
in gray to the rider.

The rider blinked his eyes and seemed to awaken from his
trance. He rubbed his chest, and then looked around, perplexed. He focused and smiled kindly at Solomon.

"You're hurt, sir. You should retire from the field."

He looked to his men and slowly pointed toward the federal troops.

"Go back, General Lee, go back!"

The rider turned his horse and quickly went back into the
thicket. The Confederate Army let out a deafening yell and
charged the Union Army.

Solomon covered his ears and muttered: "Damn!"

Herman Buchman sat, surrounded by soldiers. The President's eyes were tired and old, but as they read over the specific
charges against Herman, they became bright and mischievous.

Lincoln suddenly let out a loud laugh and began to guffaw uncontrollably. He collected his composure and grinned.

"Captain Holmes, let me see the book in question."

The President flipped open the book and began to read to himself. He laughed and looked at Buchman.

"I see you've got General McClellan burning Moscow while retreating from the Confederate advance. That explains a lot of things."

"It does?" asked Herman.

"Well, he sure wasn't anywhere close to Richmond." Lincoln closed the book and put it in the desk drawer, next to the writings by Bill Nye. He scribbled on a paper and handed it to the captain who read it before passing it to Buchman.

Buchman didn't read the page fully, but he did notice the word **pardon**.

"Thank you, Mister President."

"What you've done isn't right, Mister Buchman," said Lincoln. He then grinned broadly. "But it sure is funny. I look forward to your . . . how shall I say this . . . accurate version of recent events."

Buchman tucked the pardon into his pocket and hurried out of the office. The President's secretary, John Hay, finished taking his notes.

"The Army's destroyed the entire run of Buchman's HISTORY OF THE REBELLION," said Hay. "So, we don't have to worry about it causing any trouble. I'm curious, though. Besides its being funny, why'd you let him go?"

The President stroked his chin and answered slowly. "Not that anyone noticed. Still, somebody might, and things can get complicated. I don't want to take any chances with the German vote."

Chapter Seven

November, 1866

"As you were, Private."

Solomon lowered his hand from his forehead and sat back down at the desk. Colonel Gregory placed a stack of correspondence in front of him. "I'll need copies of the first three letters . . . there on the top . . . by tomorrow morning. The rest can wait." Captain James nodded to Solomon. Solomon liked the handsome young captain and hoped that his own dear daughter would have found a husband with his qualities. He smiled back and watched the white colonel dust off his riding coat.

"Trouble in Omaha?" asked Gregory.

"That's right, sir. Army sent in the Sixth cavalry."

"Funny. The Sixth was supposed to hook up with the Fifth."

"Don't s'pose they want us colored troops in downtown Omaha," said Captain James.

Colonel Gregory looked out the window of his office.

"No, I don't suppose they do. All the same, the Ninth cavalry is as good as any outfit in the territory. But there may be more to it than that, Captain. I heard we may get some new orders. Maybe by the end of the week. Some of the Cheyennes have been acting up. Someone's been selling them Army issue rifles. Probably whisky, too."

"Beggin' your pardon, Colonel, but where that'd be? I don't rightly know where all the tribes are yet."

"Pull down volume two of McKinney's INDIAN TRIBES OF NORTH AMERICA there. Look up the Cheyennes."

Solomon pulled the square volume off the shelf and opened it up to the title page. He wanted to make sure that it didn't have the Buchman imprint before handing the book to Captain James. He then returned to copying the official correspondence of Colonel Gregory.

"I'm not privy to the particulars of the assignment, Captain. It's going to be in the panhandle of Texas, next to the Indian Territory."

Solomon looked up from his writing. "Texas, sir?"

Colonel Gregory smiled. "Yes, Texas." He then looked to Captain James. "So, what about this trouble in Omaha?"

The captain closed the book and looked at the colonel. "Not much to tell, really, sir. You know they're puttin' in tracks there, for the railroad. Well, some man comes along and starts gettin' to all the boys workin' the track. He tells 'em to have a strike for more money and to get themselves a labor union. Nobody paid much attention, not at first, anyway. But that night, he sets out a bunch of pails of beer and gets the boys all back together again. Well, they all drank up the beer and, not having much else to do, stood there and listened while some of the boys went off and brought more pails of beer. This union fella . . . called himself an organizer . . . he tells 'em how bad they got it, and they all started to feel real sorry for themselves. 'Course, they drank up on account of feelin' so bad. Then this organizer tells them that they ought to get mad about how bad they got it. So, they drank up more beer 'cause now they're good and angry about how sad they felt. Next thing you know, they start tearin' up the town. I've heard some about what they did, but I don't know for sure, Colonel. I heard that they tore down the jail, and busted up a saloon. A teamster told me that they leveled the whole damned town. By the time the Sixth pulled in, they was all back at work, layin' down track and didn't know nothin' about it. Like it never happened."

"So, who's this fellow, this organizer?"

"Nobody knows."

"Buchman," muttered Solomon.

"Excuse me, Private?" asked the Colonel.

"Um, nothin', sir."

Buchman burped and looked down at the plate on the table. The horseradish coagulated with the blood from his prime rib, and the butter on the bits of uneaten potato had become translucent, like a thin coat of lard. The empty pails were stacked in the form of a one-dimensional pyramid in the center of the table.

"And so," said Kennedy. "The boss brings in the Chinamen."

Buchman hadn't been this tipsy since his college days in Jena. He also hadn't been paying much attention to his fellow organizers.

"Yeah," said Anderson, "so what d'ya do?"

"What could we do?" shouted Kennedy. "Had no choice but to shoot 'em. The rest ran off the next mornin'. Boss had to listen to us, then."

"You shot the Chinamen?" asked Buchman.

"Had to, Herman," said Kennedy. "Otherwise, the boss would've used them to lay down the ties and track."

"You shot them?"

"Ain't no big thing, Herman. Just Chinamen. They work for less money, and, 'cause they ain't got nothing better to do, they work too hard. Makes us look bad."

"Couldn't you have gotten them to strike?"

"My boys don't want to work with no heathen Chinee," laughed Kennedy.

"They may not be Roman Catholics, Mister Kennedy. But I've read some of their writings. They were available in Germany. And I've yet to see any English translations. Why, they have a magnificent culture!"

"If that's so, they ought to stay in China!" said Anderson, lighting his cigar.

"We had to do the same thing in Denver," said McGaw, putting down his mug of beer. " 'Cept the boss brought in niggers. And we told him, the Knights of the Union don't work with no niggers."

"You shot the black men?" Buchman no longer felt the alcohol from all the beer he'd drunk. He felt only anger.

"No, sir!" said McGaw. "Miners don't have no guns. Too dangerous. Explosives and dust. Now, railroaders. Sure. You got redskins all over the place."

"What d'ya do?" asked Anderson.

"Nothin' much, really," said McGaw, smiling. "Just strung a couple up. They got the picture and made tracks. You can be sure of that!"

"You what!" shouted Buchman.

"Defendin' rights ain't always a pretty picture, Herman," said Anderson. "You bein' a revolutionist and all, you ought to know that."

"But they are the very people the revolution is about," said Buchman. "They are the proletariat."

"Niggers and Chinamen ain't no proletariat. Hell, they ain't even people, Herman," said McGaw.

Buchman glared at the men.

"I don't think you boys understand what Herman's talking about," said Kennedy, "and I don't blame you, 'cause none of us except Herman, here, has been to a university. What he's trying to say is that we ought to quit foolin' around and get down to business. It's one thing, to print up pamphlets that explain our position on things. And you did a bang-up job on that, Herman. But the point our friend is trying to make is that, if we're going to do it right, we're going to have to go after the bosses. And maybe their families. We take down a few bosses, the rest will fall in line double quick. That's what you were trying to do in Omaha, right, Herman?"

Buchman tried to speak but didn't get the chance.

"Damn' straight," said Mahoney, commenting for the first time. "Buchman's right. Get down to the meat of it and kill the bosses. Here's to Buchman!" Mahoney raised his glass, as did the entire table. They drank and belched. Herman just looked at them.

McGaw rubbed his belly. "Hell, we get the bosses in line, we'll make them send all those Chinamen back to China."

"Why bother. Send 'em straight to hell," said Anderson.

"And them jungle bunnies!" said Kennedy.

"I'll drink to that!" shouted Mahoney.

"Excuse me, gentlemen," said Buchman. Now he felt weak and sad.

"Go ahead, Herman," laughed Anderson. "Hotel's got one of them new flush toilets down the hall."

"Yeah. And be sure to knock. Just 'cause you're a Communist don't mean you can use the john same times as everybody else!"

They laughed, and Buchman went out the back door. He steadied himself and went into the livery stable.

" 'Ev'nin, Mister Buchman," said the stable boy.

Buchman fished a gold dollar out of his pants pocket and tossed it to the boy.

"Get my wagon ready."

"But it's midnight. You shouldn't ought to be ridin' at night."

"Please."

"All right."

Within the hour, the horse aimlessly pulled the wagon past

the city limits and then stopped pulling. It didn't recognize the noises coming from the driver as meaning to go ahead, to the right or left, or even to stop. In fact, it had never heard the sound of human snoring at all. At the same time, McGaw, Kennedy, and Mahoney stepped out of the hotel and into the street looking for Buchman.

"Hey, what's this?" said Kennedy, bending his leg and looking at the bottom of boot.

"Horse puky I imagine!" laughed McGaw.

"No, look," said Kennedy.

They looked down and by the hotel's porch lights saw Buchman's entire run of *What You Should Know About the Knights of the Union* strewn about in the mud and manure.

Chapter Eight

January, 1867

Solomon sneezed and could barely see though his watery eyes. He took off the buffalo robe and covered himself with some canvas. He immediately felt better. The wind was cold, but it was worth it. He'd quit sneezing and could see clearly.

A shallow snow covered the dried grassland, and the clouds were bright, thick, and promising more snowfall. Solomon pulled back on the reins of his sway-backed old mare and looked around. In the distance, he saw a grove of cottonwoods. He looked behind. The four pack mules were content and even seemed to enjoy their burdens. He then focused on the snowy plains beyond the mules to make sure that he was still ahead of Colonel Gregory, Captain James, and eight others from his unit. Eleven to one seemed like good enough odds, and Solomon liked any plan that was simple. He was supposed to ride ahead, make sure this man was the one buying guns and whisky, wait around for an hour, and then have the colonel and some of the boys ride in to arrest him.

Solomon gently flung the reins and the old sway back moved a little faster toward the cottonwoods. In an hour's time, he could see smoke coming from the chimney of the cabin nestled in the trees. He growled when he saw a Confederate flag hanging limply on a pole ten feet away from the cabin.

He didn't have to call to the cabin. A man stepped out with a long-barreled rifle. Solomon's blood rushed through his veins, and his throat tightened when he saw the man.

"Where's Crocker?" shouted the man.

"Mister Crocker, he got the fever. They sent me in his place."

"I don't deal with strangers. Especially black 'uns."

"Suit yourself. I'll just take all this whisky and all these rifles right back where I got 'em."

The man came up to Solomon's mules and started to open the canvas packs. Solomon pulled up the collar on his shirt to cover his mouth.

"Damn. You got Colt repeaters." The man then took out a jug, pulled off the cork, took a swallow, and spat it out. "Same bad whisky, though. All right. You wait here."

The man went into the cabin, returned with a large, felt bag, and handed it to Solomon. Solomon looked in the bag and saw the gold coins.

"Count it, if you can," said the man. He squinted his eyes and studied Solomon. "I know you?"

Two Cheyenne warriors stepped out of the cabin. One of them had to steady himself on the threshold.

"Don't think so," said Solomon, nervously eyeing the warriors. Seven more warriors came from out of the grove of cottonwoods. Then twenty-five more. There were no women among them. This was a war party, and Solomon hadn't expected to find them here.

"Well, start unpackin' 'em."

"Ain't no teamster. You can unpack 'em yourself."

"Got yourself a smart mouth, don't you?"

"I just make the trade. No packin', no unpacking."

The man waved to the warriors and pointed to the mules. They opened the packs and threw the rifles to the ground.

"No, no, no!" shouted fat man. "Those are expensive." He gathered up several rifles and rushed them to the cabin while the warriors opened a jug of whisky and drank.

A warrior with a very large headdress walked up to one of the warriors putting a jug to his lips and knocked it from his hands. He shouted angry words and pointed to the guns and to the trees. The drunken warrior looked down, ashamed, and then began to carry guns to the trees. Solomon was glad that the powder was really only ground-up charcoal. Still, the odds had turned bad. He looked off to the hills.

The man approached the warrior with the large headdress. "Well, Chief. Time to pay up."

The chief frowned and waved to one of his band in the trees. He ran forward with a saddlebag. On it was written: **U.S. Post Office**.

The man opened the saddlebag and smiled. "Good."

"How many Cheyennes you got here, anyway?" shouted Solomon.

The man frowned. "None of your business."

"Is so. Crocker wants to know. Make sure you got enough. Maybe you need more."

"That so? The chief here's got forty-six men. And you're right, there ain't enough guns, so you can turn yourself right around and go get some more."

"Come mornin', sure enough will."

"Well, you stay with the chief here. You ain't comin' into my place."

The man stomped back into his cabin and closed the door. Solomon looked back to the hills and wondered how he was going to get word back to the colonel. A gust of wind blew against him and, following it, snow.

The Cheyennes had braced poles against the cottonwoods and thrown robes over the poles to block the wind. They had the beginnings of a good fire. Solomon tied down his horse and mule team and wandered over to the fire. His stomach began to churn, and his eyes began to itch. His hosts were using buffalo chips to fuel their fire. The storm was getting stronger, and Solomon swallowed hard before marching up to the fire.

Solomon toasted his front and then his back before walking away to catch his breath. The chief laughed and pointed at Solomon. Solomon scowled back. He tried to look out onto the plains, but couldn't see through the snowfall. The colonel could arrive at any moment and discover, as Solomon had, that the odds had turned and not for the better. The chief was scolding two of his band for drinking, and the fire was starting to go out.

Fire! thought Solomon. *That might do it.*

He went over to a pile of dried buffalo chips and bent over to pick some up. He stopped, thought a moment, and then picked some up. He began to fling more into the fire. The Cheyennes started to shout and mock him, and he could feel the skin all over his body burn like the fire.

" 'Achilles's wrath, to Greece, the direful spring, of woes unnumbered, heavenly goddess sing!' " shouted Solomon at the top of his lungs. " 'That wrath, which hurled to Pluto's gloomy reign the souls of mighty chiefs untimely slain,' " Solomon continued, even louder than before.

"What's all the noise!" shouted the trader from inside the cabin. Solomon took a deep breath and started to chant.

" 'Whose limbs, unburied on the naked shore, devouring dogs and hungry vultures tore, since great Achilles and Atrides strove, such was the sovereign doom, and such the will of Jove.' "

The Cheyennes began to shout and laugh. Solomon started to choke, as if some giant hands were squeezing his throat. He had to jump away from the fire and run out into the snow. He gasped for air and couldn't control his heaving.

"Private," whispered a voice. "Over here."

Solomon couldn't move.

A body crawled up to him. It was Captain James. "Follow me." The body rolled over and crawled out into the storm.

Solomon moved slowly up a hill and then down into the ravine beyond. The farther he got from anything with buffalo about it, the better he felt. He could hear the Cheyennes shouting and laughing but could see only the flickering glow of the fire. The colonel and his men were standing by their horses.

"How many?" asked the colonel.

"Couldn't tell," said the captain.

"Forty-six," said Solomon. "Forty-six hostiles."

"And is this our man?"

"Yep. Saw him do the tradin' with my own eyes."

"You get his name?"

"Nope. Didn't have to. I know him. His name's Glubb. Jack Glubb. Used to come around us colored folk in Washington City. Get us work. Actin' all nice and concerned about us, and, when he got us where he wanted us, *bang*, put us in chains and sold us for slaves down in New Orleans."

"Did he recognize you?"

"Came close."

"Corporal Salem!" said the colonel.

"Not so loud," said Solomon. "Sir."

"Salem, get back to Colonel Grierson and apprise him of the situation at once. And for God's sake, get reinforcements. With any luck, we can catch two birds with one stone. Private Freeman. You'd best get back in there before they come looking for you. Good thing they had that fire. Made us slow down and do some scouting. And we could hear your shouting. What was that all about?"

"Just recitin' something I read . . . with a real good friend,

66

a long time ago. Hoped you'd hear it."

"Rest of you, fan out. We need to keep an eye on their movements," said the colonel.

Solomon returned to the fire and sat a good way off. Even so, he was close enough to have watery eyes and itching skin. The Cheyennes sat together and sang a low chant, as though in prayer. It seemed to Solomon that they were good-looking men and as noble an enemy as a man could desire. These weren't gray-clad Rebels out to form a government or society built up on the backs of slaves, but men with genuine grievances.

When they were done praying, they passed a large skin pouch around, each taking out a piece of dried meat. They tore off pieces of the meat and chewed slowly. The chief got up and came to Solomon. He held the pouch down to him.

"This ain't buffalo, is it?" asked Solomon, reaching into the bag. He took out a piece of the dried meat and held it to his nose. When he didn't sneeze, he took a bite and began to chew. "Elk, mixed with some kind of berry," said Solomon. "And fat. Thank you."

The chief looked amused, but tenderly so, at Solomon before going back to his men.

The storm got louder, and the snow formed banks around Solomon. He couldn't just sit there, and he couldn't go to the fire, so he went over to a side of Glubb's cabin and wrapped himself in all the canvas he could find. It was going to be a long night, and the next morning even longer.

Solomon got up and started to pack his mules. The sun wouldn't come up for another thirty minutes, but the clouds glowed brightly with snow, and he could easily see his way around. Two Cheyenne sentries watched him with curiosity while the rest tossed in their blankets. Solomon slowly pulled the buffalo rifle out of its holster strapped to the horse and made sure that the charge was dry. He'd never seen a rifle this large and could barely lift it. The sentries looked on with mild interest at the size of the weapon as well.

Solomon tied the bits to each of the mules and attached the rope to his saddle horn. He then climbed up onto his horse, waved to the sentries, who in turn nodded back. His plan was to move out, before the trouble started.

He heard galloping horses. The sentries started to shout excitedly, and bodies sat up. Solomon pulled out the buffalo gun and held it firmly. The first patch of light illuminated the bright clouds. The cavalry came from all directions. The Cheyennes shouted and jumped up. Glubb opened the door, looked around, and slammed it shut. Solomon heard bolts being slid and things being thrown against the door.

Colonel Gregory shouted: "Open fire!"

The Cheyennes went into the trees. Solomon heard a volley of rifle fire from the other side, and the Cheyennes, now in fewer numbers, came back out of the grove. They went to the horses.

"Charge!" shouted the voice of Colonel Grierson.

Mounted troopers raced in and were all over the Cheyennes. The braves scurried helplessly between the soldier's horses as the soldiers threw ropes around them.

A long rifle barrel slid out between two boards in the cabin door. It fired and knocked the hat off Colonel Gregory. The colonel threw himself to the ground and reached for his revolver. Solomon grunted as he lifted the buffalo gun up to his shoulder and took aim at the door. Captain James came out from the grass with a small detachment on foot. They ran toward Solomon.

"No, don't . . . !" shouted the captain. Solomon ignored him and pulled the trigger. The rifle went off, and Solomon was knocked backward and off his horse. The cabin door splintered into three parts and disintegrated. The report startled the mules that began to bray and kick at the captain's men.

The actual battle was over as quickly as it had begun. Solomon was dizzy and tried to sit up. He heard Glubb shouting insults, and Gregory ordering that the prisoners be tied up. Solomon's arm hurt terribly, and he couldn't move it. He could hear several soldiers angrily shout at the kicking mules.

"Damn' thing broke my leg!" shouted one.

"Kill it!" shouted another.

"It kicked him in the stomach," shouted yet another.

Captain James knelt down beside Solomon and pulled him up. Solomon could not move his arm.

"My arm. It's broke."

"Serves you right, fool," said the captain. "You don't go shootin' no big gun on the back of a horse. 'Specially no big gun. Hell, another inch wider in the barrel and it'd qualify as ordinance. Damn you, old man. Lucky you ain't dead." The captain shook his head. "Looky, what you done!"

Solomon blinked and looked around. Glubb stood in his underwear, his hands tied behind his back. The Cheyennes not dying in the snow were tied to Corporal Salem's horse and were under guard. Solomon's pack mules still kicked and brayed. Around the mules, some of the soldiers rubbed bruised arms and legs, or lay in the grass with their hands on their stomachs.

"Wouldn't've had no casualties at all, if you hadn't gone off and shot that rifle," muttered the captain. "And you ain't gonna find your horse again. Not in a hundred years. Prob'ly in Saint Louis by now."

Solomon moved his arm. It wasn't broken, after all. But a surge of pain rose from his shoulder, and he fainted.

Hugh Buchman looked out the thin pane of glass in his dormitory room. The sun suddenly broke through the speeding clouds, and a fierce light glared up from the snow covering the lawns of the Harvard campus. Hugh closed his eyes and let the light warm his face. He treated himself to a full minute of the light before sitting down at the desk to finish his required reading. There was a timid but welcome knock on the door, and Hugh pushed back from his desk. "Who is it?" He waited for an answer. He went to the door and opened it. An older man scurried down the hall toward the stairway.

"Hey there!" said Hugh. "What do you want?"

The older man stopped, but didn't turn around. "I was looking for Hugh Buchman."

"Well, you found him."

The man turned around. He was pale and nervous.

"What can I do for you?"

"My name . . . my name is Herman Buchman."

Hugh scratched his head and smiled. "You're my father? My real father?"

Herman Buchman looked down at the floor.

Hugh extended his hand. "I'm real glad to meet you. Come on in. I sure have a lot of questions for you."

"I expect you do," said Herman, his voice breaking mid-sentence.

Herman went into Hugh's room. The desk was covered with papers. He fingered a book bound in black cloth. "BLACKSTONE'S COMMENTARIES," he said.

"Yeah. I've been studyin' law. It's what you do at Harvard, I guess. Still, I don't know, though."

"Don't know?"

"Well, my folks. My adopted folks, they think I should go into law. And I might just do that. But I've been sittin'

70

around reading most of my life. What with all those books you sent me. I've got a mind to go West and take a look around. Do some kind of real work."

Herman stood silently, again looking down at the floor.

Hugh waited for a while, and then pointed to a chair. "Set 'er down. You look like you've seen a ghost."

Herman sat down. "You have her eyes and mouth. And her good temper."

"My mother, you mean?"

Herman nodded.

"Well, I sure didn't get my height from you," said Hugh, smiling.

"I'm afraid you didn't get much from me at all." Herman's eyes were wet, and his hands were shaking.

"So, you've come to apologize?"

"Yes. Not just that. I'd like to. . . ."

"Make it up to me?"

Herman was silent. A tear rolled down his cheek.

"You know," said Hugh, "some gents I know . . . men who were adopted as children . . . have gone around like sour old mules about it. And I'd be lyin' if I said that I didn't sometimes wish you'd come around and take me with you. Usually when I got in trouble with my folks. But, really, it never bothered me, not like it did some fellers I know. I don't need an apology. And you don't need to make anything up to me."

Herman rose to his feet. "I shouldn't have come."

"You don't have to go. I'm not mad, or nothin'. I liked all those books you sent. And I really liked your letters. Really. It was a lot better than if you were dead, or didn't even care."

"I shouldn't have sent you away."

Hugh smiled. "You know that book you sent me on my ninth birthday, CURIOSITIES OF OTHER LANDS AND PEOPLE. I loved that book. In fact, I've been thinkin' about

that new area of study called *anthropology*. Anyway, this book
says that there are some tribes in Africa where the men raise
the children and the women run the whole show. My point is,
given your choices, the way things are here in this land and
with these people, you had to do . . . well . . . what you had to
do."

Herman hung his head. "I wouldn't trust the information
in that book."

"Why not?"

"It's a long story." Herman looked up and put his hands
on Hugh's shoulders. "How did you get so wise for such a
young man."

Chapter Nine

March, 1868

Captain James lowered his hand. His men threw the blanket over the white soldier as he stepped out onto the street. The soldier dropped his lamp, and its glass shattered on the road.

"Hey!"

They tied the blanket with rope, carried their bundle into the stockade, and gently laid it on the floor.

"Billy! Quit foolin' around!" shouted the voice in the bundle.

Captain James quickly took a key off the wall. The lamps were down low, and he had to feel his way once he got into the cell blocks.

"Who's that?" growled a drunk.

The captain fingered around the lock and, feeling the keyhole, slid the key into it. The lock clicked, and he swung back the bars. He grabbed the arm of the man inside and pulled. The man pulled his arm back. The captain reached in, grabbed, and pulled again.

"Ouch!" cried Solomon.

The captain held tight and pulled Solomon out of the cell. He threw Solomon out into the office and slapped his hands around Solomon's mouth. Solomon's eyes were wide with terror. When he recognized the captain, he relaxed. The soldier was still shouting for help, and the rolled-up blanket squirmed around on the floor. The captain put his forefinger over his lips and cocked his head toward the door. Solomon hobbled his way outside. Three of the 9th cavalry took his arms and carried him quickly into the darkness between the stockade and the barracks. Captain James looked up and down the street, and closed the door. Lamps were being turned up, and windows began to glow in all the nearby buildings.

The men left Solomon in the dark and rushed back to their barracks. A hand grabbed his arm.

"Come on!" said the captain's voice quietly.

Solomon hobbled along until he was pushed forward. He bounced off a large body that jerked and then let out the unmistakable sound of a horse snorting.

"What's goin' on?" asked Solomon.

"Gettin' your sorry old hide out of here, that's what," said the captain. "Here, put your hands up there. Got the horn? Now pull. Didn't I tell you they'd hang you for shootin' a white man? Didn't I?"

"I should have killed him."

"You in?"

"I'm in."

" 'Course he needs killin'. And they's gonna hang him. But, no, you got to go off and get some of that sweet revenge. Didn't I tell you it's against the law for any of us to shoot a white man. No matter what for. And you shootin' him in the back side . . . right there in the courtroom so everyone could see you done it with that buffalo gun. Damn you! Scatterin' his hindquarters all over me and Salem. Here's the reins. The boys and me put some greenbacks and beans in your saddlebag. Don't know why I'm helpin' you exceptin' I don't want to see no boy from the Ninth get his neck stretched. Ought to let you hang, 'cause I'm still pickin' bits of butt out of my hair. Now, get! Get far as you can! And don't come back. They're gonna be looking for you . . . looking real hard."

Solomon dug his heels into the horse and rode off in the dark. Captain James raced around to the front. Colonel Gregory stood in the doorway with a lamp in hand, still in his night robe and sleeping cap.

"Here, now. What's all this noise about, Captain?"

"I don't know, sir. I just got here myself."

Captain James rushed inside the stockade and untied the soldier, who blinked in the dim light and smiled.

"Boy, I sure am glad to see you."

"Who done this to you?"

"Don't know. But I got me an idea. Probably some of the boys from the Sixth."

"Yeah, probably."

The captain gave the lamp more wick and took it back outside. He waved to the colonel. "Just some fellers from the Sixth foolin' around!" he shouted.

The colonel frowned and closed his door. The guard stepped back outside and dusted off his pants.

"Prisoners all right?" asked Captain James.

"Yeah. They ain't goin' nowhere," said the soldier, rolling himself a cigarette.

The captain handed the guard the lamp and walked down the street. He looked around and saw the guard smoking in the lamplight.

Solomon rode through the tall grass and up the hill. His eyes began to itch. The horse was startled by the train speeding through the valley and came to a sudden stop. Solomon saw a herd of buffalo running alongside the train. He watched as heads popped out of the passenger car windows. Puffs of smoke rose from the windows, and buffalo began to fall over. In a moment Solomon could hear the distant reports of gunfire. The train was soon a spot on the horizon, and the grassland was covered with dead buffalo.

"Good!" shouted Solomon. "Serves you right! Come on, horse, take me to Saint Louis."

Mrs. Franklin wrapped a towel around her hand and then reached into the oven. She brought out a steaming pie and put it on the windowsill. She looked out the window. Her husband Joseph had his hands on his hips and was laughing at Hugh Buchman, throwing a lasso.

"You want to be a cowboy, you got to know how use your wrist!" he shouted. "Little Joe, you show Hugh how to throw. Again."

A young boy took the rope from Hugh and began to twirl it around his head. Mrs. Franklin smiled and turned around.

"Would you like some more coffee, Mister Buchman?"

"No thank you, ma'am," said Buchman. "I was thinking I should get started. I can get in a good half day's ride. Any luck, I should be back this way in time for Christmas." Buchman rose and went over to the window.

"He sure is a good boy," said Mrs. Franklin. "He'll be ready to work for Mister Goodnight come time for the spring drive, just you see. Joseph, he'll watch out for him."

Buchman smiled sadly and looked into Mrs. Franklin's young face.

"I really appreciate you taking him in. He really wants this. To work with the cows. He's got a good teacher."

"We're lucky Joseph's got a man like Mister Goodnight that'll throw him work," said Mrs. Franklin. "Ain't many ranchers west of the Pecos. And most of them don't want us colored folks hangin' 'round. Mister Goodnight, though, he's different. Even gave us this spread near his so's to keep Joe handy." She laughed nicely. "Not that it grows much. Whatever ain't sand is black and greasy." She paused and added thoughtfully: "But it's ours."

Buchman looked at the frying pan hanging on the wall, and then at the portrait of Lincoln. He smiled. Over the picture of Lincoln there was a violin hanging on the wall.

"You play? The violin, I mean."

"That old thing. Heavens, no," laughed Mrs. Franklin. "I've had that forever. Can't even tell you how I came by it. Joe put the new strings on it. Said if we're gonna hang it up, might as well make it look right."

"That's right!" thundered Joseph's voice in through the window. "Now do it again. Just like that!"

"What do you remember about that violin?" asked Herman pleasantly.

Chapter Ten

April, 1868

"And just what am I going to do with the works of Immanuel Kant?" argued Mr. Roeslin. He sat behind the counter of his bookstore, frowning at the set of books in front of him. "And it's in that fancy German script. How's anyone gonna know what it says?"

"That's the point," said Buchman. "I mean . . . ah . . . that being in the fraktur script, your German customers will snap it up. It'll remind 'em of home."

"Germans 'round here read the Roman alphabet, Herman. This . . . the binding's full tree bark calf. And it sure would look nice over the fireplace. So, what's this Kant all about, anyway?"

"German philosopher . . . around the time of Frederick the Great. Refuted the arguments of David Hume. The Scottish philosopher."

"A German arguing with a Scot? I don't know, Herman. It sounds like the transaction at hand, a great deal of discussion with nothing to show for it. For either party concerned."

Herman shook his head sadly and pulled another set out of his box.

"Then how about this set of Goethe. In English."

"Now that's more like it. Plays and novels that folks in Saint Louis can read. How much?"

"Five dollars?"

"Five dollars! I'll give you a buck fifty."

"Done."

"Oh, and before I forget, bring me in some more of those pamphlets, the tracts you wrote against the Knights of Union and Knights of Labor. The railroad boys love 'em, and the men going to Denver to work the mines buy up the rest. They say that if their bosses see 'em reading it, they get a dollar raise and are scheduled nine-hour shifts."

Roeslin spun around on his stool and pulled a volume off the shelf of books behind him. He opened the cover and took out some money from the hollowed text of THE MILL ON THE FLOSS. Roeslin then laughed. "I forgot," he said. "And I knew I would, so I put it in here to remind me." He took out a folded-up piece of paper that had been tucked in with the greenbacks. Herman was confused. "Here," said Roeslin. "Your partner, Mister Freeman, left this for you."

Herman snatched the note out of Roeslin's hand and unfolded it. His eyes became bright and face animated.

"He's here!" shouted Buchman.

"Yep. Just last week. Got himself a job down by the river. 'Cause he can read and write, he's been doing inventory for the riverboats."

"You know which one?"

"He came by Monday. Said he'd been workin' on the *Ferry Queen*." Herman started for the door. "Hey, don't you want your money?"

May, 1868

"I hate it when you do that."

"Do what?" asked Buchman.

"Smile and don't say nothin'. You passin' gas?" asked Sol-

79

omon. "And another thing. This ain't the road to Austin. And if you're thinking about getting me anywhere near a buffalo . . . !"

"No. No buffalo."

"Well, if this ain't the road to Austin, what is it the road to?"

"To that little house over there."

Solomon looked down the road and could see the house.

"You've been here before, haven't you? Hmm. Still tryin' to move that old copy of Alexander Pope's *Iliad*, huh. From the looks of all the children around there, be better if you gave 'em a deal on that run of McGUFFY'S READERs. And those are black children, Herman. They ain't got money. You sure about this? There you go again, smiling to yourself. You are passing gas, aren't you!"

The children began to shout and run up to Buchman's Conestoga wagon.

"You got the books for us, Mister Buchman?"

"Indeed, I do! Solomon, you mind gettin' in the back there. Should be a box labeled Franklin."

The children ran ahead of the wagon and into the house. Buchman pulled back on the reins when he got to the door, and the horse came to a sudden stop. There was a crashing sound inside the wagon.

"God damn it!" shouted Solomon. He stuck his head out between the canvas over the wagon seat. "You did that on purpose!" He put the box of books on the seat. "There's your dang' books."

Mrs. Franklin came out the door and smiled wistfully at Herman. "Howdy, Mister Buchman. Come on in!"

"Where's Hugh?"

"You missed him. Him and Joe are movin' the herd. Been gone 'bout three weeks now. Hugh's not comin' back, neither. He left you a letter. He was readin' to us about opportunities out West and decided he'd go on to Oregon. After they got the herd to Abilene. Said he was gonna send you another letter, care of me, when he got himself a place there. He's like you, Mister Buchman. Can't keep him to one place long enough to grow a beard."

Buchman sighed. "It's wanderlust, Missus Franklin. But he comes by it honestly. Got a healthy helping of it from both me and his mother."

"Well, don't you worry, none, Mister Buchman. He's a good-lookin' man, and some skirt's gonna tie him down. Good and tight. 'Spect you'd be long settled, too, if your poor wife hadn't gone off and died."

"I suspect you're right, Missus Franklin."

Mrs. Franklin then looked at Solomon. Her expression became concerned. "If you brung that man here to learn movin' cattle, I'm afraid there ain't no one here to teach him cowboyin'. An' I ain't got money to hire me a hand. Not yet, anyways." She then smiled brightly and threw her hands up. "Don't matter, though. You're all welcome to stay as long as you please. Come on in and I'll boil up some coffee." She turned and went back into the house.

"You go on ahead, Solomon," said Buchman. "I'll be in shortly. I'd be interested in making a trade of some books for a picture of Lincoln she's got hanging in the kitchen. Why don't you take a look at it and see what you think?"

"You want to swap some books for a picture of Lincoln? What are you going to do with a portrait of Lincoln in Texas? Last I heard, this place wasn't exactly in favor of bein' in the Union. Oh, I get it. They get that stuffy old Alexander Pope, and you sell that picture back up North. Good thinkin', Herman."

Solomon slowly climbed off the wagon and went inside.

Buchman opened the box of books.

"Now, Jubal," said Buchman to the Franklins' oldest boy, who was one of those still gathered about the wagon, "as I recall, you wanted a book about horses. Well, here's a very nice cloth edition about horses. Look at those colored pictures. Those are chromolithographs!"

Jubal smiled and took the book.

"Oh God! Oh God!" cried Solomon's loud voice from inside the house.

"And for you, Sarah," continued Buchman, "here's a book with pictures of women's dresses. Just like you wanted. I'm sorry all the women are white. Couldn't find one with Negro women. And you, Ezra. A book of fairy tales by a Danish man named Andersen."

Mrs. Franklin let out a cry, and the children looked at the house. Her sobbing was joined by the sound of Solomon's wailing: "Columbia! Columbia!"

"That's Mama cryin'!" said Jubal.

"How's he know her name?" asked Ezra.

The children ran to the house.

Buchman's eyes began to moisten. "Yes, run, *meine Kinder!* Run!"

Buchman wiped a crystal tear from the corner of his eye and listened. He looked at the horse. "That, Leibnitz . . . *that* is the kind of crying most pleasing to *Gott.*" He slapped his head. "What am I saying?"

Herman slowly led the horse over to the small corral. He heard Jubal's voice. "Can you play it?" He heard a loud sob from his friend, and then music. It was a song he'd heard the miners shout in ugly voices and with ugly words in San Francisco. The voices here were sweet. He thought about angels and closed the gate.

De Camptown races sing dis song, doo dah, doo dah,
Camptown race is five mile long.
Oh de do dah day!

PART TWO:

OF THE NEW LAND
1919–1920

Chapter One

Jack Buchman looked at the road ahead and frowned. It looked much like the road that had laid ahead for the last ten miles of his hike. His Army backpack suddenly felt thirty pounds heavier, and Jack stopped. He wondered if he hadn't somehow taken the wrong road and had come around to the very place he had started.

The herons standing in the swamps off to each side of the road looked exactly as they had the day before, when he'd started out from Burns on his way to Bang, Oregon. While the mountains looked a little closer, the rutted dirt road also looked exactly the same.

He felt at the leather patch covering part of his face and, sure that it was in its proper place, took a deep breath and continued to walk. For variety, he looked back at the road behind him. It, too, looked exactly like the road ahead, but without the dry mountains looming in the distance at the end of the road.

On the first night of his journey, Jack had camped off to the side of the road. The wetlands proved to be an unhappy campsite, and he had missed the chance of flagging down a wagon that had charged down the road in the early morning light. An hour into his trek this day, he heard the faint sound of a man swearing. The curses grew louder and were accompanied by the sounds of hoofs and rattling boards. Jack turned around and saw a very old man furiously working the reins of a horse that didn't seem to care what the old man was doing or saying and pulled a wagon at a constant snail's pace. The old man threw the reins down onto the horse and reached into his shirt pocket. He pulled out a cigarette and struck up a match on the stubble growing from his cheek.

"Excuse me!" shouted Jack. "Can you tell me how far is Bang from here?"

The old man cocked his head and closed one eye to study Jack as the wagon began to pass the man on foot. He then grinned and pointed ahead. Jack turned and saw a sign that read:

Bang
1 Mile

"Come on," said the old man, patting the seat beside him.

Jack stood and waited. The old man wasn't going to stop, and the wagon was already a short distance ahead of Jack on the road.

"I can't stop!" shouted the old man. "Took me an hour to get Kaiser Bill started, and, if I stop him now, he'll stay put till dinner time."

Jack ran double-quick up to the wagon, twirling off his backpack, and tossing it onto the bed of the wagon in one smooth motion. Without the pack, it was no trouble to get up to the front and climb aboard.

The old man looked at Jack's uniform and smiled.

"Doughboy, huh? You get over to France, or was you stuck at some base here in the States?"

"I got to France," said Jack.

"What's that thing you got on your face?"

"It's my wound. Got to keep it covered."

"Never seen a leather bandage before."

Jack looked ahead. He didn't want to talk about it and could feel the old man's eyes staring at his face. Away down the road, Jack saw a two-story brick building.

"That the hotel?" Jack asked.

"Yeah. The old Weidemeier place."

"How much for a room?"

The old man jerked his head back. "You can't stay there, soldier boy. Been closed down for forty years . . . 'cept to rats and things that crawl or slither."

"Well, can you tell me where the Blake place is?"

"Sure. Just down this road a piece. You'll have to walk up Stumbo Road about half a mile 'fore you take the fork to the left and go up the trail about another mile. Ain't nobody there, though. The hands all went into Burns for the horse show and race this weekend."

"How about the Buchman place?"

"Ain't been anybody there for forty years. I ain't sure it's even standing. Why'd you want to go there?"

"It was my grandfather's place."

The old man looked grimly at the road ahead. After a long silence, he scratched his head and reached around. He slapped an old Stetson hat on his head and looked at Jack. "Tell you what, son. Why don't you come on over to my place tonight? You can help me unload the wagon, and I'll let you take Kaiser Bill here tomorrow and you can ride around the valley. You can take yourself a look-see at things."

"I don't want to impose. . . ."

"Don't worry. You're not."

Jack looked at the road signs as they got closer to town.

"Dead Chinaman's Road?" asked Jack.

The old man didn't say a thing, but turned the horse down the road called Burnt Nutcracker Trail. They came to what had once been a fancy house. The paint had long since peeled away, and the roof was sagging inward. Several windows were broken on the second floor. The barn was leaning dangerously to the right, propped up by a number of blackened two-by-fours.

Kaiser Bill pulled the wagon to the porch and stopped. He shook his head and waited patiently for the old man to undo the harness and bit.

"Where you want these?" asked Jack, looking at the barrels and boxes in the back of the wagon.

"Just put 'em on the porch. Ain't nothin' that's gonna rot."

The old man freed Kaiser Bill from his trappings and slapped him on the rump. The horse stepped ahead and then stopped.

"Go on into the kitchen," said the old man. "I'll get the fire goin' and pull out some punch."

The house inside was as worn as the outside. The cloth covering the furniture was filthy. Jack found the kitchen to be in good working order, however. The old man went out the back door and returned with an armload of chopped wood. He began to stuff the smaller pieces into the woodstove, and then waited. When the fire was burning, he took two mugs off the cupboard. He jerked his head toward the door by way of explaining to Jack that it was time to go back outside.

The old man sat down on a broken rocking chair. Next to the chair was a half-consumed bottle of whisky. He snatched up the bottle and poured a little taste into each of the cups and handed one to Jack. Jack took a sniff at the cup and smiled.

"You know this stuff's illegal, don't you?"

"Yes. I know."

Jack took a sip and let out a cough. The whisky tasted only slightly better than gasoline.

"My supplier ain't quite got the hang of bein' a distiller yet," said the old man. "Reckon he's goin' get pretty good with all the practice he's gonna get."

Jack took another sip and winced.

"Sit down," said the old man.

Jack looked around and, seeing that there wasn't a chair, sat down on the steps.

"So, Hugh Buchman was your grandfather?"

"That's right."

"So, your father would be Herman Buchman the Second."

"Yep."

"I hear he's a pretty important fellah in state politics."

"I guess."

"How's about his adopted father, Ashton Blake? He still suckin' air?"

"Oh, yeah."

"He still a big mucky-muck in the Klan?"

Jack frowned and nodded. "Him and my dad."

The old man swallowed his whisky and lit a cigarette. He studied the young soldier. "So with your father and, for all practical purposes, his father bein' so powerful and connected and all, I reckon you got it made."

"I suppose. But. . . ." Jack let it go at that.

The old man smoked and looked over the valley. "But what?" he asked.

"We don't see eye to eye. Not any more," Jack said. "I used to think they were right. Mostly because I didn't know any better. But the soldier who found me in that trench was an Algerian, as big and black as they come. Risked his own life to save mine. And it was a French Jew who patched me up at the field hospital. And when I was in that hospital in Paris, the nurses were Roman Catholic. The way I figure it, the Klan's got it all wrong, and, what's worse, they're pretty damn' mean."

"That so?"

"That's the way I see it."

"So, you're goin' to do it on your own?"

"I guess."

The old man smiled wryly and drank more whisky.

"I was thinking I might try a little ranching on my grandfather's place," said Jack.

"I ain't so sure it belongs to your family any more, son," said the old man.

"So who's going to know I'm there?"

"You'd be surprised how much people know about each other when there ain't many people around."

They watched Kaiser Bill wander through the tall weeds. A cloud of geese appeared on the horizon and flew overhead before dropping into the marshlands a mile away from the old house. Jack began to stretch and look around, and the old man closed his eyes.

"Why don't you take old Kaiser Bill for a ride into town?"

"I'd like that," said Jack.

"I'll get some biscuits and gravy up about sundown. Best be back before it gets dark," said the old man, pulling his hat over his eyes.

Chapter Two

"Damn, these are great!" said Jack, grabbing another of the old man's biscuits.

"Don't go eatin' 'em all up before I put out the gravy," said the old man.

Jack put the biscuit back on the plate and watched the old man stir the milk and flour in the cast-iron Dutch oven. The old man took a bowl from the kitchen sink and poured in the gravy. Jack waited for the old man to take his biscuits and smother them with the sausage gravy before helping himself. The old man and Jack stuffed large forkfuls into their mouths and sat back in their chairs.

"This is even better," said Jack.

"You bet it is," said the old man.

The biscuits and gravy were consumed within fifteen minutes. The old man's idea for dessert was black coffee brewed in an old camp pot.

"That was really good," said Jack, looking down at his empty plate.

"Think so? Grab your coffee. Let me show you what's good."

Jack followed the old man out to the porch and was shocked by the darkness of the night that had fallen while they had been eating. Jack looked up and saw the stars. The sight overwhelmed him, and he sat down on the stairs.

They drank their coffee and watched as a quarter moon rose in the east.

"So," said the old man, when the moon had moved well

above the horizon, "what d'ya think of Bang?"

"What happened?" asked Jack. "All those empty build-ings!"

"It's a long story," said the old man. "And it has a lot to do with your grandfather, Hugh Buchman."

"My father didn't know my grandfather. And Grampa Blake refused to talk about him."

"Doesn't surprise me."

"Was my grandfather against the Klan?"

"I can't say that he was, 'xactly," said the old man. "Mostly 'cause he didn't know much about the Ku Klux Klan. In them days, the Klan was a real secret society. Not like it is now. Heck, it's downright fashionable to be a member of the Klan these days. Blake and your pappy must be sitting mighty pretty, what with all them university boys joining up and just about every city father in the whole Willamette Valley running in the door right behind them. But addressing your question directly, from what I know about Marshal Buchman, I think I could say that he was against the Klan and the kinds of things that the Klan stands for."

"So, can you tell me about my grandfather, Hugh Buch-man?"

"Well, since I'm the only man fool enough to live out here by myself, you might say I'm the local historian. And there ain't anybody else out here to contradict me, so I can tell you as tall or as lean a story as you please. Your grandfather, Hugh Buchman, was a pretty important figure in the story of Paradise Valley, and to understand his story you're goin' to have to hear the whole story. Of Bang and the whole of Para-dise Valley."

"I got all night," said Jack, looking at the moon.

"Well, son, I got to prepare you for the worst. But your

bein' a soldier who fought the Hun and all, I guess you ain't no pink-faced baby about the ways of the world. There comes a time when a man sees that the game is rigged against him. No lucky draw is going to change the course of the game. He's going to lose, and about the only thing he's got a say in is how he's gonna take it. Some fellers go down cursin' and hollerin', others go down with grins like a clown. Others still go down tight-lipped, squintin', and keepin' it all to themselves. Now, sometimes you see what's coming along before the losin' hand. You sign up to go off and fight a war . . . and sure as shootin' you get into a battle where you find yourself in a real bad spot. Well, you should have seen that comin'. That's what you signed up for. But sometimes that losin' hand kinda sneaks up on you. Other times, what's gonna get you is all around you, and you just don't see it. Well, that was the case with Hugh Buchman.

"Hugh wasn't one of the original settlers of Paradise Valley. Nope. Far from it. The Paiutes and other Indians that lived in the upper part of the Great American Basin never spent time in the valley. They believed the place to be haunted by powerful skookum. Whatever business they had hunting or fishing in the valley, they did *pronto* and then hightailed it out as quick as they could.

"The next folks to come to the valley came piecemeal at first. Old Frenchy, who most folks said was probably a runaway slave, claimed to be a Dominican national. And he had just enough accent to make you believe that it could be so. He became a guide for a number of the wagon trains headin' West. In fact, he brought the Reverend Catley and his family to Paradise Valley in the train of 'Fifty-Nine. And it was the right reverend who named the valley. After the war back East, the Campbells, a family from Mississippi who'd lost everything in the battle for Jackson, came along with a host of other

Southern families who'd also lost their farms and plantations to the war.

"There was considerable work to be done those first few years. Barns to be put up, fields to break in, boundaries to be set. But the mainstay of the region was without a doubt the bountiful game to be found in the hills and juniper forests of the High Sierras of eastern Oregon. After the snows of winter, there'd be plenty of water. But in the heat of the summer sun, it dried up quick. It wasn't exactly good farming country, but it was just fine for cattle and horses.

"Early on, the Reverend Catley used a tent on Sundays and called it the Paradise Valley Church of Christ. In those lean and building times, those Sunday get-togethers were the glue of the community. Everybody would wait for the reverend to open the flap to his tent. The men would talk business, and the women would put out a fine picnic dinner.

"The reverend had slated this Sunday afternoon to baptize one of the new babies in the valley and hoped that this gathering would also give, with the co-operation from the residents of Paradise Valley, the emerging township a name. This item on the agenda had been carried over from the weekly meeting the Sunday before as the residents had gotten too involved with the renaming of the sulphurous geyser that lay three miles out of town from The Devil's Cesspool to Angel Fountain.

"Old Frenchy, who'd come and pray and sing with the rest of them, even if he was a Roman Catholic, was admiring a new Colt revolver he'd ordered in the mail. Everybody saw how he was fooling with his new toy, but there was no way to suggest anything sensible to the Frenchman. He'd get all riled and swear in French, calling on the name of the True Cross or the Virgin to invoke a misfortune upon the recipient of his wrath. Well, Frenchy looked down the barrel and spun the fool thing around in his hand, and it doesn't take a genius to figure out what happened next.

"The pistol's discharge scattered some of Frenchy's right ear all over the reverend's tent. The pistol's report going off startled a team pulling a wagon full of children, and its driver jumped for his life, leaving the kids to scream for the mercy of great God above. They got the ride of their life. Most of the men in the town set off on their mounts to chase that wagon. The womenfolk had been setting out a larger selection of food than usual for the large picnic dinner after the Sunday preaching. The shot startled Haddie Montbatten, who was no small woman. It was said you could ride to Portland in about half the time it took to walk around this gal. Well, the shot made Haddie jump, and somehow or another she managed to stumble over Missus Weidemeier, who was about four foot tall and easy to miss. Well, Haddie Montbatten fell onto the end of the picnic table. The spread flew into the air, some of it flying halfway to Idaho.

"The womenfolk had to spend a great deal of time cleaning off the food and had few kind things to say about Haddie or old Frenchy. It's next to impossible to pull dirt from a pie and a roast chicken that's landed in the roadway, and, after setting in the mud where the horses had been, the food didn't smell too good, neither.

"All the same, the wagon full of children was recovered thanks to the eldest and best of them, Johnnie Campbell. Johnnie had climbed out of the wagon, jumped onto the backs of the team, and brought the whole parade to a standstill . . . as though he'd been trained in the circus. The right reverend cut out his usual hour of talk of fire and brimstone to a short and pointed thanks to Him above.

"Just before serving up the picnic, a few of the men decided that it might improve the general appetite to have

Frenchy dress up the side of his head. Jake McCaffrey, a butcher, was a self-taught surgeon and physician, fresh from the war back East. Old Jake just loved to cut off human limbs. His eyes glazed over, and he breathed mighty heavy while he removed the remnants of poor Frenchy's ear. Jake McCaffrey was the only man who had near ecstatic memories of the Battle of Gettysburg and especially its aftermath. Being a man from the South, he had plenty of limbs to crop. Once the ear was cropped, Haddie bandaged up Frenchy's head, and Frenchy went around looking like an overgrown cotton swab for several weeks.

"When everybody sat down at the table and looked over the meager rations that had not been ruined laid out before them, nobody seemed to have anything to say. Not even the right reverend. It was a sad-looking picnic dinner and hardly enough to feed a fasting monk, much less a hard-working township. Just then the little baby, Jessie Lang, who'd been born on the trail coming out, piped up loud and clear . . . 'Bang!' And so the township got its name.

"Well, there was hard work, prosperity, and before long Bang was a burg of no small importance to the State of Oregon. A family that had come from the German city of Hamburg, the Weidemeiers, had built up a two-story brick building that served as the general store, and hotel, and restaurant for the eastern part of the state. Just about everybody had a major ranch, and there was a big drive every year up to Pendleton to move the herds onto the trains for Portland or Spokane. There was even a newspaper, and we almost got us a bank.

"After a few years of profitable horse tradin' with the horses bred by Frenchy, the Mississippi man, Owen Campbell, was able to build the reverend a church, finance a good road north to Pendleton, and became the region's representative in the Senate of the State of Oregon. In fact, there was even talk, before all the trouble began, that Owen Campbell could have made it to the Governor's mansion. He began to spend less time in Bang and more time in Salem. It should come as no surprise that the right reverend kept an eye on the Campbell family while old Owen was away.

"But if Owen Campbell was the most important man in the valley, the fact is that the reverend was the most powerful and pretty much ran the whole corner of the state. You didn't get to live in Bang until the reverend gave you the permission. It wasn't that he'd tell a man he couldn't stay, but he wouldn't introduce a fellow he didn't like to the ranchers, and so a man ended up leaving town to find work. Bang didn't really need a government, thanks to the right reverend, but the reverend understood that it was in good form to have some kind of a city council, mayor, and all the political trimmings. And over a period of twenty years, he set this up like a maiden aunt puts together a high tea on a Sunday afternoon.

"Hugh Buchman rode into Bang in July with about twenty other men looking for ranch work. The Langs, Montbattens, and the rest had sent out word that more hands than usual would be needed for the cattle and horse drives to commence in early August. Buchman was a thin man and clean-shaven and easy to look at. He said he was the son of a bookseller back East, and from talkin' to him you knew him to be a soft-spoken and truly well-read gentleman. He and Johnnie Campbell became good friends and took to hunting elk together.

"On one of their hunting trips they set up their evening camp a little too late, after the sun had already set. They weren't paying much attention to the lay of the land and threw down some bunch grass and twigs to start their fire. The grass and twigs started to writhe and move around, and they came to understand that they had started their fire right on top of a rattler. The old rattler moved off some, but the two of them knew that they had to find and kill it now as it would come back into the camp to find its night-time lair. So, they lit up some bunch grass and chopped around the chaparral for an hour. Well, Hugh was bent over, looking through some moss and grass, and felt a sting on his behind. He jumped up swearing, sure that the rattler had given him a million-dollar bite. But it wasn't a snake, but his friend with a blunt knife who'd poked him in the butt. They laughed for hours, but never did sleep well that night 'cause they never found the snake in question.

"Whether it was that Hugh was a good hand with a team of horses or impressive with his ability to quote the sweet Bard of Avon, there was little doubt that the Reverend Catley took a liking to the young man and, sure enough, there was always going to be plenty of work for Hugh. The reverend even went so far as to offer the boy the sheriff's job.

" 'I don't know,' said Hugh. 'I'm not sure I'm cut out for law enforcement.'

" 'Relax, son,' said the reverend sternly. 'It's just a little something to keep the money rolling in during the months you're not cowboyin'. Besides, about the only crime in Bang is the occasional drunken brawl. If you can rope a cow, you can surely pull down a drunk.'

"And so Hugh Buchman strolled around Bang with a shining silver star hangin' on his chest. One of the advantages to the position was that with his new job, Hugh seldom got coated with dirt or animal hair from tip to toe. When he walked down the three streets of Bang, the womenfolk of all ages made sure that they had business outside.

"The gals would talk about Hugh at the soda fountain in Weidemeiers', and, if they weren't eligible to catch old Hugh at the altar themselves, they'd plot out just who was. Jessie Lang was Haddie Montbatten's nomination for the position of Hugh's wife.

" 'Jessie Lang's the one!' said mountainous Haddie.

"She slurped down the last of her soda and handed the glass back to the young Weidemeier boy. The other ladies at the fountain at Weidemeiers' wiped their chins.

" 'Excuse me?' asked Missus Campbell.

" 'The pretty young Lang woman,' said Haddie, pointing out the picture frame window at Buchman, who was standing on the porch of Weidemeiers' General Store. 'I've been going over and over in my mind, who shall we get for that fine young man. And the answer is as obvious as the nose on your face. Jessie Lang.'

" 'Jessie Lang? She's a proud one and thinks no small portion of her worth,' said Missus Catley.

" 'And she'd ruther be living with the high society in the capital,' suggested Missus Campbell. 'Or at least she should ruther be living in Salem. Such a flower is wasted out here.'

" 'I'd have been as happy as anyone if I had a catch like Sheriff Buchman,' said Haddie.

" 'There's no denyin' it,' said Missus Catley. 'They would be a pretty couple. And the children. What gorgeous children they would have. Still, Jessie's got a bushel of men to choose from. And it's gone to her head.'

" 'Being beautiful is a terrible hardship,' sighed Haddie.

" 'And you vould know?' said Missus Weidemeier, who was a few feet away at the counter, cutting a measure of cloth from the bolt.

" 'Still, Haddie has a point,' said the reverend's wife. 'The sooner Jessie's found her true place as a woman, all the better for her disposition and her eternal soul. And Hugh Buchman . . . my, a glorious match for Jessie. Or any woman. It wouldn't be sinful to help the Lord by doing a little of the footwork for him.'

"And so it was that the conspiracy was launched, and before the end of the week Jessie and Hugh were formally introduced. By the end of the month, Haddie and her co-conspirators had the Langs inviting Hugh over for one of their large Sunday dinners. Jessie and the other womenfolk had started to serve up the dinner, and, as was expected, Senator Campbell butted right in there with a political opinion to get everybody either all riled up or to jump on his bandwagon of the moment.

" 'Hugh, what do you think of all this suffrage business?'

"Hugh hadn't said a word all night and was now on the spot. The women paused in their serving and passing platters of food and focused their eyes on Hugh.

" 'Well, Senator Campbell, I seem to remember reading that history is chock full of very capable queens. Like Elizabeth in England. And Isabella of Spain. So, it seems to me that, if a woman can run a country, and it's been shown that they can, a woman could as easy take a part in a democratic government.'

"The womenfolk all smiled, especially Jessie, who was just about to place a full gravy boat in front of Johnnie Campbell.

" 'Women? Vote?' scoffed Johnnie. 'They got too much say in things already if you ask me.'

"Jessie released her hold on the gravy boat, and it landed right on Johnnie's lap. The Campbell boy let out a yowl and fell backwards in his chair, his feet kicking the table and rattling the works all around.

" 'Oh,' said Jessie sweetly. 'It wasn't boiling hot, was it?'

"As Johnnie was trying to dust the hot gravy off his pants, Jessie looked over to Hugh and saw him grinning like a beaver. He looked up at her, and their eyes locked. They quickly glanced away from each other, not willing to put their antes on the table. At least, not right then and there.

" 'Here, Rex!' shouted Johnnie.

" 'Rex is outside, like a dog should be,' said Missus Lang.

" 'I was gonna have him lick the gravy off my pants,' said Johnnie, smiling.

" 'Not at the dinner table, you don't!' said Johnnie's mother.

" 'That's disgusting!' said Missus Catley.

"Hugh and Jessie laughed and exchanged glances again. Johnnie looked at Jessie and let out a laugh.

" 'Butterfingers!' said Johnnie, looking at Jessie. He then went outside, shouting for Rex.

"The rest of the dinner went on with the senator speaking out against suffrage and the reverend adding the Lord's two cents' worth. All that Hugh and Jessie could do is try to take a look at one another when the other wasn't looking.

"It was plain that Hugh was plenty interested in Jessie, but no one could tell just what Jessie was thinking. The conspirators realized that dinners and introductions were no substitute for Cupid's arrow, and, for nature to take its course, Jessie and Hugh would have to have some time together. Alone, but not without a touch of chaperon. The solution presented itself when Senator Campbell announced that he would be taking a group of Oregon legislators into the hills around the valley for a good hunt.

"The hunting party had set up its camp, and the old men set about to the real point of their coming into the hills . . . to drink and talk politics. The women chased children in and out of camp and did the chores. That left the young folk free to do the hunting. Hugh and Johnnie began to saddle up, when Jessie strolled over to them.

" 'I don't see why the men get to do all the hunting,' said Jessie.

" 'Can you use a gun?' asked Hugh.

" 'Sure.'

" 'Then come on.'

" 'Hunting isn't proper for a young . . . ,' started Missus Lang. A severe blow in the back from Haddie's elbow knocked the breath out of her. Missus Lang looked accusingly at Haddie. Haddie furled her eyebrows, and Missus Lang suddenly got the picture.

" ' 'Scuse me,' said Haddie.

" 'Can I go?' asked Jessie.

"Missus Lang gasped for breath and waved her hands good bye.

"As Jessie and Hugh got to their horses, Haddie called out to Johnnie Campbell . . . 'Oh Johnnie, could you help old Aunt Haddie for a minute?'

" 'But I was just startin' out!'

" 'You can catch up to them,' said Haddie. 'You can track, can't you?'

" 'Jessie, you go ahead and take Peanut,' said Johnnie to Jessie. Johnnie winked at Haddie.

"One of the small children got a bee sting and began to wail, startling Missus Campbell who dropped the sandwiches. Missus Lang caught her breath, but tripped over the firewood.

" 'Let's get!' said Jessie, applying the spur.

"Well, some two hours later, Jessie and Hugh were hunting, moving along from tree to tree. A very large five-point buck was standing in the meadow, alert to their movements.

" 'I got him,' whispered Hugh.

"Hugh jumped out from behind a tree, but before he got his shot off, the buck began to prance away. Jessie came out from behind the tree and let go her shot. The buck bolted a few more times, and then collapsed.

" 'Great shot!' said Hugh.

"They stood over the buck pondering just what to do next.

" 'Why don't you go on back to camp and have them bring down some pack horses?' suggested Hugh.

" 'It'd be more fun if we just hauled it into camp ourselves.'

" 'Not a good idea, draggin' your kill. Tears up the meat and leaves a trail for cougar and wolf.'

" 'I'd just like to show them that I can hunt like a man.'

" 'Well, you've done better than that. You've proved you can hunt like a woman. But the proof ain't doing you any good out here in the pine trees. We've got to get the buck back to camp.'

" 'Let's flop it over Peanut.'

" 'But Peanut's a hunter, not a pack horse.'

" 'Just like a man! To put somethin' in a place and keep it there. How do you know Peanut won't pack the buck until you try?'

"Hugh scratched his chin and watched while Jessie brought Peanut over to the dead buck.

" 'Give me a hand,' said Jessie.

"They pulled up the buck and then pushed it onto Peanut's back. Just as they got the buck slumped up and over the saddle, Peanut reared back and jumped ahead. The buck fell off onto Hugh and Jessie, knocking them over and pinning them to the ground. Jessie started to laugh.

" 'You all right?' asked Hugh. He tried to push the buck off his chest but had little success and then began to laugh himself. Jessie continued to laugh until tears welled in her eyes. Just how long they laughed, who's to say? But like all good things, it had to end.

"They began to push at the buck together, but found that their arms alone didn't have the power to get very far, so they began to twist and turn their way out. At once they were face to face and real close together.

" 'Well,' said Hugh, 'your idea would've worked except for one thing.'

" 'What's that?'

" 'You didn't ask Peanut.'

" 'Didn't ask Peanut what?'

" 'His permission. Horses are more human than most people. And the first time you do somethin' with a person, you gotta ask permission.'

"Jessie smiled and looked thoughtfully into Hugh's eyes. 'Well, Hugh Buchman, would you mind terribly if I kissed you?'

" 'Here?'

" 'Shut up and kiss me!'

"When Johnnie Campbell caught up to them, he found them smooching under the buck. 'Well I'll be damned,' said Johnnie, surprising the lovers. 'I can understand your wanting a buckskin blanket. But you got to clean and tan it first.'

"As they walked back to the camp, the buck safely strapped to Peanut's back, Hugh nervously broached a subject with Johnnie.

" 'You ain't gonna tell everyone, are you?'

" 'That you both got stuck under a buck and started up to sparkin' and pettin?'

" 'That's right.'

" 'Hmm. Well, my silence don't come cheap, Hugh.'

" 'What if I agree not to whup you right up side the head?' said Jessie.

" 'That's good,' said Johnnie. 'But it's gonna cost you more than that. Let me think about it.'

"Hugh and Jessie spent the rest of the hunting trip out looking for firewood or out scouting for more game. The conspirators had succeeded! And as far as either Hugh or Jessie knew, Johnnie had kept his trap shut about what he'd seen. But they learned otherwise at their wedding shower.

106

" 'Why, goodness,' said Jessie, casting a mean look to Johnnie. 'Another buckskin blanket. Thank you, Missus Campbell.'

" 'By the Virgin!' cried Frenchy, coming into the room with a very large box. 'That will go very well with this, my present to the bride.'

"Jessie opened the box, and Hugh pulled out the mounted head of the buck they'd landed just six weeks before.

" 'Gee, thanks, Frenchy,' said Hugh.

"Jessie looked about the room. Among the guests were her gifts . . . a table top held up by buck legs, four buckskin blankets, a mop and bucket, the usual cookware, an envelope from Senator Campbell with the words . . . **Enclosed: A Hundred Bucks** . . . and a brand new Winchester rifle. She also saw Johnnie Campbell beating a hasty retreat to the kitchen.

"After the presents were all opened, cake was served, and the men folk all yanked Hugh aside to render him their congratulations and advice.

" 'You're going to want to put in more time on your sheriff's job,' said the reverend to Hugh.

" 'I don't know. The pay is awful slim.'

" 'Oh, don't worry about that, boy,' said Senator Campbell. 'As you know, I know some of the right people in Salem. Even as we speak, the papers are being drawn up to make you a deputy state marshal. By the end of the week, you'll be getting paid for working the entire county. Maybe several of them.'

" 'That's a large spread.'

" 'Look at it this way, son,' said the reverend. 'You'll be driving criminals, instead of cattle.'

" 'I ruther do cattle,' mused Hugh. 'They don't cuss back, and they don't shoot at you.'

" 'Now don't be cynical, son,' said the reverend. 'There hasn't been a drop of blood shed here since old Frenchy purchased that Colt revolver.'

"And so Hugh Buchman became a deputy state marshal as well as the sheriff for the township of Bang in the State of Oregon. Nobody had a sour word for Hugh, either. Hugh took his job seriously. His father, although a bookseller, didn't send much in the way of forensic science for Hugh to study, with the exception of the many books on the subject of archaeology. However, the supply of fiction which was instructive to a new lawman was endless. Hugh delighted in the Uncle Abner stories and the works of Austin Freeman. Hugh's father also sent along as many of the books of science as he thought might be instructive to his son.

"Hugh's first summer tour around the county fell on the heels of his wedding. As much as he might have enjoyed a longer honeymoon, he didn't want to have to ride in the fall rain. Since this was his first set of rounds about the county, Hugh enlisted Frenchy to show him the particulars of the terrain. Hugh had gone over the country, but he'd always had one eye on the lead cow and the other on the stragglers in the back and had never looked at the land like a marshal has to see it. What might be a troublesome hole for cattle to get stuck in could be an outlaw's entrenchment, for example.

"Frenchy started off by introducing Hugh to the Lo family who lived five miles out of town. Being the only Chinese in Paradise Valley, the Lo family kept pretty much to itself. Hugh had seen Mister Lo selling ducks and duck eggs in town and had seen Missus Lo picking up wagon loads of laundry from Weidemeiers' store . . . which also served as a laundering drop off and pick up point. The spring lakes proved a perfect swamp for the Los to plant the rice that sustained their diet. In fact, Mister Lo sold any extra he'd harvest in town. Mister and Missus Lo were delighted to see Frenchy riding up the trail and began to chatter excitedly, but were tight-lipped and reserved the instant they noticed Hugh.

" 'Mister Lo!' shouted Frenchy. 'I want to introduce you to my friend, and our new country marshal, Mister Hugh Buchman.'

"The couple bowed as if in the presence of the Emperor.

" 'Oh, by the Holy Cross, man,' said Frenchy. 'He's my friend.'

" 'But he white,' said Lo, struggling with the only common language he shared with Frenchy.

" 'That makes no difference, man,' said Frenchy. 'Now if you ever have a problem, you can call on Hugh here just as you can me.'

"Missus Lo approached Hugh and studied him as closely as a small woman may study a tall man on a horse. 'He smile nice,' she announced at last. 'You most welcome, Hugh Buchman,' she added.

"The visit was short, with Mister Lo introducing all eight of his children and twelve of his precious ducks. Hugh was given a tour of the swamp and shown the laundry tubs. The Los beamed with pride and, rightly so, for there were a good many Chinese who had far more work and a lot less to show for it at the end of the day . . . especially in the Far West.

"Beyond the Lo homestead, there were a million lakes teaming with birds. Frenchy paused to point out to Hugh the shallower points and the endless variety of waterfowl. 'All that water gonna dry up come summer,' said Frenchy. 'By then, these creatures, they'll be up in north woods.'

"They camped on the edge of a small forest of junipers and pines. As Hugh and Frenchy set up camp, they were sere-naded by rutting elk.

" 'No man ever need go hungry in these parts,' said Frenchy.

"Every so often, Frenchy would introduce Hugh to the occasional homestead, small ranch, or Mormon settlement. At the edge of the county, Hugh and Frenchy sat upon their mounts overlooking a ranch spread out in the country below.

" 'That is the Butler spread,' said Frenchy. 'You should stay clear away,' he added quickly.

" 'Why's that?' asked Hugh. 'I met Mister Butler last year on one of the Campbells' drives, and he and his wife . . . dang, if I can remember how to pronounce her name . . . but they were very nice.'

" 'I have a difficult time with Indian names myself,' said Frenchy. 'And, yes, Hugh, Mister Butler and his Paiute wife are nice. Still, you should stay clear of here, if you can.'

" 'Why?'

"Frenchy pointed off to a group of riders racing toward them. 'If I am not mistaken, you will know the why very shortly.'

"Two of the four riders were on them as fast as storm clouds. One of straggling riders was on a stout Percheron, good for hard work but not much on speed. The rider was as big and tall as Haddie Montbatten, and as ugly as a week-old dead steer all bloated from the sun. Hugh got a good look at the four of them as they pulled back their reins and came to a sudden stop. The two closer to the fat one were thin as posts. Their faces were like leather tanned by anger, fear, and too much sun. One sported a *killer* mustache.

" 'I told you never show your face on this property again!' said the big one.

" 'They's just across the county line, Heff,' said the mustached one.

" 'It don't matter,' said Heff. 'He's close enough to spit on

110

the boss' property, and that's enough for me.'

"The last rider came up. He was an older man with golden, flowing long hair and was dressed in a clean vest. He wore a distinguished beard and mustache that were equally clean and groomed. 'No gettin' yourself all riled up, Heff,' said the vested gentleman. He looked over Frenchy like one looks over a bad cup of coffee. 'Frenchy, you know that you are not welcome here. But since you are here, and since I see that your escort is wearing a badge, I would like to know your business.'

" 'Name's Hugh Buchman,' said Hugh. 'I am the appointed marshal of Harney County. Frenchy has been showing me around the country. Actually I rode with the Campbell drive last year. I've met Mister Butler. He is a fair businessman and a lot friendlier than you gents.'

" 'Marshal,' spat the mustached rider.

" 'Nathan!' scolded the vested man. He turned and smiled at Hugh. 'It is my great pleasure to meet you. I am Ashton Blake. Foreman for the Butler Ranch. This is my crew. Claiborne, Nathan, and Heffner. You, Marshal Buchman, are most certainly welcome. Would you like to accompany us to the Butler household? I am assured that they will welcome the establishment of constabulary regulation in this wild and savage land. I don't believe that our county has a marshal as yet, so I hope that we can count on you for assistance, should the need arise.'

" 'You ain't lettin' the nigger go down to the Butler place?' asked Nathan.

" 'I appreciate the offer, Mister Blake,' said Hugh. 'But we've got a terrible lot of country to ride before dark.'

" '*You,*' said Ashton Blake with particular emphasis toward Hugh, 'are always welcome. Come along, boys. We've got work to do.'

"The riders sauntered off, and Hugh couldn't help but notice that nasty glare that Heff kept shooting back at them.

" 'You see what I mean?' asked Frenchy.

" 'That I do.'

"The Oregon high desert was host to dozens of families who wanted to leave the rest of civilization behind them. There were Indian men with white wives, white men with Indian wives, black men with white wives, white men with black wives, men with multiple wives, men with men, and women with women. Out in the middle of nowhere, there is only the land, sky, and God to judge you, and that is considerably more comfortable than having neighbors.

"Once Hugh had been shown the people in his jurisdiction and the essential roads, Frenchy led him to his favorite hunting hills and fishing holes. It takes a great deal of riding and silence with a man to become his friend. These commodities Hugh and Frenchy had in abundance. On the trail back they got around to asking personal questions.

" 'Tell me, Frenchy,' asked Hugh over some strong camp coffee, 'is it true what they say . . . that you were a runaway slave?'

" 'By the Holy Cross, man!' swore Frenchy. 'Because my skin is full of color, I am of slave stock? I will have you know that I am a free man. I am fully American. My ancestors include the Seminole, the Spanish, and the French. You Northern people,' Frenchy spat, 'are newcomers to my land. And by the Virgin, I have family in the free and independent Santo Domingo. Yes, there is black blood in my veins. Free black blood! Not one drop of slave!'

" 'Don't be so touchy,' said Hugh. 'I don't particularly care. Just curious.'

" 'Curious like a girl lifting up her dress to a gentleman.'

"Hugh let out a chuckle.

" 'And you, is your heritage so much better than mine, man?'

" 'Not at all,' said Hugh. 'My ma died when I was little. She and my father came over from Germany. After she died, he went to sell books out of the back of a wagon. And me? I was put up for adoption.'

" 'I am so sorry,' said Frenchy.

" 'No need to be,' said Hugh. 'They were a good family and took good care of me. It could have been a lot worse. In fact, it worked out fine because I finally got to meet and know my real father. He's plenty smart. Given a choice of roads, he always takes the hardest trail, but he's got a good heart.'

" 'Does he know you're married?'

" 'Well, I sent him a letter all about Jessie and all. I didn't get a letter, but he did send me a book to read to Jessie.'

" 'A book!' scoffed Frenchy.

" 'It's a grand book, Frenchy. LOVE SONNETS FROM THE PORTUGUESE. A true first edition, published in Reading, England.'

" 'And by the Chalice, what would the Portuguese know about love? They can't even make a decent wine.'

" 'That's just the title, Frenchy. It's poetry by an English-woman.

" 'Love sonnets! English!' Frenchy wiped his face with his left hand and looked Hugh in the eyes. 'You profane the name of love by speaking of the English in the same breath.'

" 'And what about Shakespeare?'

" 'What *about* Shakespeare?'

" 'The great playwright. You know, *Romeo and Juliet, Hamlet,* and *Macbeth.*'

" 'I don't know this Shakespeare,' said Frenchy. 'But if his writing was any good, it's not because he was English.'

"The two travelers feasted on the geese and ducks that

covered the silver lakes in fluttering black flocks. There were plenty of larger animals, but they had no need or time to properly clean and transport bigger game. When they returned home, they were given a hero's welcome, and the right reverend gave a fine sermon on the good and faithful servant. The summer and fall were good seasons for the folk of Paradise Valley and very profitable for the residents in Bang. The Lo family brought up more rice than anyone could or would eat, and Mister Weidemeier sold it to Mister Campbell who, in turn, sold it to one of the railroad lobbyists from the Oregon Road and Navigation Company that, in turn, sold it to the Chinese who worked on his track. The rice would have cost the poor Chinese rail men a lot less money, if they had only known to buy it from Mister Lo directly.

"And the Los weren't the only folk to have a good year. The fall hunting was so good that the Langs set up an extra smokehouse, and all that meat was sold to hungry folk in Portland and Spokane for Christmas dinners. A number of folk moving to the Pacific Northwest, looking for their own little stake of heaven, stayed in the Weidemeier rooms and bought plenty of Weidemeier goods. So much money poured into Bang that year that the right reverend had to get himself a bigger collection plate.

"Hugh enjoyed married life and his responsibilities, or lack thereof. But there is always a price to be paid with marriage, and that price tag for Hugh was the monthly dinners he had to endure with his in-laws, the Langs. At least, Hugh got to fool around some with his friend, Johnnie. But without fail, the right reverend and his missus, and the Campbells were always in attendance. The after-dinner discussion with the older men folk was always a matter of being bored to tears and knowing better than to say so. Mister Campbell would talk about the politickin' he was up to in Salem. Mister Lang would talk about how the Republican Party was a danger to the Constitution, and the reverend would put the Almighty into the discussion.

" 'Reverend,' announced Mister Campbell, puffing on his cigar, after one such dinner, 'and you'll find this to be of interest, too, Hugh. It's a mite early to be makin' any announcements, but I have, thanks to the support of Lang here, a deal in the making that will put Bang on the map, nay, on the globe itself.'

" 'And that would be?' inquired the reverend.

" 'Thanks to that rice deal, and our bountiful year, and what promises to be a good year this year,' said Campbell, 'the Oregon Road and Navigation Company has taken an interest in Paradise Valley. They have proposed building a railroad from Carson City to Spokane, putting Bang as the midway point between the two. That, my friends, would put Bang in the dead center of a great deal of commerce. Because of all the hunting our valley provides, we would be a natural point for tourists and sightseers from all over the world.'

" 'Praise God!' said the reverend.

" 'Praise God, indeed,' said Campbell.

"Hugh smiled in agreement, but knew in his heart that God didn't give a damn about commerce in Bang, Oregon.

" 'When will we know?' asked Lang, his eyes already showing the reflection of a great many greenbacks.

" 'The survey teams are already working from Reno north and Spokane south,' said Campbell, puffing his cigar even more vigorously. 'Sometime next summer, we should expect some representatives from Oregon Road and Navigation to give our little hamlet a good look-see. But the railroad won't be here for some time.'

" 'That gives us time to make more money and get things really spruced up,' said Lang.

" 'What do you think, Marshal?' asked the reverend.

"Hugh had wanted to stay out of the conversation. He looked over to Johnnie Campbell, who was asleep in a big red chair. 'Have any of you ever been to Abilene or the railroad and commerce towns in Kansas or New Mexico?' he asked.

"The men looked at one another with dull eyes.

" 'Well, I have,' said Hugh. 'Commerce brings money, money brings people. If one cow goes mad and runs around, it's no big problem to put an end to it. If a whole lot of cows go mad and run around, you got yourself a stampede. And that is a big problem. Abilene . . . so many folks that keepin' things right is no easy job. They've gone through a lot of law men. Mostly the good ones.'

" 'You've got a point,' said Campbell. 'But look at Portland. A sizable city. And very orderly. The city council has made one sensible move after another. First of all, they have made it impossible for the riff-raff and sub-species to live there. And second, and no less important, they have given their police the numbers to enforce these ordinances.'

" 'What exactly do you mean by *sub-species?*' asked Hugh.

" 'You are a man of learning,' said the reverend. 'Modern science has affirmed what the Good Book has said all along, that the fruit of Cain and Ham are accursed by God. The Chinese, the Negroids, and the Semites. While they are in most respects much like the white race, they are nevertheless inferior and cannot help but succumb to the workings of the devil more easily.'

" 'Well, Reverend, if all these groups are sub-species, they might be the best evolved of the race,' said Hugh. 'We owe gunpowder and paper money to the Chinese, for instance. And if I'm not mistaken, Jesus was a Jew, and therefore a Semite. If they are sub-species, they may well be the best adapted to the world and its environments. Have you ever

116

gotten your hands on a copy of the works of Charles Darwin, Reverend?'

"The reverend chuckled to himself. 'I have read of him,' he said. 'But I haven't had the luxury of having a kind father who happens to be an extraordinary bookseller. They say that he has proposed that God is not the Creator, and that the Earth and all of its inhabitants are some kind of accident. But I have not read his works, Hugh. I'm afraid that, once again, you've out-flanked us with your splendid education.'

Hugh realized that it was he who had been out-flanked by the reverend's turning the conversation away to the personalities involved in it and by feigned humility.

" 'Who in the hell has time to read books, anyway,' said Campbell. 'When it comes to the Legislature, I can tell you this, we don't waste any time with books or studying. When you build an empire, son, you don't have time to sit around reading.'

"Hugh thought about Thomas Jefferson, but held his tongue.

" 'You'd be a good schoolteacher,' said Mister Lang. 'And when Bang really starts to grow, that'd be your best callin.'

" 'We need a man of your education right where you are,' said Campbell. 'But I think you'd be better suited in Salem representing our state.'

" 'Gentlemen,' said the reverend in a patronizing voice, 'our discourse has digressed. Why we are no better than the women at a quilting bee.'

"There was chuckling. The image even brought a smile to Hugh's face.

" 'We have much to do, in light of Senator Campbell's pronouncement this evening,' added the reverend. 'And we are agreed, that this information must remain in this room.'

"They all nodded.

"Well, the information didn't stay in that room, because each of the men told their wives, and the wives told their friends, each one promising to keep the secret. The winter was cold and brought plenty of snow. Besides the talk of the railroad, the only story of interest was that old Padover, one of the lamest cowhands to ever work any valley, got sent by the Weidemeiers to Portland to pick up a shipment of toys for the Christmas season. When he came back, he had neither the money nor the toys, claiming that he had been trapped in a blizzard and had been forced to use the toys to start the fire that kept him alive. Fortunately for the children of Paradise Valley, the Stumbo brothers, besides being good wheelwrights, were able to carve and assemble plenty of doll bodies, rocking horses, Quaker rifles, and toy trains in short order.

"In late winter, Hugh and Jessie knew that Bang would have a brand new resident come late June or early July. But Jessie had decided to keep it a secret from the town until Hugh was back from his patrol so that he could be with her at the general announcement and share in the gaiety it would bring.

"Jessie being with child gave Hugh a good reason to get his county rounds done early in the spring. The work around the homestead that he would have liked to do would just have to wait. He could do all of it while staying close to Jessie and home. So with freshly baked cakes and candies still hardening, Hugh waved so long to his young wife.

" 'Hugh!' she cried. 'I almost forgot. The buggy's right front wheel is broke.'

" 'Aw, honey,' sighed Hugh. 'You know I got to start my rounds. I tell you what, go and borrow ole Frenchy's rig. He don't use his hardly, except for his drinkin' nights at the Hog Farm. I'll fix it when I get back.'

" 'Why don't we take it over to the Stumbo brothers, like my parents do?' objected Jessie.

" 'I'd as soon save the money to add on a room for the baby,' said Hugh. 'Besides, I'll take great comfort in knowing that old Frenchy will be dropping in . . . if not for your cookin', to check up on his property.'

"I expect that Jessie smiled bravely and wiped a small tear from her eye as Hugh started off. Their little house was on the high ground, so she could look around the small ranch. The sky was a perfect blue, the clouds billowy and tall. Just at the edge of the property, on the side of the mountains which jumped right up into the clouds and hung there, were two families of elk strolling cautiously among the junipers and tall grass. Suddenly they bolted, and Jessie saw a gray wolf come running out of the trees. The elk were faster and soon out of danger. The wolf skulked into the trees once more. Jessie wished that the wolf would come in closer so she would have the excuse to use her new Winchester rifle. But things were always just a bit out of range for poor Jessie. She was born just too soon to enjoy the right to vote, and she was a little too young to have a big voice in the goings-on in Bang. She got her husband, all right, but he had a job that took him away from her side.

"She had been quite taken with that book of love sonnets that Hugh's father had sent. In fact, she had set out to write up a sonnet of her own. But words didn't always come easy to Jessie, and she had to ask Haddie Montbatten what rhymed with buck. Perhaps it was because she was still a young bride, but Jessie could only think of two words that rhymed, and one wasn't the sort of word a good woman put down on paper. And for the life of her, she couldn't think of what to do with the word duck. Of course, Haddie didn't keep what Jessie had asked her in confidence to herself, and there was plenty of subdued tittering by the women of Paradise Valley for a few weeks about that question of rhyme.

"Hugh's rounds were at first quite routine. Most of the homesteaders talked about a wolf, and how hard the snow had been on them that winter. One of the families had lost a child during the hard winter. Hugh promised that he'd send the reverend along to offer his services and comforts.

"Around the middle of his journey, he found himself riding into the Butler Ranch. While the Butlers weren't in his county, they were close enough. He hoped that the foreman, Blake, and his boys were out on their rounds or, even better, that Mister Butler had gotten some sense and cut them loose.

"As he approached the ranch house, Ashton Blake came out of the front door.

" 'Marshal Buchman,' said Blake, courteously enough. 'On patrol, I see.'

" 'You could say that,' said Hugh. 'Is Mister Butler home?'

" 'It is my regrettable duty to inform you that there has been a tragedy at the ranch,' said Blake.

" 'Tragedy?'

" 'Mister and Missus Butler were murdered early last month,' said Blake.

" 'Murdered?'

" 'That's right,' said Nathan, coming out of the ranch house behind Blake.

" 'I hadn't heard.'

" 'In fact, Heff started out yesterday . . . toward Paradise Valley for that very purpose, Marshal Buchman,' said Blake. 'I sent word to *our* county seat in Redmond as soon as we learned of the crime.'

" 'But that's a longer ride,' said Hugh. 'And I didn't know that your county had a marshal just yet.'

" 'I don't make the laws, and I certainly didn't draw up the county lines, Marshal Buchman,' said Blake.

" 'What are you boys still doin' here, then?' asked Hugh.

" 'We have remained here to keep an eye on the place until some of the Butlers' kinfolk come along and make their lawful claim to the ranch,' said Blake. 'Surely there is no law nor commandment against protecting thy neighbor's property.'

" 'No, there ain't,' admitted Hugh. 'Any idea who murdered the Butlers?'

" 'Was some of them prairie niggers,' said Nathan. 'And they sure as hell got theirs.'

" 'What does he mean?' asked Hugh, looking to Blake.

" 'The Butlers were generous to a fault, Marshal Buchman,' said Blake. 'Why you yourself have told me of their hospitality. Some of the local vagrant Indians came to the Butlers, presuming upon this hospitality. The Butlers made the terrible mistake of letting the savages stay on the premises. While the boys and I were out looking for strays in the snow, the guests became hostile and murdered their kind hosts.'

"Hugh wished that this were in his jurisdiction for it was a situation that cried for a thorough investigation. All the same, he wasn't about to let the circumstance go un-noticed. 'It's mighty unusual for the Indians to go off and kill one of their own,' he said. 'Especially a woman. And I haven't heard that they've ever killed a white man married to one of their womenfolk. What did you mean, about them getting theirs?'

" 'We found some of the band,' said Blake. 'Blood still on their hands. I suppose we should have contacted the Department of the Army. But it seemed to us at the time that it was better to dispose of a danger at once rather than let them live to kill another innocent family.'

" 'I sure hope you haven't made a mistake,' said Hugh. 'A number of the recent wars with the Indians have started by the likes of this. You should have called in the Army. Just don't be surprised if some of the Bannocks don't come along lookin' for you.'

" 'Don't you worry about us old Confederates,' spat Nathan.

"Claiborne came out of the house with a rifle. 'I hope they do come a-lookin' for trouble,' he said. ' 'Cause I'll give it to 'em ag'in.'

"Hugh sat thoughtfully for a moment and decided that he'd better put this on the trail behind him. 'Well, if you have any trouble, don't send off to Redmond, you send word to me in Bang, and I'll be up here double-quick.'

" 'Thank you, kindly, Marshal Buchman,' said Blake.

"Hugh rode up to the hills overlooking the Butler place and got into a thicket of junipers. He watched and waited. Before an hour was out, he saw Heff squeeze through the door of the Butler place.

" 'He lied,' said Hugh between his teeth, remembering that Blake had said that the fat one had gone down the trail to Bang. Hugh would send a report of this to the state marshal and be done with it. He'd been gone over a month, and the trail home seemed to take forever. Even his horse Butternut seemed anxious to get home.

"Hugh had lost two whole months on his rounds and was in a hurry to catch up with things around his own piece of heaven. He gave the roof over the kitchen a fresh splash of tar and some new wooden shingles. What's more, he repaired the family carriage wheel and returned the borrowed carriage to Frenchy.

"Not much to his surprise, Bang had remained lawful and quiet during his absence, with the exception of the Stumbo brothers. And there wasn't much to be done about them. He'd sent a letter to the attention of the state marshal about the Butler business and had gotten a nice letter back from the governor himself, thanking him for looking into the matter and saying that, given time and resources, something more would be done. From this letter Hugh inferred that the current state marshal for that county was between jobs, and that the governor hadn't gotten around to appointing a replacement. That all being a problem on the other side of the state, Hugh washed his hands of it. He enjoyed a season without having to pry into anyone's else's affairs.

"Hugh was in his woodshed chopping kindling to start up the morning ovens. It never ceased to amaze Hugh how even the most straight-grained woods would turn out to have the most pernicious knots hidden inside. He braced the troublesome log with his foot and started to swing his hatchet when he heard the sound of a horse galloping up to the homestead. He looked and swung, and then looked down at his foot. The hatchet had gone into his boot as well as the log. He gently pulled out the hatchet and was relieved to see no blood on the edge.

" 'Hugh, you in there?' shouted a voice with an unmistakable accent. 'You better be in there. Your wife thinks you're in there, and you don't want to make her a liar, do you?'

"Hugh stuck his head out of the shed and looked around. A one-eared man was dismounting from a nut-brown quarter horse.

" 'Frenchy!'

" 'By the Virgin, I will kill them!' Frenchy swore as dramatically as possible.

" 'Kill who and why? Calm down, Frenchy.'

" 'All spring long, you are doing these rounds of yours in the county! I watch the town for you! I look after your wife and your homestead! No trouble when old Frenchy is in charge! You come back, Hugh. My best horses stolen. I will cut them to pieces!' said Frenchy, in a little over one breath.

" 'What are you talking about, Frenchy?'

" 'Horse thieves, by the Virgin!'

" 'Somebody stole your horses?'

" 'That's why I'm here.' Frenchy's eyes seemed to bulge out from his face, and he was sweating. 'You're the deputy marshal. Do something!'

" 'Give me a minute,' said Hugh.

" 'Every minute, the thieves, they ride farther away!' cried Frenchy.

"Hugh carefully took off his boot and saw that he had put a small razor-sharp cut on the side of his right foot. He took off his apron and hung it on the back shed door. He then stepped outside and pulled a two-by-four across the door as a way of locking up the shed.

" 'Ready? Let's go!' shouted Frenchy.

" 'Frenchy,' said Hugh. 'Just hang on. I'm moving, I'm moving.'

"He went into the farmhouse. His front room served as a dining room and library. Jessie was brushing her golden hair in front of her vanity mirror.

" 'Hugh,' she said, lighting up as he entered. 'Did Frenchy tell you about his horses?'

" 'Are you kidding?' said Hugh.

" 'I'll be glad to ride around the road and ask some questions,' Jessie volunteered.

" 'No, honey,' said Hugh, looking at Jessie's belly, now showing signs of the life she carried within. 'Not this time. Wait until after the baby comes.'

" 'A little ride won't hurt him,' she said. She smiled and added . . . 'Or her.'

" 'It's not the ride I'm worried about,' said Hugh. 'I just don't want to think about what might happen if you by some chance found the thieves, if there are thieves, instead of the horses.'

" 'You don't think they were stolen?' asked Jessie.

" 'Let's put it this way,' said Hugh. 'I wouldn't be at all surprised if one of Frenchy's hired hands left the gate ajar and didn't want to 'fess up to it. At least, not until the horses were found. You know how Frenchy is about his horses.'

" 'I do, indeed.'

" 'Well, there you go,' said Hugh. 'I don't want to be havin' to put our friend into jail for murder, now, do I?'

" 'Don't stay out too long, sweetheart.'

She wrapped her arms around his neck and planted a lover's kiss on his lips.

" 'I think I'd better go out and take a look at his place this instant, before you get my mind entirely off Frenchy's dang' horses,' sighed Hugh. 'And I'll probably be late for dinner.'

" 'In that event,' said Jessie with just a little irritation in her voice, 'I'm going into town tonight.'

" 'But you went last week, honey,' said Hugh.

" 'And I'm gonna go every week until the baby is born,' she announced sweetly. 'You can't expect old sawbones McCaffrey to come out here every week. And, besides, I miss my friends. I wish we had a house closer to town.'

" 'Aw, honey, you know I don't like neighbors,' whined Hugh.

" 'Well, then, my darling,' said Jessie, planting a peck of a kiss on his lips, 'you'll have to put up with me going into town from time to time is all. Besides, I bet you'll be gone most of tonight anyway, 'cause if you don't find the horses, Frenchy will make you keep looking, and, if you do find them, you'll have to celebrate with Frenchy because you found them.'

" 'I tell you what,' said Hugh. 'If I don't find them soon, I'll go right into town and use that brand new telegraph at

Weidemeiers. I might find 'em faster that way than by riding around in circles on this old high-desert plain. Maybe one of my father's book's come in at the Weidemeier store. I'll look for you there.'

" 'Well, if I'm not there, I'll leave word. I'm not sure I like bein' stood up for a horse,' teased Jessie, lifting her nose up into the air as if highly offended. She smiled at her young husband and then added thoughtfully . . . 'Oh, I'd like to take the surrey. Can you get it ready?'

" 'The surrey? You ain't that big with the baby yet.'

" 'I thought I might stop by Haddie's,' said Jessie. 'If she wants a ride into town, well, you know, Hugh.'

" 'I know, I know. Mount Hood with two legs. We don't want her breakin' no innocent horse's back.'

" 'That's not very kind, Hugh.'

" 'My wife, mover of mountains to Mohammed.'

" 'You stop it.'

"While Jessie put herself together for her trip into town, Hugh took off his boot and washed his cut thoroughly with vinegar and soap. He wrapped it up with some fresh cloth that had been brought into the house for Jessie to sew into diapers. Jessie came out of her bedroom with the coat she'd ordered through the catalog at Weidemeiers. She was prettier than a Virginia City show girl, and Hugh wished that they could just stay at home.

" 'Well, is the surrey ready?' she asked.

" 'Not hardly,' said Hugh.

"Frenchy was sitting on his horse in front of the doorway.

" 'Well! You goin' to help old Frenchy, or not?' he asked.

" 'I got to get the surrey ready for Jessie,' said Hugh, almost swallowing his words, embarrassed at having kept his friend waiting for so long.

"Frenchy rolled his eyes in disgust. 'For the first time, a

crime in this valley, and the sheriff has to fix up the surrey for his wife!'

"Hugh went out into the corral to put together a matched team. Jessie came out and stood on the steps.

" 'Madame Buchman, you are more beautiful than ever,' said Frenchy from atop his mount.

" 'Thank you, Pierre,' said Jessie.

" 'The baby? All is well?' asked Frenchy.

" 'Doc McCaffrey seems to think so,' said Jessie softly.

" 'Hey, Frenchy!' shouted Hugh from the corral. 'The sooner I get this rigged up, the sooner we can get over to your place. Give me a hand, will you?'

" 'I will do this, but only because I want my horses back, not because you are a fool and couldn't rig a carriage to save your life!' shouted Frenchy, dismounting.

"Before too long, Hugh had a team together, and Frenchy helped harness them while Hugh put together the surrey.

" 'Got everything?' asked Hugh, lifting his wife into the driver's seat.

" 'I think so, honey,' she replied.

" 'OK, then,' said Hugh. 'I'll catch up with you in town.'

"She was down to the road in short order.

" 'The rains that are coming will make driving that surrey very difficult,' mused Frenchy. 'I think you are going to get covered with mud sometime soon.'

" 'Ground sure is wet,' said Hugh. 'One more rain, and nobody's gonna be pullin' wagons at all.'

"The day was disappearing fast, so Hugh prepared his own mount and followed Frenchy out and over the pastures.

" 'You see this!' swore Frenchy, showing Hugh where the wooden fence had been pulled apart. Hugh studied the ground, and, sure enough, there were plenty of boot tracks accompanied with the prints of shod horses. There was even a print from the wolf that had been hunting in Paradise Valley.

"The fence had been taken apart carefully, even methodically. Hugh had seen older fences come down when cows had been boogered and had charged them, but this was not the work of a cow, or horse.

" 'Isn't this where you kept your brood mares?' he asked.

" 'Of course. Why else would I show this to you?'

" 'How many did you lose?'

" 'Napoléon and Belle.'

" 'Oh, oh,' cursed Hugh under his breath.

"Belle was about thirty years old. She had foaled most of Frenchy's favorite stallions. To say that Frenchy was extremely fond of her would have been treating his affections lightly. As for Napoléon, he was the prize stud of the ranch and had made Frenchy a considerable and tidy sum of money.

"Hugh could see blood rushing to Frenchy's face at the thought of his two favorites being missing and attempted to get his friend thinking on issues related to the case but off the fact of the missing horseflesh.

" 'Isn't Belle just a little too old to be . . . ?' said Hugh. 'Well, you know.'

" 'You are never too old,' laughed Frenchy. 'The trick is to start young and keep on brooding, no?'

" 'But Napoléon is so young.'

" 'All the better for Belle, no? Every mature woman dreams of a young man.'

" 'I don't think it works for horses the same way,' said Hugh.

" 'That is because you are so white,' said Frenchy.

" 'I don't see what that has to do with anything,' said Hugh.

" 'Horses take after their owners. You know this to be true. The passions of France and Spain flow through me. Therefore, they also flow through my horses. We know how to love.'

"After Hugh finished grinning from ear to ear, he took a slow ride around Frenchy's spread to look for the missing horses or some clue as to their whereabouts.

" 'You got anything else missing, Frenchy?'

" 'No, by the grace of God,' swore Frenchy.

" 'Nobody touched your cuttin' stock?'

" 'No, Hugh.'

" 'No cattle missing?'

"Frenchy shrugged his shoulders.

" 'Nobody broke into your place, took anything?'

" 'It is all as I left it,' said Frenchy. 'Except for Napoléon and Belle.'

" 'Damned strange. It don't make sense. Listen, did you know that a wolf's been prowling around? Getting awful close to your horses?'

" 'I seen the big wolf,' said Frenchy, unimpressed. 'He runs away. He knows better than to bother me.'

"Hugh dismounted so he could study the tracks around the broken part of the fence a little more carefully. 'Frenchy,' he said with finality, 'we've got some good clear tracks in the mud here, and I want to make up some molds.'

Hugh reached into Butternut's saddlebags while Frenchy looked on with no small amount of suspicion.

" 'What in the hell are you doing? Pouring flour into the tracks!'

" 'It ain't flour,' said Hugh. 'It's calcimined gypsum.'

" 'Plaster?' asked Frenchy incredulously. 'You carry plaster with you? By the Holy Cross, I don't believe this that I am seeing.'

" 'I read this in one of my father's books a year ago,' said Hugh.

" 'Your father wrote about this?'

" 'No,' said Hugh. 'I told you he was a bookseller. And he always has books about everything.'

"Hugh mixed up more plaster in the bag and poured it into another series of tracks. 'In about two hours, I'll pull up these plaster molds and take them back to the office,' he said. 'If I'm not mistaken, we'll at least have some kind of evidence about whose horses were here and the size of boot the fellers wore who took down your fence.'

" 'But we should be out after them!'

" 'No, Frenchy. They've been gone since morning. There's no point to it. We won't find them. The thing is, two horses won't fetch a large enough price for a man to risk putting his neck in a noose. They're still out here, probably figurin' on just whose horses they're going to steal next.'

" 'You are not going after them?' pleaded Frenchy.

" 'No, Frenchy. I have a feeling that they will find their way to me.'

" 'By the prayers to the Virgin Mary, I just can't sit around here and do nothing at all!' cried Frenchy.

"He cursed in French, Spanish, and threw in a little Dominican besides, and then charged off toward the hills, stopping every so often to look for tracks. While waiting for the plaster to dry, Hugh watched Frenchy zigzag all about the cañon looking for a trail. Darkness was settling over the valley, and a storm was coming over the high desert.

"Hugh dug the plaster out of the dirt and poured the rest of his gypsum into some similar tracks around the fence. He could come back for these another day. He stuffed the plaster molds into his saddlebag and took them back to his office in Bang.

"He put the plasters on his desk and sat down to study them. After a few minutes of intense observation, he began to sketch out patterns and makes notes. His study was interrupted briefly by a visit from the Reverend Catley and Johnnie Campbell.

" 'Reverend,' said Hugh. 'Johnnie.'

" 'Whatcha got there, Hugh?' asked Johnnie, coming up to the desk.

" 'Evidence,' said Hugh.

" 'Evidence?' inquired the reverend.

" 'Somebody's gone off and stolen two of Frenchy's horses,' said Hugh. 'These are replicated copies of the prints around the fence where the horses were taken.'

" 'What a great idea!' said Johnnie. 'Now tell me, did you think of that? You are one of the true geniuses of our times, Hugh Buchman.'

" 'Thank you kindly, Johnnie,' said Hugh. 'But I can't take credit for it. I read about it a year ago in one of my father's books about those fellers who were diggin' up dinosaurs in Colorado and Wyoming.'

" 'I don't understand. Dinosaurs and horse thieves. What are you going to prove?' asked Johnnie.

" 'Well, dinosaurs and horse thieves have one thing in common. They like to make themselves real scarce. You have to dig up dinosaurs and piece 'em together to get enough evidence that you do, in fact, have a dinosaur. By a-lookin' at what you built, you can figure out what kind of critter it was. Well, in the case of the horse thief, you also have to piece together enough evidence to figure out just who the critter was. That's the point of these plaster prints on my desk, here. I can show them to some of the stable hands around the county. They might recognize the shoe or the work put into the shoe.'

" 'I see, very interesting,' said the reverend. He paused

131

and began a speech that was obviously rehearsed. 'Very interesting, indeed. And it brings me around to something I've been wanting to talk to you about. Hugh, you've been doing a grand job as deputy marshal.'

" 'That's right, Hugh, a grand job,' repeated Johnnie, unaware that he was sounding like a parrot.

" 'I learned of an opportunity that just might be the ticket for you, Hugh. I was going to talk to you earlier, but you were out, a-huntin' horse thieves from the sound of things. And doin' a bang-up job by the looks of it. To start off, I want to say it's high time you stepped up in the world some, son.'

" 'What do you mean?' asked Hugh.

" 'I have learned from my friends in the state capital that there is soon to be an opening for the position of superintendent for all the state deputy marshals,' announced Reverend Catley. 'And I think you would be best suited for the job.'

" 'I'm glad you like my work, Reverend,' said Hugh. 'But I hardly earn my keep out here in the high desert. This horse theft today is the first real work I've done in the time I've had the job. And the county's big enough. I don't know that I could cover the whole state.'

" 'Think of Jessie,' said the reverend. 'She deserves more than the life you can offer her here. And think of yourself. A man of your learning, a rancher, and a county deputy marshal? I see bigger things for you, my boy. And, besides, you wouldn't be the one doing all the rounds, although you'd travel around the state from time to time to supervise. You'd make all sorts of new friends and important connections, Hugh. It could lead to a better position in the state capital. Why, you could take this as far as you wanted to take it.'

" 'I'll think it over,' said Hugh.

" 'You are a sober and thoughtful man,' said the reverend. 'But don't think too long. Some opportunities only last a short while.'

" 'I promise I won't,' said Hugh.

" 'Oh, Hugh,' said Johnnie. 'Dang it all, I almost forgot. Jessie is visiting with my mother. You're all invited for dinner.'

" 'Thank you kindly, Johnnie,' said Hugh. 'I've got a little work to do right now, but I'll be around shortly.'

"After Johnnie and the reverend had gone their way, Hugh made a pencil rubbing of the boot print on the plaster. He tacked that onto the wall and then made a pencil rubbing of several of the horseshoe prints. He noticed that time was moving right along and so turned off his lamps and made his way to Weidemeiers' store.

"The Weidemeiers building was the tallest and proudest in Bang, which truly amazed Hugh as the dear Weidemeiers were the shortest and humblest folk in town. From the second-story windows, you could see for miles in every direction and just about every little thing in town. In turn, you could see what the Weidemeiers had in storage and what they were doing if they left the blinds up.

"It seemed like half of the Weidemeiers' many children lived on the second floor. Some of the children attended the Reverend Catley's services on Sunday, but Ma and Pa Weidemeier encouraged the others to quietly observe their own heritage on Saturdays. Hugh could see two Weidemeier children looking out the windows and doing nothing at all . . . which constituted observing the Sabbath as he understood it. But whatever religion the Weidemeiers encouraged their children to observe, there was no question that they believed in hard work, Sabbath or no, and were going to put together a fortune for their children even on Saturdays.

"Hugh went into the store. Anna Weidemeier was serving sodas to the usual crowd.

" 'You've got a package from your father, Hugh,' shouted Missus Weidemeier.

"Hugh looked around but couldn't see her. What he saw was a large female mannequin, dressed in the fashionable long dresses that the women on the East Coast were sporting, moving to the left, then to the right.

" 'Missus Weidemeier?'

" 'I've pinned myself to this god-dampt mannequin,' cried Missus Weidemeier.

"Some of the more proper customers left the store in a huff at this slightest hint of profanity. Hugh, however, lifted up the dress of the mannequin and found poor Missus Weidemeier, needle and thread in hand, repairing one of the underpinnings of the dress. Sure enough, suffering from a lack of light, she had sewn part of her dress to the mannequin's under garments.

" 'Your package is behind the counter,' said Missus Weidemeier. Then, gathering up a tremendous breath, she shouted coarsely . . . 'Anna, get the marshal his package. And bring me a pair of scissors.' Hugh smiled and gently dropped the skirt, enclosing Missus Weidemeier in the dark once more.

" 'Hey!' shouted Missus Weidemeier. 'You just lift up my dress right now, young man!'

"Haddie Montbatten charged around the corner to see what was happening and probably in high hopes. She glared at Hugh. The mannequin jumped to the right. Haddie squealed and ran off like a boogered cow.

"Anna came around the aisle with a square package wrapped in paper.

" 'Here you are, Hugh. Where's Momma?'

"The mannequin jumped forward. Anna let out a high-pitched shriek.

" 'I'm down here, *Dummkopf!*' cried Missus Weidemeier.

" 'You all right?' Hugh asked of Anna. Plainly exasperated, Anna nodded and lifted up the dress of the mannequin.

" 'Thank you kindly,' said Hugh.

"He tore open the little package.

" 'Dear Son,' started the note. 'Hope all is well. Here's a little book I think you'll like. If all goes as planned, I should be on the West Coast within the next few months. I hope to be able to come and meet your wife. Congratulations. You'll be a good father. Much Love . . . Father.'

"Hugh opened the book slowly and read the title and author aloud. 'THE MOONSTONE by Wilkie Collins.' He tucked the book into his riding-coat pocket. His father might not have been a plentiful sight in his life . . . in fact, far from it. But he always had great books which he gave freely."

Chapter Three

The old cowboy stopped, stood up, and arched his back. He picked up his mug.

"Coffee? Or something a little stronger?"

"No, thanks."

The old man went into the kitchen, and Jack could hear him pushing more blocks of wood into the stove, followed by the sound of the whisky being poured from a large jug. Jack smiled when he heard the old man choke on the first swallow of the nearly lethal brew, and, presently, the old man took his place in his old chair.

"So, did Marshal Buchman find out who stole the old Frenchman's horses?" asked Jack.

"Well, if I told you the end of the story, there wouldn't be any point in telling you the beginning," complained the old cowboy. "It's just like us to accept historical facts on a convenience level. It is convenient to know what happened to one man or one this or one that. We forget that there are a good many other things, great and small, which bear down upon the consequence or have the consequence bear down on them. They say that General Lee held up his entire Army for a day, looking for a favorite hen. Now what do you suppose it might have meant iffen he'd gotten to Gettysburg one day earlier?

"You see, Hugh had much to consider and reconsider on his ride to the Campbell homestead. Besides all of the ideas about career possibilities swirling around like May flies in his head, he couldn't help but think of old Frenchy riding around the hills looking for his beloved Napoléon and Belle. And why didn't the thieves take all of Frenchy's horses? It would be no more work for Hugh to track a few than it would the whole she-bang. He then realized that he hadn't been marshal long enough to understand the criminal mind and smiled at the thought, for now he knew just how to graciously decline the supervisory position the reverend had been offering him.

"The dinner went just fine. Much to everyone's delight, old man Owen Campbell had come for the week and, while the food was being passed around, gave a long oration on the threat of socialist thought.

" 'We must be ever vigilant not to let these godless socialist principles invade our community,' bellowed Campbell.

" 'I concur, Senator,' said the reverend. 'Dispense with the notion of private property, and the next thing you'll know, you will have theft and, in short, continual violation of one of God's great Commandments . . . thou shalt not steal.'

" 'What do you think, Hugh?' asked Campbell.

" 'Well, I've had some readin' in the area, and I've given it a little thought,' said Hugh thoughtfully. 'To start with, socialism hasn't really been practiced much. And by that I guess that I mean it has the virtue of not having been tried.'

"The reverend laughed. 'Then you would try murder, say, to see if it might work?'

" 'I'm not sure that socialism and murder are exactly the same,' said Hugh. 'And, no, I'm not sayin' that socialism should be tried. There's a lot to a community, besides its economical operation. You've got to take into account the sophistication of its jurisprudence. I am not sure that any society, socialist, or capitalist, or whatever there may be, can work if it doesn't have a system of laws and enforcement, rights and responsibilities to match up. Socialism would have to be highly organized to work . . . too many people and too many ideas and just so much property to share.'

" 'That's why I like you, my boy,' said the reverend. 'You are truly an intellectual in cowboy clothing. If I could only get you dressed up and in the Legislature, where you belong. . . . But, still, don't you think that giving the laborer more say in the factory and more power in its operation than the owner is dangerous?'

" 'Well, Reverend,' said Hugh, 'it's not my job to be butchering Scripture, and certainly not to my preacher, but didn't the Lord tell of the master who gave out his property to his hired hands? Ain't that socialism, in a sense?'

"The reverend almost applauded. 'And right you are, Hugh Buchman. But as you will recall, only one of the laborers produced any results for his master.'

" 'And so you have it, Reverend,' said Hugh. 'It's easier to make serious results for your own self than it is for someone else. And if socialism has a broken spoke, that's surely it.'

" 'But there are other serious problems with socialism,' said Senator Campbell. 'When you have no clear sense of property, you are likely to lose the sense of propriety. Everybody would be equal to everybody else. You'd have black men with white women. Indian men with white women. The great white race would be ruined in a generation.'

" 'Amen to that,' said the reverend.

" 'Well,' said Hugh, 'you'd be knowin' more about the future than I would. But from what I've seen out in the countryside, you got plenty of white men and white women with other races, as you call them, already. And you know, maybe they like the country out here 'cause everybody leaves 'em alone about it.'

" 'I'd like a list of those folks,' said Campbell sourly. 'You know, there exists legislation about that.'

" 'I'm sure that's so,' said Hugh. 'But just whose job is it to enforce it? Most folks out here can't read, much less provide documents to prove their relationship to someone who happens to be on their spread. The only way to know for sure whether these folks are married is by looking at their kids. And they're so dirty from playin' in this desert sand, you can't be sure. As for the list, sure, I suppose I could put one together, Senator. But it seems that the state is going to waste a lot of money to make a case that it can't prove in court.'

" 'Don't you worry about that, son,' said the senator. 'There exist groups who serve the interest of the capital who might be helpful.'

" 'Fine,' said Hugh. 'But if that means vigilance committees, they're going to get a fight out of me first.'

" 'Oh, no, son, nothing like that,' assured the senator, glancing over to the reverend.

" 'I think this is all very interesting,' said Missus Campbell. 'But whether it's a socialist or capitalist world, it's we women who are going to end up doing the dishes.' She turned to Jesse and the reverend's wife. 'Shall we get to work so the men can earn their keep by settling the world's problems over cigars?'

" 'Don't impress them too much,' said Jessie into Hugh's ear. 'Or you *will* get a job in Salem.'

"Hugh shuddered.

"After the women had scooped up the dinner, the senator ignited a monstrous Cuban cigar. The reverend abstained, as did Hugh.

" 'Say, where's my pal Johnnie?' asked Hugh. He'd noted that the senator's son was absent during dinner.

" 'He's out looking for that wolf,' said the senator.

" 'Alone?' asked Hugh. 'From the size of the tracks, I'd just as soon meet up with it with a friend or two.'

" 'Johnnie's not got your learning,' said the senator. 'But he's got the sense to be out with his friends on this one.'

139

"Hugh wished that he had been able to go out wolf hunting with his friend, rather than to endure the company of these old men. He also wondered if Johnnie and the hunting party wouldn't run into Frenchy out in the hills.

"Owen Campbell and Reverend Catley, having pinned their opinion to every issue of the day, eventually led Hugh to the library where the women and children were playing auto-harps, the piano, or singing at the top of their lungs. Hugh watched his Jessie, who simply glowed at things like this. In fact, she glowed most of the time. He hated to even bring up the subject of leaving because he knew that he would be ordered, ever so nicely, to stay overnight in one of the many rooms at the Campbell household, and Jessie would plead with her biggest eyes to stay. Hugh was no fool. He knew that a man can either do it his wife's way at once, or fight with his wife and end up doing it her way.

"In the midst of the singing and carrying on, there was a knock at the front door. Whoever it was didn't come in, but the voice sounded familiar to Hugh.

"Missus Campbell beckoned the reverend to the door. He stepped outside for a moment and then returned.

" 'You will have to excuse me, I'm afraid,' said the reverend to his hosts. 'From time to time, I must perform the Lord's duty at his convenience and not my own.'

"The reverend got his coat, kissed his wife on the forehead, and took his leave.

"Within the hour, Hugh was shown to a bedroom that had been made up by a servant just for himself and Jessie. He got to the room well enough ahead of Jessie so he could change the bandage on his foot without her seeing it.

"Jessie slept in late and would rise for the large breakfast with the family. Hugh, on the other hand, used the excuse of his investigation to get an early start. He was intercepted on the front porch by the good senator who'd also risen early.

" 'Tell me about this situation,' said Senator Campbell, lighting his morning cigar.

" 'You know Frenchy,' said Hugh.

" 'Pierre Lematrie,' corrected the senator, observing at all times the formalities. 'Yes. One of the originals in Paradise Valley. A lively character and a fine breeder of horses. And were it not for his complexion, a very welcome member of our community.'

" 'Well, the long and short of it is that someone's made off with Belle and Napoléon,' said Hugh, ignoring the senator's final remark.

" 'Belle?' asked the senator. 'She's older than the hills. She was one of the original settlers of Paradise Valley, too. The dam of many of the finest mounts in the eastern part of the state. Now who'd want to steal her?'

" 'That's just one piece of the puzzle.'

" 'Was anything else taken?'

" 'Not one single thing more, Senator.'

" 'If you ask me,' stated Campbell, 'it's plainly not a case of theft for resale. Probably a case of someone needing a horse. A vagrant, or the like.'

" 'I wondered about that,' said Hugh. 'Take one to ride and have the other handy to do freight or to switch on if the ride ahead was a long or a fast one. But it wouldn't take the thief long to learn that Belle was a brood mare and had never done any kind of other work. Not even pulling a light wagon.'

" 'True enough, son,' said Campbell. 'Pierre would rather pull a wagon himself than make his darling Belle do the work.'

"Hugh knew that if he stayed in this conversation any longer, the senator would change the subject to either the goings on in Salem or to a pressing issue at the nation's capital, either of which was of little consequence to Hugh at the moment. 'Well, sir, I'd best be on my way.'

"As he started out to the stable, Johnnie Campbell came riding in with three men.

" 'Did you find the wolf?' shouted the senator.

" 'Wolf?' shouted Johnnie, bringing his horse to a full stop as if that would help him think. He looked down, and then at Hugh with a peculiar expression. 'Oh, yeh,' he answered his father, 'the wolf. No. No luck.'

"Hugh froze when he saw that two of the three men were Claiborne and Nathan from the Butler spread.

" 'Senator,' he said, 'do you know those men with Johnnie?'

" 'Well, of course, I do,' said the senator. 'Jake's been with us forever. And those are two fellahs I hired on this week. Nathan and Claiborne.'

" 'I need to talk to you about them, right now,' said Hugh.

" 'I don't worry myself with the hands much, Hugh,' said the senator. 'If you have some concerns about them, let me introduce you to my new foreman. And speak of the devil, here he comes.'

"From around the Campbell house came Ashton Blake, leading his horse. Behind him was Heff, more dragging than leading his horse.

" 'Under the circumstances, I need to talk to you, in private and right now,' said Hugh.

" 'Sure, son,' said Campbell. 'But I need to talk to Blake for a moment.' He shouted and waved for Blake to come over. Blake sauntered toward the senator, leaving the reins of his horse with Heff.

" 'Marshal Buchman,' said Blake slowly and deliberately. 'It is truly my pleasure to meet you again.'

" 'You've met?' asked Campbell.

" 'Why, yes, sir, yes, we have,' said Blake. 'The marshal was kind enough to drop in on me and the boys after that unfortunate business at the Butler home. His attention was above and beyond the call of duty, and I owe him, that is, you, Marshal Buchman, my sincerest thanks.'

"The senator shook his head sadly. 'Nasty business, that,' he said. 'But you boys did the right thing. And I'm not surprised to find out that Hugh came by to help. I'm proud of this one, Blake,' said Campbell, slapping Hugh on the back. 'Hugh, Blake here served with the Confederate cavalry in the late war. He's quite a hand with the horses, and I need to talk to him for a moment. A big deal. A really big deal.'

" 'Would you like me to go?' asked Hugh.

" 'Heavens, no, boy,' said Campbell. 'It ain't gonna be a secret for long. Blake, I want you to go out and buy up every steer in Paradise Valley. Let the seller have his price, if it's not too far out of bounds. The Oregon Road and Navigation boys need meat for their survey teams, and I intend to sell it to them. When you got 'em together, we'll set up a route to Spokane for a summer drive.'

" 'What if the owners do not wish to sell?' asked Blake.

" 'Then let 'em keep their animals,' said Campbell. 'Just be sure to tell 'em it's me that's buyin' and that I will have their money in short order and, if I'm late, with interest.'

" 'That's right dandy,' said Hugh. 'But just what are we going to eat here in Paradise Valley?'

" 'The booty that walks the hills around us, Hugh,' said Campbell. 'There's enough elk and moose and ducks to feed the federal Army in our hills. And with the money from this deal, we can buy up all the steers in Texas to replenish our stock.'

" 'Senator,' said Hugh, 'I really need to talk with you.'

" 'Yes, I know,' said the senator with a tone of exasperation, as if interrupted in the midst of a speech. 'You can express your concerns here and now, can't you?'

" 'Mister Blake,' Hugh said slowly, 'you told me that you had sent the big guy, Heff, to tell me about it. Well, I saw Heff with you there after I rode off a ways.'

" 'I fully understand your concerns, Marshal,' said Blake with a polite smile. 'I turned out to be quite the liar, didn't I? But if you will permit me, I can explain.'

"Hugh nodded.

" 'You see, Marshal, I had, in fact, asked Heff to come down to Paradise Valley. And from what he told me, that is exactly what he had intended to do. But poor Heff is mighty in body and weak in mind. The poor boy got lost. He got back to the ranch but hid himself from me for some time, fearing that I might be angry. Well, it's not easy to be angry with a dumb animal, now, is it, Marshal?'

" 'Hmm,' said the senator. 'I can see why you were concerned, Hugh. But you see, the truth will out, and there's no harm done.'

" 'I guess not,' said Hugh. 'I'd better be looking into where harm has been done.'

" 'Yes, poor Frenchy,' said the senator. 'Let me know what you find out, will you? I'll be going back to Salem soon, so I hope you and your lovely wife will be joining us for supper on Sunday.'

" 'Thank you,' said Hugh, trying to think up a good excuse not to.

" 'A married man,' said Blake. 'Splendid. I, too, am a married man. I have just sent my beloved a letter and the money to come to Paradise Valley to join me. I may be a bit hasty, but I think that this community will suit her just fine. Much better than the Butler homestead, bein' so far out and all. That country's fine for lookin' at, but not living in. She's a Birmingham belle, you understand.'

" 'She will be most kindly welcome,' said the senator.

"Hugh realized that he had spent far too much time listening to wagging tongues. 'Gentlemen,' he said, 'if you will excuse me. I have some marshaling to do.'

"The senator was expounding upon his deal to make Paradise Valley the center of Western commerce as Hugh got on his horse. He saw Johnnie Campbell brushing down his horse and rode over to say hello to his friend.

" 'Hey, Johnnie, next time you go out hunting the wolf, let me know.'

" 'Oh, sure, Hugh,' said Johnnie. 'I always tell you when I go huntin'.'

" 'Yes, you do,' said Hugh.

"Johnnie avoided Hugh's eyes and kept brushing.

" 'Well, later, Johnnie,' said Hugh, and to himself as he turned Butternut away he thought . . . *Now that's damned strange.*

"When Hugh got into town, he found the door to his office ajar. He looked around the room and didn't see anything of importance missing, at first. The old hunting rifle and his pistol in its holster still hung on the wall. The papers were on his desk just as he'd left them. But something was gone, and in a heartbeat he knew what it was. The rubbings he'd made of the plaster molds had been torn off the wall, leaving the tacks still in place. He looked over and around and through his desk. Sure enough, the molds were gone, too.

"Hugh wrapped the belt of the holster around his waist for the first time since taking on the job as lawman. He stepped outside. A dark cloud had come in over the valley. Wild ducks circled about the sky, enticing the thousands of ducks in the nearby lakes and waters to join them for a trip to Klamath Lake. He noticed Anna Weidemeier on the second floor of the store building looking out the window. She pulled two curtains together rapidly and modestly, as if caught in the act of dressing. This gave Hugh an idea, and he strolled up to the Weidemeier store.

" 'What can I get for you, sir?' asked the oldest Weidemeier boy, Joseph. Joseph was a chemist and had become a very reliable pharmacist's apprentice and a miracle worker at the soda fountain.

" 'How's about a cup of coffee,' said Hugh, 'and a little of your time.'

" 'Sure thing, Marshal.'

" 'Any of your family see anybody going in or out of my office last night?' asked Hugh.

" 'Well, I know I didn't,' said Joseph, and then shouted at the top of his lungs across the floor. 'Esther? Did you see anybody in the marshal's office last night?'

" 'Joseph, I wouldn't be shoutin . . . ,' Hugh started to say.

"Clarence Davenport, the editor for the *Paradise Valley Chronicler* and about the nicest busybody that had ever put ink on paper, came around the stationery aisle. 'You have a break-in, Marshal?' asked Clarence.

" 'Anything missing?' somebody else over in sundries called out.

" 'No!' shouted Esther. She in turn shouted Hugh's question to an older sister across the store. That other sister ran upstairs to find Missus Weidemeier.

Hugh just shook his head. He'd brought it down on himself. Still, a mistake can be turned to advantage. Clarence sat down next to Hugh on a fountain stool, a pad and pencil in hand, ready to take notes. 'So, tell me what happened?' he asked.

" 'Well, Clarence, as you know, old Frenchy had two horses stolen yesterday.'

" 'Two horses stolen,' said Clarence as he wrote. 'No kiddin'. I ain't heard 'bout that.'

" 'I'd made some plaster of Paris molds of the tracks,' said

146

Hugh. 'And today I was going to show 'em to some of the stable boys and the blacksmith, to see if they could recognize the horseshoes in questions. I'd made some pencil rubbings, too.'

" 'That so!' said Clarence, scribbling wildly.

" 'Marshal!' came a shrill cry from upstairs, right through the ceiling. It could be none other than Missus Weidemeier. Hugh engaged his cup of coffee, and Clarence was writing the beginnings of an article. 'Marshal!' came the shrill cry again, but this time from the other end of the store. Before long, Missus Weidemeier stormed through the aisle. 'Marshal!'

" 'Yes, ma'am.'

" 'I didn't see you come in. Your office. There were men in your office! Looking for you,' she stated, almost out of breath from her long run down the stairs and across the floor.

" 'Did you see who?' asked Hugh.

" 'The Campbell boy,' said Missus Weidemeier.

" 'And when did you see him?' asked Clarence.

"Hugh sat back and let the editor do both their jobs.

" 'It was before daybreak this morning,' said Missus Weidemeier in one breath.

" 'You always up that early?' asked Clarence.

" 'I have to get the breakfast, you fool,' said Missus Weidemeier. 'Any virtuous woman's up that early. Christian or Jew.'

" 'You sure it was him?' asked Clarence.

" 'The men he was with,' said Missus Weidemeier, 'they fired up lamps so they could look around. I saw them. If you don't believe me, ask Lewis Benchley.'

" 'The barber?' asked Clarence.

" 'That's right,' Missus Weidemeier announced with finality. 'He was driving into town early and came down Main Street while the Campbell boy was still out in front of the door to the marshal's office.'

" 'Why didn't you tell the marshal sooner?' asked Clarence.

" 'Because I didn't know where he was, you nosy little man,' said Missus Weidemeier. 'And I don't have time to be riding all over the valley looking for him. Oh, and there is one other thing. A strange thing. When Johnnie and his friends rode up to the marshal's office, they all had funny hats on that covered their faces. Is this a Christian holiday? Should we carry these hats?'

" 'Ain't no Christian holiday ceremony I ever heard,' said Clarence, scribbling wildly.

" 'If they had their faces covered,' asked Hugh, 'how did you know it was Johnnie Campbell?'

" 'They went in your office with the hats on,' she said, 'but when they came out, the hats were off.'

"That made sense to Hugh. If you were going to snoop around a dark room, you'd have to uncover your face first. Johnnie and the others had made the mistake of not covering up again before leaving. Like all thieves, they'd been in a hurry.

" 'I'll square up on the coffee later, Joseph,' said Hugh, then remembering an item on his shopping list. 'Oh, Joseph, you have any more plaster of Paris?'

" 'Sure thing, Marshal.'

"Joseph left his post at the fountain and within a few minutes offered a plain brown box of plaster to Hugh. Hugh nodded solemnly. Joseph sat down at the fountain next to his sisters.

" 'You gonna arrest Johnnie Campbell?' asked Clarence like a five-year-old boy.

" 'Depends,' replied Hugh. 'Depends. The door to my office ain't ever locked, so it isn't a clear case of illegal entry.' He lowered his head and quietly made his way out of the store.

"He was getting even more edgy uncomfortable about

Frenchy's absence and hoped that Frenchy had found Belle and Napoléon wandering beneath the mountains and that Johnnie's fooling around with the molds might be some practical joke. But this was the hope of his heart. His belly told him otherwise. He saddled up and went back out to find his old friend.

"Frenchy did not maintain a large crew, and the men he did employ he kept at a distance from his own home, figuring that they would be better off without the boss breathing down their backs. Hugh found the hands easily enough, out drinking at the Hog Farm, but not a one of them had seen old Frenchy. The very next piece of riding took Hugh to Frenchy's home. The fire had gone out entirely in the stove and fireplace, and the place was the same as ever, unkempt, unused, and cold. Hugh rode up the foothill not a hundred yards away from Frenchy's cabin and looked over Paradise Valley. He knew the direction Frenchy had headed out and figured by starting at the place where the search would have ended he might save the most time. He went to the lakes.

"He saw no sign of Frenchy, but he did find Napoléon. The stallion was jet black with silver lightning-shaped markings along the withers. He was as proud as they come, but he was ready to go home and happy to follow Hugh, 'though he certainly never let it be known that he was tired and hungry. Hugh figured that he'd find Belle soon enough. Horses stay close to their own and show a loyalty to one another of the purest form. The two horses wouldn't necessarily be side by side, however. Napoléon was young and could run. Belle could only mosey.

"After riding less than a mile, Napoléon began to snort and pull back on the line Hugh had tied to the horn of his saddle. They found Belle . . . or what the wolf had left of her.

"Hugh took time to fix the location. Frenchy's hired hands would need to come out and move the carcass. There was no sense in leaving it out, as it would only serve as an invitation for all the scavengers in the state. He'd have tried to do it himself, but he was now more than ever in a hurry. He was silently praying that he'd find Frenchy like he'd found Napoléon, proud, tired, and ready to go home.

"He passed through the lakes district and came to the bottom of the mountain. He'd have to give up his search for the day in short order. Jessie would give him hell for being late, but surely she'd understand his wanting to find Frenchy.

"Much time had been lost working into each little cañon or going to the top of each little hill. In one of the valleys, Hugh found a long-dead campfire with the charred remains of what had been a brightly colored nutcracker. This added credibility to old Padover's story about the time he'd been sent to bring back the toys for Christmas, had gotten stuck in one of those instant and furious blizzards, and had been forced to make a fire with the whole purpose of his trip out of the valley.

"After a few more turns on the mountainside had been explored, the sun was 'way down. Hugh took his fix of location and gave up for the day. The trail took a fork that offered him the choice of going into town or toward Frenchy's ranch. He figured that he'd missed dinner and was in for it as it stood, so why not make one more pass at Frenchy's ranch . . . in high hopes that his friend had given up and gone home.

"It is easy to understand the belief in ghosts and such. Just take a ride on the trail at the edge of night. Hugh saw a hundred shapes to make him pause and call out for Frenchy. It was when one of the shapes moved and snorted that Hugh jumped up in his saddle. Even his horse reared back.

"The shadow was certainly one of the four-legged variety, and, when it got close, it smelled enough like a horse to take the supernatural out of the experience. The moon was just hovering over the eastern horizon and was very large. In the new but dim light, Hugh lit two matches at once so as to get a quick flash of light. The horse was Frenchy's favorite hunting mount, General Bertrand . . . named for one of General Napoléon's marshals. The matches went out, but in the moonlight Hugh saw a human form lying to the side of the trail.

"He got down.

" 'Frenchy?' he said to the motionless form. He reached down to the face and knew it was Frenchy. The ear was missing. And so was the life in the rest of the body.

"Hugh never realized how deep the well of his feelings ran. He was grateful that he was allowed to shed a few tears and shout in rage by himself. But he couldn't indulge in his emotional inventory for very long. Something had to be done.

"He searched the ground for any large rocks so he could make small piles around the body. This would mark the location of the body for a later look-see around the area. This was another trick he'd learned by reading up on the recent archaeological digs in Wyoming and Colorado. He then made a very large pile of small stones on the trail so he wouldn't ride on by the other stones during the light of day. He snapped a stick where the feet lay nearest the trail. As he gathered poor old Frenchy up into his arms, he took a moment to feel whether the hands were turned up, down, or in a fist. They were flat and open, which meant to Hugh that Frenchy hadn't recognized that there was danger.

"Putting Frenchy on top of Napoléon was no easy task. Napoléon didn't care for the smell of death and didn't want it tied on his back.

" 'Come on, Napoléon,' pleaded Hugh. 'Give him one last right ride. Please.'

"Napoléon stood still and watched carefully as Hugh flopped poor Frenchy over his back. Napoléon lowered his head as Hugh tied Frenchy down. To make things worse, Butternut was none too easy with any of this and had moved off some. Hugh had to find Butternut to get some rope to put around Napoléon, who'd in the meantime moved off some while Hugh was looking for Butternut.

"While stumbling about in the moonlight, Hugh discovered a campfire. Two large timbers, pre-cut with saws by his reckoning, were still smoldering. If Hugh hadn't known better, it looked like Frenchy had set up a big bonfire with the cross on top of the old reverend's church.

"It was closer to Frenchy's cabin than to town, so Hugh made his way there in the moonlight. Two of Frenchy's hired hands had come home and were starting up their evening fires in their quarters. Hugh called out to them, and before long they were gathered around the body of Frenchy slumped over Napoléon. They asked a lot of questions that Hugh couldn't answer, swore revenge on the party responsible for the murder, and then started cursing about the back wages they weren't likely to collect.

"Hugh had them help get the lifeless body into the cabin and then sent them into town so as to bring some pertinent folks to Frenchy's cabin and to get word to Jessie about what had happened. He filled the wait for their return by bedding down the horses, starting up a roaring fire in Frenchy's place, and laying out the body for a closer examination. The first of the hands returned with a basket of dinner, still warm, sent by Jessie. From his recounting, Jessie was fully understanding of Hugh's absence and only worried about his general nourishment. The next hand to return brought Sawbones McCaffrey.

" 'Yep, he's dead, all right,' announced Sawbones, having viewed the body for a moment and having lifted up the arm to let it drop stiffly to the side. 'Let's find out why,' he continued, turning the body over and starting to take off Frenchy's clothing.

" 'Well, this looks like a pretty good reason for death,' he announced, pointing to a large hole in the back of Frenchy's head. He rolled the body over and pointed to a small hole in Frenchy's forehead.

" 'Some kind of projectile. Without a doubt, a bullet,' said Sawbones. 'Bring me my bag and I'll dig out whatever there is left of the bullet. And get me some towels and a basin, or jar, somethin' to put the brains in. This is gonna be good and messy,' he added, his eyes glassing over with a perverse ecstasy.

" 'Was there any kind of fighting?' asked Hugh.

" 'Well, I don't see any bruises, cuts, scrapes, or the usual indicators,' said Sawbones. 'No mushy parts of the head bone. Let me see those knuckles again.' Sawbones picked up Frenchy's right hand, dropped it, and then picked up the left hand. 'No swelling in the knuckles, or any other indication of fist fighting.'

" 'I'll get out to where I found the body first thing in the morning,' said Hugh.

"Hugh couldn't watch as the doctor started to scoop out Frenchy's gray matter, but decided to stay near the cabin. The moon was but a bright spot buried in the clouds. Hugh drank coffee on the porch and watched as the lightning shed its instant and ghostly light about the valley. Eventually Sawbones emerged from the cabin, smelling of blood.

" 'Well, I didn't find much,' said Sawbones. 'Here, you can take these, Marshal.' The doctor placed some bullet fragments into Hugh's palm, saying . . . 'There ain't enough there to tell what kind of gun did it.'

"Suddenly there was the crack of gunfire from less than a mile away, and plenty of it.

" 'Sounds like the Stumbos ag'in,' said Sawbones.

" 'Probably so,' sighed Hugh. 'But in light of Frenchy's death, I'd better ride along to make sure if it is them. Thanks, Doc.'

"It took some time to saddle up Butternut in the dark, but gunfire still continued. Hugh's heart pounded as he sped the horse in the general direction of the noise. The clouds became a blanket overhead and began to flash with sheet lightning. Riding in lightning isn't easy on a horse, and it's not particularly a safe thing to do. But it helped Hugh make his way in the darkening night. The gunfire was slowing down. Hugh was certain this racket was related to Frenchy's murder, but much to his disappointment and also relief the gunfire turned out to be routine.

"John and William Stumbo had come to Pleasant Valley after the War Between the States. With nary a wife nor child between them, they lived and worked together in absolute disharmony. As wheelwrights and carpenters, there was no questioning the quality of their workmanship, but their continual bickering with one another made their company altogether unpleasant. Even the blue jays avoided their place.

"Their house was really nothing more than a cabin, and, considering they were extraordinary workers with wood, it displayed with crystal clarity their mutual problem with alcohol. On certain anniversaries meaningful only to veterans of the War Between the States, the Stumbo brothers would start to drink whisky. They then would start remembering how things had been in the conflict. This was always a sad mistake as it resulted in fist fighting. But when the Stumbos played that game of theirs, invariably Hugh had to get out of bed and put a stop to it before it caused the death of one or both of them.

"Sure enough, they'd closed the damper to their fireplace and shuttered the windows. Hugh got off his mount and carefully approached their hut. There was a Rebel yell, and an Enfield sang out. Splinters of wood showered on Hugh's head. William Stumbo shouted . . . 'Glory!' A moment later, the wall again splintered, this time to the report of an old Harper's Ferry musket. Dim firelight and smoke shot like jets out the holes. Hugh waited a moment to see if they were slowing down any.

"The general idea of this game was to fill the house with blinding, eye-blistering smoke so as not really to see your target, and then call out and shoot at your brother. The Stumbos called the game Antietam. While the gunfire might keep the valley folks awake, it usually resulted in only a mild wound to one or both of the Stumbos. All the same, Hugh didn't want one of them to get lucky. Bang needed their talents, and to lose one would be to lose the other.

"Hugh slowly pulled out his revolver and let go a round in the air.

" 'What was that?' shouted William.

" 'That wasn't you?' shouted John.

" 'Stumbos, at ease!' shouted Hugh.

"The cabin door opened. Smoke billowed out as from a terrible battlefield.

" 'You hurt?' asked William of John.

" 'Nah,' said John. 'You hurt?' asked John of William.

" 'Nah,' said William.

" 'What can we do for you, Marshal?' asked John.

" 'For one thing, you can quit playin' that damned game,' said Hugh.

" 'I told you we shouldn't be playin' at night!' said William.

" 'Damn if it wasn't your fool idea!' bellowed John.

" 'Was not.'

" 'Was, too.'

" 'Was not.'

" 'Stop it,' shouted Hugh. 'Now sit down and get some air. And then fix up some coffee. You're keepin' me awake.'

" 'Sorry, Marshal,' said William.

" 'How many times am I going to have to come over here and get you boys to quit?' said Hugh with anger and authority.

"The Stumbos just looked down at the ground like bad schoolboys.

" 'You gonna arrest us again?' asked John.

" 'No, I ain't gonna arrest you boys,' said Hugh. 'But you're going to give me those old rifles of yours.'

"The Stumbos looked down sadly at the ground.

" 'I know the war was a terrible experience for you,' said Hugh. 'And maybe by playing this game you're gettin' something out of your souls. But one of these days, one of you is going to get killed. And that, believe it or not, would grieve me, and my missus Jessie would cry about it for days.'

" 'She would?' asked William, looking up.

" 'She would,' said Hugh. 'You are good boys. You just got to quit that drinkin' and horseplay with guns. The war is long over. If you start to feel bad about that war, come on over to my house and talk about it. Get it out in the open that way.'

" 'You mean it?' asked John.

" 'Damn' right I do,' said Hugh, starting to think that maybe he'd made a bad mistake. 'Now get some coffee and get to bed.' Hugh was about to get back on Butternut when it dawned on him that maybe the Stumbos might know something about Frenchy's murder. 'Just one more thing,' he said. 'While I've got your attention. You boys see anything unusual last night?'

"The Stumbos shook their heads.

" 'Well,' said Hugh, seeing that the cabin was now half full of breathable air, 'if you think of anything, let me know. And

I'd like you to check your firearms in town at my office first thing in the morning, you understand?'

"Hugh already had several muskets of theirs in his office. They'd collected plenty of souvenirs on the fields of Mars.

" 'Hey Billy,' said John. 'I just thought of it. Didn't you say you saw Bedford Forrest's boys last night?'

" 'Well, I might have,' said William. 'But we was both pretty drunk.'

" 'We're drunk 'most ev'ry night,' said John. 'You was out at the back house and you came in and said you saw Bedford Forrest's cavalry, and I said you was a damn' fool 'cause you never saw action with Bedford Forrest no how, and you said you'd read about them in *Harper's Weekly* and how they sometimes put hoods on their heads when they went to places they didn't want to be noticed, and I said how the hell you not gonna be noticed when your shootin' everybody in sight, and you said that I was a damn' fool 'cause it was the way Forrest was fightin' after the surrender at Appomattox. Don't you remember, Billy?'

" 'No,' said William. 'But that don't mean I'm callin' you a liar.'

" 'Well, you might as well be,' argued John.

Hugh slowly backed away and got over to Butternut.

" 'I was not callin' you a liar, Reb.'

" 'No, you wasn't, but it was the way you wasn't that was callin' me a liar, Yankee.'

"Hugh gave up on the Stumbos for the night. As he rode away, he heard the unmistakable sound of knuckles running into jawbones.

"In the morning, Hugh went out to the fence where he'd taken the original casts. Two of the molds he'd left were still in place and hadn't been fooled with, outside of a little rainfall. Hugh carefully took his knife and pulled them from the ground. Then an hour's ride took him to the place where he'd found Frenchy. Again, he poured the plaster into some nearby prints that he was certain were not either his own or Frenchy's. He got back to town in time to see the good doctor hauling Frenchy's remains in.

"The body of a murder victim was a rare enough sight in Bang that a small crowd gathered outside of Doc McCaffrey's office.

" 'What happened to Frenchy?' asked Missus Weidemeier.

" 'He doesn't look well,' added Haddie.

" 'Looks like old Abe Lincoln after a night at Ford's Theater,' said William Stumbo, shaking his head sadly.

" 'Damn,' swore John Stumbo, 'look at his head!'

" 'I have an announcement to make,' said Hugh loudly. 'Pierre Lematrie is dead. And I have reason to believe that he was murdered. That's all I have to say upon the matter for now.'

"Hugh had an uneasy feeling that he knew who had murdered Frenchy. All that was needed was some confirmation. He went to the Western Union office, which was, of course, in the Weidemeier store, and gave one of the Weidemeier girls a message to send to the biggest city in the state, Portland. He was going to need some help from the outside.

"He went to his office and set about to trace the hoof prints from the plaster casts he'd been smart enough to leave behind. The horseshoes had several distinct nicks and worn edges, and, if these matched the casts he'd set at the murder scene, he'd be that much closer.

"He reluctantly climbed into the saddle of his horse and went straight away to the Campbell Ranch. He was going to have to ask his friend Johnnie some hard questions about his whereabouts the night before, and he hoped that Johnnie would have some good reasons for getting into his office.

"As Hugh was no stranger to the Campbells, nobody thought much about his going into the barn and looking over the shoes on the horses there. Johnnie's favorite mount, Peanut, swished his tail, annoyed with Hugh lifting up his hoofs during a fine lunch of dry hay. Hugh took out his tracings to compare the shoe on Peanut to the shoe on the mold. Hugh's heart soared when he saw that none of the tracings matched Peanut's shoes. But there were still a good number of horseshoes to look over.

"Missus Campbell found Hugh out by the hands' quarters, lifting up the legs of horses and studying the shoes. 'Gone to black smithing?' she asked.

" 'No, ma'am,' said Hugh, embarrassed.

" 'Well, whatever it is you're doing,' she said pleasantly, 'you're welcome to stop and join us for lunch.'

" 'Missus Campbell,' Hugh asked, 'are any of the horses out workin' right now?'

" 'No,' she said. 'The men are all in the kitchen, washing up. Oh, but Johnnie's new horse, Ornery, is tied up out front. He's goin' into town after supper.'

" 'Well, I thank you for the offer,' said Hugh. 'I'm just doing some marshalin'. You can tell Johnnie that I'll be back in town tonight, and I need to talk to him.'

" 'Well, you can talk to him right now if you want,' said Missus Campbell.

" 'No, ma'am,' said Hugh. 'This is pretty serious, and I want to talk with him private-like, man to man.'

" 'Is he in some kind of trouble?'

" 'Maybe,' said Hugh. 'I hope not, anyway. But I'll be danged if I'm going to interrupt my friend's supper. Besides, I've got to get some riding done yet. Oh, one thing, could you send word off to Jessie that I'll be in town tonight.'

" 'Gladly, Hugh,' said Missus Campbell, plainly disturbed.

"Missus Campbell went off to the back house while Hugh finished examining the horses. Much to his dismay, none of the hand's mounts had the matching marks on their shoes.

"He was about to get back up on Butternut and be on his way when he remembered that he hadn't yet looked at Johnnie's new horse. It bothered Hugh that Johnnie hadn't said anything about a new horse. Johnnie wasn't one to keep secrets. Hugh's heart sank as low as it had ever been when he had found Frenchy's body. It didn't take much of a look at Onery's shoes to realize that there was a match to the tracings taken from the plaster molds.

"Johnnie had been a party to the theft of Napoléon and Belle. That left Hugh with a sickening feeling in his gut. He went back out to get the plaster casts he'd set up at the murder scene, which kept him from getting back into town till after dark. He wanted to inspect the molds from the murder scene but was afraid of what he would find.

"It was not a good day for Hugh, and, moreover, he thought as he went into his office, there would be some sharp words from Jessie.

"The door to the office flew open, and Jessie charged in with a basket covered with cloth.

" 'Do you want to tell me what's going on?' she asked

"Hugh looked up from his desk, and she met his eyes.

" 'What is it, Hugh?' she asked more tenderly.

" 'Here's the plaster molds of the horseshoe prints from Frenchy's gate,' he said, showing her the molds. 'See those marks?'

"She nodded.

" 'These are the molds I took from where I found Frenchy,' said Hugh sadly.

" 'Oh, my God!' said Jessie, covering her mouth. 'They're the same.'

160

" 'And they're from Johnnie's new horse. I've already sent word for a judge from another county to come to Bang for an arraignment.'

" 'You're going to arrest Johnnie?'

" 'I have to,' said Hugh.

" 'But he's one of your best friends.'

" 'I know that, Jessie. I know that.'

" 'I can't believe he'd kill Frenchy!'

" 'Well, if he didn't, he knows who did,' said Hugh.

"Jessie stood silently, and Hugh could see that she was thinking. She broke the silence. 'Couldn't you just let this be, Hugh?' she wondered.

" 'I can't do that . . . even if Frenchy hadn't been a good friend of mine . . . and yours.'

" 'But if you arrest Johnnie Campbell, we'll have no friends left in this valley,' she said, her eyes welling up with tears.

" 'I know that,' said Hugh.

"There was a knock at the door.

" 'Come on in,' said Hugh nervously.

"Johnnie Campbell came in with his father, mother, and the reverend.

" 'Hugh,' said Johnnie, grinning broadly, 'Ma said you needed to see me.'

" 'That's right,' said Hugh. 'But I'd rather just talk to you alone, Johnnie.'

" 'Missus Campbell indicated that there might be trouble,' said the reverend. 'If you don't mind, I would like to hear what you have to say.'

" 'And I'm his father,' said the senator. 'I have every intention of staying.'

"Hugh sighed. 'All right, then. Johnnie, I've got me some witnesses that say you got into this office last night.'

161

" 'That's right,' said Johnnie. 'I came by to see if you wanted to go out wolf huntin'.'

" 'No, Johnnie, that ain't why you came by,' said Hugh. 'You knew about me takin' plaster molds of the prints at Frenchy's, so you came in and stole those plaster molds.'

" 'Have you got proof of this?' demanded the senator.

" 'No,' said Hugh. 'But what you didn't know, Johnnie, is that I had some other plaster molds out in the ground at Frenchy's.'

" 'So?' said Johnnie. 'What's this got to do with me?'

" 'The markings on your horse's shoe, where it's worn, I mean, are the same as on the molds I took from Frenchy's gate, and from where I found Frenchy's body.'

" 'This is ridiculous,' said the senator.

" 'Be careful, Hugh,' advised the reverend. 'You are in danger of swearing false witness against your neighbor.'

" 'I don't think so, Reverend,' said Hugh. 'Johnnie, we can do this easy or we can do this hard. You can tell me why you stole those plaster molds and who killed Frenchy, or I can arrest you and make you tell the whole damn' world about it in a trial.'

" 'How dare you!' shouted the senator.

"Missus Campbell burst into tears.

" 'Well,' said Hugh firmly.

" 'There's nothing to tell you,' said Johnnie.

" 'I'm afraid, then, that you are under arrest for horse theft and murder.'

" 'Olivia,' said the reverend to Missus Campell, and to Jessie . . . 'Jessie. We'd better step outside.'

"The reverend opened the door. Missus Campell fled to the street, but Jessie held her ground.

" 'Jessie?' asked the reverend. She shook her head and went over to Hugh's side. The reverend shook his head and closed the door behind him.

" 'Come on, Johnnie,' said Hugh, taking a large key off the wall and pointing to the one-room cell in the back of his office.

" 'What if I don't want to,' said Johnnie.

" 'Do as he says, Son,' said the senator firmly. 'I'll not have you breaking the law by resisting arrest. It would only give credence to the marshal's case.'

"Johnnie strolled proudly back to the cell.

" 'You have just made a big mistake,' said the senator. He left the office and slammed the door behind him.

"Hugh stood in silence.

" 'He'll get over it,' laughed Johnnie from inside the cell, the door still wide open. 'We're still friends, Hugh. You just don't know what's goin' on yet.' Johnnie's confidence bothered Hugh.

" 'Would you like to tell me?' begged Hugh.

" 'Can't, partner,' said Johnnie. ' 'Least, not yet.'

" 'What do you mean, not yet?' asked Jessie.

"Hugh thought a moment and whispered to Jessie . . . 'Maybe it's something he doesn't want to talk about in front of. . . .'

" 'A woman? That'd be so typical of a typical man,' muttered Jessie softly. 'But if you think he might talk if I leave. . . .'

" 'I'd just as soon you stay. But maybe. . . .'

" 'I'll be back,' she said. 'Now that I think about it, I'd better get over to Weidemeiers' and head off as many of the rumors as I can.'

"The flow of visitors for Johnnie Campbell started out as a trickle, but by the next morning it became a flood. The girl friends and school chums avoided Hugh's glance as they entered, or left, his office. Senator Owen Campbell and his missus came to the office around dinner time, bringing with them a fine dinner for both Johnnie and Hugh. The reverend was with them.

" 'We figured you'd both be mighty hungry,' said Missus Campbell.

" 'I would have preferred to dine in the comfort of my own home,' said the senator. 'But I'm with my family and my friends, so where we eat doesn't really matter.'

"Hugh's morale jumped up from the valley to the peak. 'I'm glad you feel that way,' he said.

" 'You are a part of our community,' said the reverend. 'And it is a good community, and we take care of our own.'

" 'There you go,' said Missus Campbell, pulling out the last of the fare from her giant basket.

"Hugh let Johnnie out of the cell, and the reverend stood over the desk and pronounced grace. There was only one chair in the office, and Hugh offered it to Missus Campbell. They all began to eat.

" 'This reminds me of the old Sunday meetin's' said the reverend. 'Just enough chairs for the women and children while the men stood and partook of God's glorious bounty.'

" 'I miss those times,' said the senator.

" 'Well, I don't,' said Missus Campbell. 'I didn't particularly like the rain coming through the canvas and drippin' down on us while we were praying together.'

" 'Yes, the new church is just grand,' said the reverend gratefully.

"They ate happily and silently until the reverend had had his fill and took to talking. 'You surely got everyone upset, Hugh,' he said as he passed the sliced meats to Johnnie, who was still eating.

" 'I'm sorry,' Hugh said.

" 'At first, I was very angry,' said the senator.

" 'We even had to call Sawbones for a sedative,' added Missus Campbell.

" 'But I realize now that you were only doing your job,' said the senator. 'From time to time, I, too, have had to make a stand, a stand that is not popular with my colleagues or constituency. I understand that you've wired for a judge.'

" 'Yes, sir,' said Hugh, smiling at the realization that you can't keep a secret in a small town.

" 'A good idea,' said the senator. 'I understand that Judge Lane is on his way and should be here by morning.'

"Hugh nodded as he took a bite of potatoes and gravy.

" 'We'll get this over with once and for all,' said the senator.

" 'Oh, before I forget,' said Missus Campbell, 'Jessie's over at the Montbattens'.'

" 'She sure does get on with Haddie,' said Hugh.

" 'She's very upset by all this,' said Missus Campbell. 'And it's not good for a woman in her condition.'

" 'It ain't so easy on me, neither,' said Hugh.

" 'I know that,' said the senator. 'You were fond of old Frenchy, after all. And Frenchy was a good hand with the horses. A credit to his race.'

" 'Credit to his race?' interrupted Hugh.

" 'Come, now, Hugh,' said the senator. 'You know as well as I that old Frenchy had Negro blood.'

" 'So what if he did? What if he'd been black altogether? That doesn't mean we get to go around killing colored folk!' said Hugh.

" 'You're right,' interrupted the reverend, looking sternly at the senator who was beginning to get angry. 'We are all God's creatures. But remember, Hugh, this is not the kingdom of God. Not yet. Here, the order to things sometimes doesn't make sense and doesn't seem fair. I need go no further than the

Gospel . . . just look at what happened to the Son of God.'

" 'What's your point, Reverend?' asked Hugh.

" 'Frenchy's death is most unfortunate, Hugh,' said the reverend. 'But Frenchy was of the unfortunate race we call the children of Ham, while Johnnie Campbell is Senator Campbell's son.'

"Hugh slumped back in his chair disgusted. He studied his benefactors. They all waited for his next words. He thought carefully because what he was about to say could easily ruin the atmosphere of reconciliation. He looked at Johnnie. 'I want to know why, Johnnie,' he said. 'I figure you lured Frenchy out into the hills by taking Belle and Napoléon. I know about when he died and pretty much how he died. He probably thought you'd come to help look for Belle and Napoléon. He wasn't expecting a bullet in the head. I can see it all pretty clear. But what I don't understand is why?'

" 'What do you mean?' asked Johnnie.

" 'I think the question is straightforward enough,' replied Hugh. 'Why did you kill Frenchy?'

"Johnnie looked to his father and mother.

"The reverend hung his head, silent. The senator and his son tightened their lips. Only Missus Campbell looked Hugh in the eye, and her gaze could have cut steel rail.

" 'What I done, I done for the good of the community,' said Johnnie. 'And especially for you, Hugh Buchman.'

" 'I fail to see how this killing benefits the community, or me in particular,' said Hugh.

" 'I've tried to be pleasant about this,' said the senator, getting up from his chair. 'But I guess I have to lay it on the table.'

"Missus Campbell got up and started to whisk away the picnic dinner.

" 'Then what's this all about?' asked Hugh.

"The senator put a coat around Missus Campbell.

" 'Wait a minute, son,' said the reverend to Hugh. 'There's some things men need to say in the company of men. Alone.'

" 'She knows, though,' said Hugh.

" 'I keep no secrets from my wife,' said the senator.

"Missus Campbell gave her son a kiss on the cheek and planted one on Hugh as well. 'It'll be all right, Hugh,' she whispered. 'But you'd better sit down.'

"Once Missus Campbell was on her way out the door, the senator lit a cigar and posed as if to give a long political speech. 'Women are perhaps the greatest creation of God's for the benefit of man,' he stated.

"The reverend nodded.

"Hugh looked to Johnnie, who was stuffing carrots in his mouth and rolling his eyes.

" 'But they are weaker than men,' added the senator. 'And more easily avail themselves to the temptations of the devil.'

" 'Amen,' said the reverend.

" 'It was Eve, after all, who could not resist the evil one's promptings, was it not?' said the senator.

" 'So I've heard,' said Hugh quietly.

" 'What I've got to tell you, Hugh, isn't easy,' said the senator. 'So I'll get to the bone right off. While you were out doing your job, making your way through the county, putting your very life on the line for the benefit of your fellow man, your wife was in the intimate company of Pierre Lematrie, also known as Frenchy.'

" 'What do you mean . . . in the company?' asked Hugh.

" 'You know what he means,' said the reverend.

" 'You're crazy!' said Hugh.

" 'It's God's truth,' said Johnnie. 'I seen Frenchy's carriage out back of your place nearly every day and night, while you was gone.'

"Hugh buried his head in his hands.

" 'I know this is hard,' said the reverend, putting his hand on Hugh's back. 'But don't you worry, son. Like I said, we take care of our own.'

" 'It . . . ,' stammered Hugh. 'You thought. . . .'

" 'Now, we've taken care of everything,' added the senator smugly. 'Jessie will be taken care of. Haddie knows all about this.'

" 'But . . . ,' started Hugh. 'You don't . . . ?'

" 'After the baby is born,' said the senator, 'we will have one of two choices. If, by the grace of God, the baby is white and yours, then this will blow over like nothing had ever happened. But if the child is not yours, we can make arrangements which will protect you, Jessie, the unfortunate child, and, most of all, the community.'

" 'Damn it, man!' shouted Hugh. 'The carriage you saw at my place! That was borrowed.'

" 'That may be,' said the reverend. 'But Frenchy was seen around your place.'

" 'Did it ever occur to you that he might have just been checking in on Jessie?' asked Hugh.

" 'It wasn't his place to do that,' said the senator. 'Jessie was well attended by her friends.'

" 'Take it easy, Dad,' said Johnnie to his father. 'We've just told Hugh some powerful bad news. Naturally he's going to be sore.'

" 'Damn' right, I'm sore,' said Hugh. 'If I were half a man, I'd shoot you where you stand for saying what you just said about my wife.'

" 'Under the circumstances, not a soul would blame you, son,' said the senator softly. 'We're going to take our leave now, and let you think this over. Johnnie, get your things.'

" 'Johnnie, you stay here,' said Hugh.

168

"Johnnie looked to his father. 'I think I ought to stay with him for a while,' said Johnnie. 'Even if it's in that cold cell.'

" 'A true friend,' said the reverend, patting Johnnie on the back.

" 'I'll be sending some folks around,' said the senator. 'To check in on you.'

"The reverend and senator left the office without a word more. Hugh sat with his face in his hands, and Johnnie went back to his cell. After a long silence, Hugh went out to the boardwalk and looked up at the sky. His spirits were as dangerous as the storm that was brewing overhead.

"Another cold set of clouds had flown in over the valley and began to pelt the ground with a hard rain. Hugh stepped out into the street and let the cold rain soak him to his bones. He focused on the feeling of the pounding rain and, for that moment, forgot his troubles. But that instant in time was brought to a close when there was the sound of a coach coming into town. An exhausted team of white Percherons yanked and tugged at a black Studebaker coach. Hugh hadn't seen such a rig since a visit to Saint Louis many years before. The canvas coverings for the windows were blue silk. The driver was a black man in fancy brown boots that looked more like a fisherman's waders.

"The coachman slowed the team when he saw Hugh.

" 'There's rooms at Weidemeiers' store,' shouted Hugh, pointing.

" 'Thank you, sir,' shouted the coachman. 'But I've been instructed to find a Mister Johnnie Campbell.'

" 'Well, sir, he's in here! Guest of the county,' said Hugh.

" 'You must be Marshal Buchman.'

" 'I am.'

"The coachman pulled in the reins and stopped the team completely. He jumped down onto the street, which was rapidly turning into mud. He opened the door. A tall and full-bosomed woman stepped down and hurried into Hugh's office. No doubt about it, she was something to look at. Hugh followed her into his office.

" 'Martha!' said Johnnie from his cell, plainly delighted.

" 'Oh Johnnie,' said Martha, rushing to his cell. After planting a very wet, and perhaps deep, kiss on Johnnie, Martha pulled back, her eyes beaming, and sized up Johnnie. 'Well, what have you done this time, Johnnie?'

" 'Marshal Buchman . . . I mean, Hugh, here . . . says I murdered a man,' said Johnnie.

" 'Well, did you?'

" 'You know me, Martha,' said Johnnie. 'I wouldn't just go off and kill some feller. Not unless there was a damn' fine reason.'

"Martha studiously looked over Johnnie's cell, pondering his words, before turning to Hugh. 'How much?' she asked Hugh.

" ' 'Scuse me?' asked Hugh.

" 'How much will it take . . . for you to release Johnnie to me?' she asked.

" 'Bail ain't been set, ma'am,' said Hugh.

" 'It ain't no use trying money on him, Martha.' Johnnie laughed.

"Martha looked around the office, went over to Hugh's desk, picked up one of his books, and then smiled gently at Hugh.

" 'I've grown accustomed to the West, Marshal,' said Martha. 'Forgive me, but I quite forget myself at times. There aren't many men with books out this far. You are a gentleman, so allow me to introduce myself. I am Martha Huskems.'

" 'Martha Huskems, the . . . ?' Hugh caught himself.

" 'Courtesan,' said Martha with a smile. 'Or, if you prefer, whore.'

" 'You came all the way from Portland?' asked Hugh.

" 'I was in Pendleton this afternoon, and I came as soon as I heard you were in trouble, baby,' she added, cooing to Johnnie.

" 'You can't step in a horse cookie in this state without everyone knowin' about it,' laughed Johnnie. 'My dad's just gonna be cooked when he finds out everybody knows.'

"Hugh stood in amazement. Martha Huskems was a living legend. It was said that, if she had made it to Cashtown, Pennsylvania, as she had planned in her youth, Lee's Army would never had moved on to Gettysburg. It was also said that the route of the transcontinental railway followed her crib from East to West. At present, she was running a floating bordello in Portland. It sat smack dab in the middle of the Willamette. When the constabulary of west Portland wanted to bring Martha in, her boys would pull the barge close to the east Portland side. And when the east Portland law men wanted Martha shut down, the boys on the west side would pull her over. The recent merger of the two sides of the city had been accomplished on account of the law-abiding citizens of Portland wanting to bring Martha to justice. Hugh wondered if a visit to Pendleton wasn't an exploratory venture to find new quarters for her girls. It was no surprise that she had heard about Johnnie, as it was widely known that more of the state's commercial and political activities were settled in her rooms than at the capitol building in Salem.

" 'I make friends easily, Marshal. I should like to make you one of them,' she said to Hugh. 'If money can't buy Johnnie's freedom, I'm sure we can come to another arrangement.'

" 'I'm a married man, ma'am,' said Hugh.

" 'How adorable! You must be newly married.'

" 'He is,' laughed Johnnie.

" 'Perhaps some champagne would help,' said Martha, gesturing for her coachman to retrieve some from the Studebaker. 'What the artillery does for the infantry, champagne does for the businesswoman.'

" 'No, ma'am, I can't,' said Hugh.

" 'Marshal,' said Martha firmly, but sweetly, 'I like getting my way, and I have been known to go to very great lengths to get it.'

" 'That may be so,' said Hugh. 'But not here in this office and not today you don't.'

" 'Come now, Marshal,' said Martha. 'I'm an educated woman. If I cannot interest you, allow me to return to my initial offer. How much?'

" 'I can't do it,' said Hugh.

" 'Ten thousand dollars?' said Martha.

" 'Ten thousand dollars?' said Hugh almost wistfully.

" 'Hell, man, take it!' shouted Johnnie. 'It ain't often a man gets paid by the woman. Ten thousand dollars. You could buy half the state.'

" 'Ten thousand dollars,' said the coachman, his eyes glazing over at the thought of the sum.

" 'I'm sorry, ma'am, but I just can't,' said Hugh.

"Martha frowned. She looked around the office disapprovingly.

" 'Perhaps if I freshen up a bit. And this is no place for a woman. I'm going down the street to get myself a room,' said Martha. 'But I will keep the oil burning late. Jacobs, here, will see that you can find your way to my room with absolute discretion. Who would know?'

" 'I will,' said Hugh sourly. 'I will.'

"Martha Huskems and her coachman went out the door.

"The rest of the evening was quiet. After a few hours,

The Buchmans

Hugh began to wonder why he hadn't heard from Jessie. Doc McCaffrey came to the office around midnight.

" 'Everything all right, Hugh?' asked Sawbones.

" 'No,' said Hugh flatly. 'I suppose you've heard everything.'

" 'More than I wanted to,' said Sawbones. 'Say, the rain's stopped. Why don't you walk over to my place. I've got some fresh coffee on. Take a few minutes to relax.'

"Hugh looked over to the cell and saw Johnnie snoozing in the corner.

" 'Maybe I'll just do that,' said Hugh. 'Say, you heard from Jessie?'

" 'Nope,' said Sawbones. 'But I'm sure she's all right. If she'd broken water, I'd've been the first to be called.'

" 'True enough,' said Hugh.

"Hugh strolled over to Doc McCaffrey's office and found a pot of camp coffee, as fresh as old Sawbones had promised. But before he poured a cup, he sat down on the doctor's couch. He never even got close to the coffee. He lay down and fell fast asleep.

"The next morning a red leather stage quietly rolled into Bang. It passed a black Studebaker coach with mud baked on the wheels, going out of town. Judge Lane, an older man, strained his neck from the coach window to see if who he thought was in that carriage was, in fact, in that carriage. She was.

" 'Martha!' shouted Lane.

"The black silk curtains were pulled back, and Martha smiled. Both coaches slowed, and Lane jumped from his before it had come to a complete stop and fell into the mud. The Studebaker picked up its pace, leaving the judge alone and in the middle of the road.

" 'I'll be back this afternoon!' shouted Martha happily to

the judge, her head sticking out of the coach. The judge stood in the mud, looking forlornly at the Studebaker, making its way down the road.

" 'Had enough of the ride, Judge?' shouted the driver wryly over his shoulder. The shotgun driver sliced apart a few granny knots with his Bowie knife, pulled out a carpetbag, and tossed it to the ground. It landed with a sickening *squish* in the mud, making a sound suggesting there had been glass inside and intact at one time.

" 'Yes, quite enough, thank you,' replied Lane.

"The driver jumped down in front of Weidemeiers' and began to unhitch the exhausted team. Three boys, like summer flies, came out of nowhere, gawking and offering to help for a small service fee. From the curses directed at them from the driver, they knew they were not wanted and ran down the road to the judge.

" 'Can you direct me to Marshal Buchman?' the judge asked one of the boys.

The boy pointed to a door on a plain one-story building. **SHERIFF** was painted on the door in gold leaf with green and cream backing. There was no missing it. Judge Lane dragged his carpetbag along behind him and waddled to the door, stiff from having slept over a very rough road.

"Hugh, still brushing the sleep dust from his eyes, came up behind Judge Lane at the door. 'Hey there,' he said.

"The judge was startled and dropped his bag.

" 'You must be the judge I sent for,' said Hugh, opening the door and offering his hand. 'Hugh Buchman.'

" 'Marshal,' said Lane. 'I got here as soon as I could. As soon as I heard it was Senator Campbell's boy that was in trouble, anyways. Give me a hand with my things, will you?'

" 'Sure,' said Hugh.

"The judge looked down the road, squinting. 'What was

Martha Huskems doing out here?'

" 'She wanted me to let Johnnie Campbell here go.'

" 'Why didn't you?'

"Hugh cocked his head, unsure that he'd just heard the judge's remark. Meanwhile, the judge looked at Campbell, sitting in his cell and bored out of his mind. The judge then looked over at Hugh.

" 'What kind of man are you?'

" 'A married man.'

" 'And a new one, I reckon. Tell me, son, where can a feller get a shave and bath?'

" 'You might as well head on down to Weidemeiers',' said Hugh. 'When you're ready, just send up for your bags.'

" 'I'll send a boy along for 'em, don't worry 'bout that,' said the judge. 'I'll be down, after I clean up, to review the particulars of this case with you. Have it put together best you can.'

" 'Thank you, Judge,' said Hugh.

"Hugh opened the drawer in his desk. His eyes bulged with disbelief, and he pulled the drawer all the way out. He went over to the bookshelf and pulled the books forward so as to look behind. He opened his saddlebag and poured the contents out onto the desk. He then went over the cell and glared in at Johnnie Campbell.

" 'Where are they?'

" 'Where's what?' asked Johnnie.

" 'The plaster molds and the drawings?'

" 'Well, I can't be sure,' said Johnnie. 'It's not too well lit up in here and all. But the doc was foolin' around with some stuff, when you was out last night. And he woke me up doin' it.'

"Hugh ran out the door and into the street. He grabbed a boy walking down the road and shook him.

" 'Where's Doc McCaffrey?' shouted Hugh.

" 'I don't know,' whined the kid.

"Hugh ran across the road to the Early house, and he frantically ran into every building in the town. The folks present whispered quietly into one another's ears, keeping their eyes on Hugh the whole time. Eventually Hugh spotted Doc McCaffrey's old chestnut in front of the stable.

" 'Where's the doctor?' roared Hugh, coming into the stable with his hand on his pistol.

" 'Why, I'm right here,' said the doc, standing up.

"The doc and the blacksmith were by the forge, which was in a full white heat. Hugh came up, and on the coals he could see his plaster molds. The blacksmith poked at a mold like a camper pokes at a log in an evening fire. The mold broke in half. The remnants of the other molds glowed white hot among the coals and ashes, and with each stir of the blacksmith's poker more of the hard-gained evidence broke into smaller pieces.

" 'Get 'em out of there!' Hugh ordered the blacksmith.

"The blacksmith looked to the doctor for instructions.

" 'I said get them out of the fire!'

"The smith used his prongs to pull the plaster molds out of the fire and let them slip. They fell to the dirt and shattered into a thousand glowing shards.

"Hugh locked eyes with the doctor. "So, you, you're in on this, too!'

" 'Hugh,' said the doctor, 'there's more to this than you know, my boy. Just let it be, son.'

"Hugh felt the blood rush to his face. He wanted more than anything in the world to pull out his gun and inflict injury on old Sawbones and the smith. But then he'd be no better than the rest of them.

"He went into his office and slammed the door. He began

to clean his pistol and fit cartridges into his belt. The town was as quiet as a tomb. The usual traffic hurried, rather than sauntered, along, and the children were kept indoors.

"Mid-morning, Hugh heard a knock on the door.

" 'Who is it?' he shouted.

" 'John Stumbo!' bellowed a voice.

" 'William Stumbo,' bellowed another voice.

"Hugh opened the door. The two brothers stood shoulder to shoulder and held out their rifles.

" 'We're here as ordered, sir,' said William.

" 'Thank you,' said Hugh. 'I've changed my mind, though. You can keep those dang' rifles.'

" 'Thank you, Marshal,' said John.

"The brothers started on their way, but John stopped in his tracks.

" 'Say, Will,' he said, 'don't forget to tell the marshal about Forrest's men.'

" 'Dang, I almost forgot,' said William. 'Marshal. You know how I told you about Bedford Forrest's men?'

" 'Yes,' said Hugh.

" 'Well, here's that *Harper's Weekly* I was a-tellin' you about,' said William, pulling out a half torn up past issue of the magazine. 'I get this, even if it gets here two months late. I got hooked on 'em at Vicksburg. Weren't much to do back then but dodge old Whistling Dick's cannon balls, read *Harper's Weekly*, and listen to the Rebs slurp up stewed pussy cat.'

" 'Thank you, boys,' said Hugh. 'Now you'd better be gettin' to your work. I know I've got to get to mine.'

"The Stumbo brothers saluted Hugh, turned an about-face as though in formation, and marched away. The children on the street giggled at the sight. Not long after the brothers had left, Judge Lane came along to visit with Hugh.

" 'Well, son,' said the judge, 'I've come a mighty long way

and in a hurry. Train from Portland to Pendleton and by coach all night to Bang. Let's see this evidence you got.'

" 'I'm afraid that the evidence has been destroyed,' said Hugh. 'But if you can get the men who destroyed the evidence on the stand, you'd be able to get them to tell you that it *did* exist.'

"The judge's expression soured. 'That's not so easy as it sounds, Marshal,' he said. 'You got any witnesses to the alleged murder?'

" 'No,' admitted Hugh.

" 'Well, god damn it,' cursed the judge. 'You've run me all the way out here for nothing, then.'

" 'But I can testify that I had the evidence and against those who destroyed it,' said Hugh desperately.

" 'And everybody else sayin' you're a liar,' said the judge. 'I ain't going to waste my time, nor anybody else's.'

" 'But a man was murdered!'

" 'A black man,' said Lane. 'You didn't tell me *that* when you wired me, neither. I wouldn't have made the trip if you had.'

" 'Black, white, what's the difference? A crime has been committed.'

" 'If he was murdered, it's a shame,' said Lane. 'But it's not a crime of consequence, Marshal.'

"Hugh stood silently. It was plain that there was going to be no justice for poor old Frenchy.

"The judge shook his head. 'Don't call me out to Bang again,' he said, and slammed the door behind him.

" 'What you goin' to do?' asked Johnnie.

" 'I guess I'm going to let you go, Johnnie,' said Hugh. 'I'd sure like to know why you killed Frenchy, though.'

" 'I didn't kill Frenchy,' said Johnnie.

" 'Then who did?'

" 'I can't tell you yet,' said Johnnie. 'But I will, Hugh. I will. Right now you got to sort it out. Why don't you come a-huntin' with me? We'll track down that wolf and give it what for.'

"Hugh opened the cell. 'You're free to go, Johnnie. I'm droppin' the charges. At least for now.'

"Johnnie slowly left the cell and went outside, squinting at the sunlight on the street. Hugh watched him walk up the street to the Weidemeier place.

"When Hugh got home, he found the fire out and the cookware cold. He decided to go over the to the Mont- battens' to see if Jessie was there. The wide Missus Montbatten and her short and thin husband hadn't seen Jessie, so Hugh swung by the Lang place.

"With all of the trouble, it would be natural that Jessie would stay at her parents' home for the night. As he rode up, Mister Lang stepped out on to the porch.

" ' 'Evenin' Mister Lang,' said Hugh, not yet in the motion of dismounting.

" 'Hello, Hugh,' said Lang sadly.

" 'Is Jessie here?'

" 'She is,' said Mister Lang.

"There was a long silence.

" 'Well,' said Hugh. 'Can she come out to play?'

" 'I'm afraid not, son,' said Lang.

" 'What do you mean . . . I'm afraid not?'

" 'You know I'm fond of you,' said Lang. 'You know that, don't you?'

" 'I guess so,' said Hugh, now confused by the course of the conversation.

" 'This ain't easy for me, Hugh, but we're keepin' Jessie inside until she has the baby. And she's not to have visitors.'

" 'You'd have to tie her down before she'd give up her friends,' said Hugh.

"Lang looked down at the porch.

"Hugh felt sick to his stomach. The Langs probably had tied Jessie up. 'You don't believe this nonsense about Frenchy and Jessie?' he said.

" 'I don't know what to believe, son,' said Lang, his eyes welling with tears. 'Now get on your way, Hugh. I'll keep you posted about Jessie and how she's doing.'

" 'You can't do this, not to my wife,' said Hugh.

" 'I wished I didn't have to,' said Lang. 'But it's for your own good. And the good of Paradise Valley.'

"Suffice it to say that Hugh was mighty upset. He wanted to get his wife and leave that valley, *pronto*. But that wasn't what happened. He went to all of his friends and tried to get them to intervene. Everybody felt bad for Hugh, but nobody would do a thing. The reverend would only say that after the baby was born, if all was well and as it should be, Jessie could come home.

"A few days later, Hugh left his badge on his office desk and quit. He didn't even bother to tender a formal resignation. He pretty much stayed at his homestead, tending to the stock and biding his time. The only incident which I'll tell you, as it pertains to this story, is that one night Hugh heard a wagon bouncing up the hardened mud road to his house. It was William Stumbo, and he was crying.

" 'What's the matter?' asked Hugh.

" 'It's John,' said William, pulling a limp body out of the wagon.

" 'Is he dead?' asked Hugh.

" 'Don't know,' said William.

"They got John into the house, and Hugh saw that his shirt was covered with blood. 'What the hell happened?'

" 'We got drunk and played Antietam.'

" 'And you got lucky,' sighed Hugh. 'You'd better go get Doc McCaffrey.'

" 'He's out of town,' said William. 'He left last week.'

" 'I'll do what I can, then.'

"Hugh found that William's Springfield had placed a neat hole in John's chest. It seemed the natural thing to do to cut open the wound and pull out the Minié ball. William wept and held John's hand while Hugh gored the limp body. Fortunately the lead ball had lodged itself in a rib, but the rib was shattered. All that Hugh could think to do was to pull out the shattered bits and dislodged portion and then sew John up like a worn pair of work pants.

"The next morning John regained consciousness. He was sure enough weak and none too well. Hugh couldn't tell if it was the effects of the drinking or the shootin' which caused poor John the most misery.

" 'Now,' said Hugh, 'are you boys ever gonna play that damn' game again?'

" 'No, sir!' said William.

" 'Well, get into town and get some ointments and soup from Weidemeiers,' said Hugh.

"William flew off to town like the cannon balls over Atlanta. When he returned, Hugh forced Missus Weidemeier's chicken broth down John's gullet and covered the wound with the greasy ointments and salves that Mister Weidemeier kept in stock. It was easier for John to fall back into a deep sleep than it was to eat. Hugh sat on his porch, rubbing his eyes, and was joined by William.

" 'Marshal . . . ,' started William.

" 'I ain't the marshal no more,' interrupted Hugh.

" 'Hmm,' said William. 'That's why you ain't been in town for a month.'

" 'That's right. And you can tell that to everyone who asks, if you like.'

" 'Maybe I will. But what I came out on the porch to tell

you is that if you ever need anything . . . anything at all . . . we'll be there for you.'

" 'I might just take you up on that,' said Hugh. 'But to start, you make sure you and your brother get that war behind you. I've met other veterans, and I know that the fighting seems to have hit 'em hard. And I can always tell them that didn't really see the fightin' 'cause they talk proudly about it. It was mighty honorable of you to fight against slavery. And no less honorable for your brother to take a stand for his beliefs, misguided as they might have been.'

" 'Oh, hell,' said William. 'We didn't join different sides 'cause we believed different. You see, Marshal . . . I mean, Hugh, we both hail from Missouri. We was gonna both join the same Missouri unit, no matter what side it was. We didn't have no slaves, and we didn't care about that. We just wanted to get our belly full of fighting and get paid for it.'

" 'I see,' said Hugh, rubbing his chin.

" 'When the war broke out,' continued William, 'John was off to Hannibal buyin' some wire hoops and joiners shipped up to us from New Orleans. And me, I was up north. Well, we both joined the first recruitin' station we could find. It never occurred to us that Missouri would be sending units to each side of the war.'

"Hugh almost laughed.

" 'We spent half the war lookin' for each other,' added William. 'And we finally met up at Jonesboro, at the end of the war. This damn' Reb kept shootin' at me and me at him, and we was both off the mark. So he charged, and we got into fisticuffs right off. Well, that Reb got me down and started to re-arrange my nose, and then he stops and shouts to heaven . . . "Lord, I'm whippin' my older brother." '

" 'That must have been a terrible thing, that war,' said Hugh.

" 'We wanted a fight,' said William contemplatively. 'But I seen things I ain't never seen before and never want to see again.'

" 'All those dead bodies,' said Hugh, shaking his head.

" 'That wasn't pretty,' said William. 'But what really made me sick was all them dead horses. During the fightin', you'd hear 'em screamin' and watch 'em get their legs blowed off. Men, we deserve what we get. But them horses, what did they ever do to deserve that? There ain't nothin' so botherin' to my soul than to see the look of terror of a shot up horse tryin' to get through the thick of a fight.'

"The conversation turned to thought. By and by, they checked up on John and found him to be recovering slowly, but surely. In the evening, Hugh and William sat on the porch, watching the moon rise over the mountains in the east. A large glow of firelight filled one of the small vales of Pleasant Valley.

" 'The Langs must be burning some swamp clearing,' said Hugh.

" 'The Langs live two miles off that point,' said William. 'It's probably them Bedford Forrest boys, havin' one of their times.'

" 'What do you mean?'

" 'Ain't nothin' to tell. Those hooded cavalry boys all circle around and burn a wooden cross, shout out a bunch of mumbo jumbo, ride around, and then go their ways.'

" 'I think I'll go take me a look,' said Hugh. 'Unless you want me to stay here, in case something happens to John.'

" 'Thanks to you, John is goin' to be just fine,' said William. 'You go ahead and take yourself a look. John and me watched 'em several times. It doesn't settle well with us, but we couldn't tell you why.'

"Butternut wasn't particularly interested in a moonlight ride. He resigned to do his master's bidding, but all the same he wouldn't give Hugh much speed. He didn't understand why this ride was necessary, until he got as curious as Hugh about that glow in the ever-nearing valley.

"Before long, Hugh was in a thicket of juniper trees watching a curious sight. There were a dozen men in white hoods standing around a bonfire. They had guns in hand, but by the smell of it they weren't ready to use them tonight. The horses were relaxed and looked in his direction. They could sense Butternut's and Hugh's presence, and, as the scent was just of curiosity, they were not alarmed. All Hugh said was . . . 'What the hell?' Butternut didn't understand the words, but he knew the sentiment. After a while, they headed back to the homestead."

The old man started to chuckle. "Here I am, talking from the horse's point of view."

"Actually, I rather liked it," Jack said.

"Now, where was I? Oh, yes. What Hugh was seeing that night, but didn't know, was the very beginnings of the Ku Klux Klan in Oregon. You know that Oregon has one of the larger Klan memberships?"

"Yes, sir. But I thought that it came more recently."

"Well, it's probably in full bloom," said the old man. "But it had small beginnin's. Things like that always start small so you don't notice it, like a pretty little sage plant on the side of the trail, and then by the time you look at it again it's as big as a cow and blowin' all over the hills and valley and gettin' in the way of everything. But I'm gettin' off the story."

Chapter Four

"John Stumbo fully recovered, and he and his brother were very grateful to Hugh. As for Hugh, he started to pack up his family's things and get ready to take Jessie out of the valley forever. It wouldn't be long before the baby arrived, and Hugh knew that it would be his. He rather looked forward to seeing the whole valley eating crow about it. All the same, he had no desire to stay any longer than that one moment of satisfaction. He planned to head to Portland, find out where his father was, and perhaps hook up with the old man.

"One morning, as Hugh was tying down some furniture onto the wagon, a fancy surrey came down the road.

" ' 'Morning, sir,' said Ashton Blake. Hugh noticed right off that Blake was now wearing the marshal's badge. Beside Blake was the only woman Hugh had ever seen who was prettier than his own Jessie.

" ' 'Mornin' yourself,' said Hugh.

" 'If I'm not mistaken, it looks as though your intentions are to move,' said Blake thoughtfully.

" 'As soon as I get my wife back,' grunted Hugh.

" 'Get your wife back?' asked Blake's female companion. 'Ashton, whatever does he mean?'

" 'My dear,' said Blake slowly, drawing out words, 'this is not a matter for general public discussion.'

" 'Hell it ain't!' Hugh said. 'The whole damn' valley talks about it every day. They've judged and convicted Jessie and me for somethin' Jessie didn't even do. And in the meantime, I can't even see my wife.'

" 'Ashton, honey,' said the woman, 'what crime exactly did the poor thing commit?'

" 'And now,' interrupted Hugh, 'even strangers are askin' and talking about it.'

" 'Ashton,' scolded the woman, 'where are our manners?' She graciously rose from her seat and delicately came down from the carriage like a leaf descending from an autumnal tree. She extended her small, white hand. 'Allow me to introduce myself, sir,' she said. 'I apologize for my poor manners. I know your name already, Mister Buchman. I am Mary Blake. And I understand that you have already met my husband, Mister Ashton Blake.'

"Hugh smiled and found himself honestly enchanted by the beauty and grace of Mary Blake. He wondered how she had ever hooked up with a man of dubious character like Ashton Blake.

" 'Now tell me,' said Mary, turning to her husband, 'since you are the newly appointed marshal of this territory, what crime did Missus Buchman commit?'

" 'It isn't a matter of law,' said Blake, shifting nervously in his seat.

" 'Then why on earth can't this man be with his wife?' demanded Mary.

"Blake looked down. 'I said that this isn't for public discussion.'

" 'Well,' said Mary, 'if it isn't a crime, and since there isn't anything to talk about, I think I will take it upon myself to right this grievous wrong.' She turned to Hugh. 'Now, just where is your precious wife?'

" 'At her folks',' said Hugh, realizing that he was under Mary's spell. 'The Langs.'

" 'Oh, that lovely family Ashton introduced me to on the way over,' said Mary. 'Well, now. You just get your horse, and you get right over there. Ashton, honey, will you be so kind as to drive me back to that family?'

Blake shook his head and rattled the reins to get the team moving. Hugh stood in amazement.

" 'Well?' said Mary sweetly to Hugh.

" 'I don't know,' said Hugh. 'The Langs can be head-strong.'

"Mary laughed melodically. 'Honey, so can I. Now get along and get over there.'

"Hugh hurried off to the pasture, convinced Butternut that it was time for a ride, and saddled up. By the time he got to the Langs', he saw his very swollen and pregnant wife weeping in Mary's arms. Mary herself was covering her eyes in grief. The Langs wouldn't look Hugh in the eyes. Blake looked dispassionately on from his carriage.

" 'Hugh!' cried Jessie.

"In his excitement, Hugh jumped from his horse before he'd come to a full stop. He got up from the dust and rushed to Jessie. She laughed at the sight and cried with joy in his arms.

" 'Oh, Jessie!' cried Hugh. They both began to weep heavily. Mary wiped her eyes and came over to the couple.

" 'Now, it's not a good thing for a woman to have too much excitement when she's in the motherly way,' said Mary to Hugh, and, turning to the Langs . . . 'And we'll have no more of this nonsense. It's as plain as the nose on my face that Jessie would never have done such a thing. You owe her, and her cute little husband, an apology. Now,' said Mary, looking to Hugh . . . 'since I know that all your things are on that wagon of yours, you'd both better be coming over to our spread for the night. And Ashton,' she added sharply, 'I'll be having you stay out with the boys tonight.'

"Hugh did not want to stay under Blake's roof, but Mary

was dead on right. All their things were in the wagon, and from the looks of things Jessie could drop the baby in a heartbeat.

" 'Now Jessie, honey,' said Mary sweetly, 'you ride with me. Ashton, you can borrow a horse and show Hugh the way.'

"Jessie with tears in her eyes quickly got into the carriage, not once looking back to her parents, hanging their heads. Hugh wondered how Mary could accomplish his wife's liberation when he could not. He was then ashamed of himself for having only confronted the Langs but once!

"The carriage shot down the dusty road, leaving floating dust for Blake and Hugh to ride through.

" 'I hope you don't hold it against me,' said Blake, riding up beside Hugh. 'That I'm the marshal, now, I mean.'

" 'Not hardly,' said Hugh. 'As soon as I can, I'm taking Jessie out of this god-forsaken valley.'

" 'I'm sorry you feel that way,' said Blake. 'You're a good man and true. The community needs men like you.'

" 'You sound like the reverend,' said Hugh.

" 'That is high praise,' said Blake. 'He is an outstanding citizen. And though I have not been a member of his congregation for very long, and I am certainly a new arrival to Bang, I can tell that the reverend is responsible for the wonderful spiritual and economic development of the area.'

"Hugh could have kept up the conversation, but didn't like the company. He kept quiet and let Blake do all the talking.

" 'Hugh, what are your feelings about the Ku Klux Klan?' asked Blake finally.

" 'I've read some old *Harper's Weekly* articles on 'em,' said Hugh. 'But I don't know that I have any feelings one way or the other, except that I think that men who cover their faces have something to be ashamed of.'

" 'There is a spiritual power to anonymity,' said Blake. 'It removes the existing social ranks and makes every man an equal. And it provides a certain amount of protection.'

" 'Be that as it may, Blake,' said Hugh, 'I don't see what equality has to do with it. If I understand it, men of color, the Jews, and even the Roman Catholics are not welcome in the Klan.'

" 'The white race is at a critical turning point,' said Blake. 'If we allow the inferior races to control us in any way, we are doomed.'

" 'I wasn't aware that being Jewish or a Catholic was a matter of race,' said Hugh. 'Look at the Weidemeiers. They don't look much different from us.'

"Blake frowned and said nothing more on the ride to his own small ranch. The ride was not a long one, as the Langs had sold some of their spread to Blake. Hugh noticed a sizable herd of steers on the Blakes' land, and it occurred to him that he hadn't seen many cattle, or horses, on the Lang place. Lang had sold them all to the railroad company to make an impression, Hugh reckoned.

"Blake's hired hands were all standing around, smoking cigarettes.

" 'Gentlemen,' said Blake sharply, 'haven't I given you enough work to do?' They all glowered at Hugh and went their way, except big Heff who stood his ground and kept glaring at Hugh. Hugh paid no mind and went into the house.

"Mary already had water boiling.

" 'Where's Jessie?' asked Hugh.

" 'She's laying down,' said Mary. 'I think that tonight is the night. Poor thing, her water broke on the way out here. Ashton, honey, go into town and get Doctor McCaffrey.'

" 'I'll send one of the boys,' said Blake.

" 'You will not,' said Mary. 'You have taken this poor man's job. The least you can do is help him out in his hour of travail.'

" 'But I just put the horse up,' whined Blake.

" 'I don't care if you put up the whole bunch of horses,' scolded Mary. 'Now you git to Doctor McCaffrey's this instant. You hear?'

"Blake sulked out of the house. Hugh, while delighted at Blake's getting the hard end of his wife's tongue, knew that Mary was a force to be reckoned with. You just can't argue with grace and beauty, even when they come on real harsh.

"Hugh found his wife laying down.

" 'Hold me,' said Jessie.

" 'I'm so sorry, Jessie,' said Hugh, feeling his eyes well up with tears.

" 'It's not your fault,' said Jessie.

" 'I tried to get you,' said Hugh, his voice breaking.

" 'I know you did, Hugh,' said Jessie, now crying. 'I know you did the right thing.'

" 'I wanted to shoot my way into your folks' home and take you out, but I just couldn't,' said Hugh, now crying.

" 'You did right, Hugh. You did right.'

"He held her in his arms, and they cried. Suddenly Jessie flinched and groaned.

" 'Oh, my God!' exclaimed Hugh.

"As Mary had predicted, the baby was on the way. Hugh waited outside as darkness covered the valley. He heard Jessie scream and wanted with all of his heart to be at her side. However, Mary had ordered him outside, grumbling about the fact that she was going to have to deliver the baby without the doctor. Hugh's eyes desperately searched the darkness for sign of riders, but it was his ears that brought him the good news. He could hear the creaking wagon that old Sawbones McCaffrey favored inching its way down the dark country road. Jessie's screams were getting louder and more frequent.

The Buchmans

"The doc pulled up just as Mary came out onto the porch. She was covered with blood and was weeping.

" 'Oh, Hugh,' she said softly. Hugh shot to the bedroom and found a crying infant in the arms of his wife. Her eyes were closed, and her expression grim.

" 'Jessie!'

"Jessie lay still, not opening her eyes. The bed was soaked with blood.

" 'Jessie!' cried Hugh, grabbing her shoulders.

"McCaffrey and Mary came into the room without a word. Mary scooped up the tiny infant and carried it out of the room. Doc McCaffrey matter-of-factly took Jessie's wrist and felt for a pulse while looking at his pocket watch. The doctor laid Jessie's hand back down gently on her chest and with a sad expression in his eyes looked to Hugh. There were no words to be said, so the doctor pulled a sheet up and over Jessie's head. Hugh fell to his knees at the side of his wife's bed and sobbed so hard he choked.

"When Hugh came out of the Blake bedroom that next morning, he found Mary spoon feeding the infant milk and adoring his child. The Reverend Catley sat quietly with Blake. Hugh stood, speechless.

The reverend slowly rose. 'I'm so sorry, Hugh,' he said, as he came up like a storm over the mountains.

" 'Well, is it white?' growled Hugh.

" 'What?' asked Blake.

" 'Is the baby white?' demanded Hugh.

" 'As a snow petal,' said Mary.

"Hugh stared accusingly at the reverend, who for the first time in his life looked down with shame.

" 'I'm sorry, Hugh,' said the reverend quietly. Looking up to meet Hugh's rage, he added . . . 'My intentions were only to protect you, and Jessie.'

" 'And your little lily white community,' said Hugh. 'Now give me the baby.'

"Mary approached Hugh and handed him the bundle in her arms.

" 'You have a son, Hugh,' she said, trying to offer some small comfort. 'A fine baby boy.'

"Hugh looked down at the squinting little face and headed for the door.

" 'Where are you going?' asked Mary.

" 'I'm riding my son out of hell,' said Hugh.

" 'Hugh,' said the reverend.

" 'Reverend,' Mary commanded, 'you best go pray for the dear and departed. Ashton, you go get the carriage ready. Sit down, Hugh.'

"The reverend obediently went into the bedroom, Blake went outside, but Hugh stood his ground. Mary came to him and gently took the bundle from his arms.

" 'Now, Hugh,' said Mary firmly, 'I don't blame you one bit for being angry. Not one bit. And you have every right to leave this town. I've never been so angry with a town, any town, in all my life. But you can't go taking this baby out on the road just like that. You've lost your precious wife. And if you take this baby now, you'll lose him, too.'

" 'What am I going to do, Mary?'

" 'Leave town if you want,' said Mary. 'But let me take care of the baby. At least, until it's grown enough to travel.'

" 'How long is that?'

" 'Until it can walk,' said Mary.

"Hugh thought for a moment. 'Mary,' said Hugh, 'I appreciate your offer and I really appreciate your wanting to help. And God knows, I sure could use a woman's help when it comes to takin' care of a baby and all. But I ain't leaving Paradise Valley without my son. And there's something I have to say to you, and I might as well tell you now as later.'

Mary's eyes searched his.

" 'I don't much like your husband,' said Hugh.

" 'Why?'

" 'I don't intend to spread dirt on a man's reputation in his own house. I just don't trust him, that's all,' said Hugh.

"Mary sat down and rocked the baby and had a look of grave concern on her face. Finally she said . . . 'You have your reasons for that, I'm sure,' she said. 'And you're a brave man to tell me that openly. If there's anything I've done to . . .'

" 'Oh, no,' interrupted Hugh. 'It's a long story. Maybe I'll tell you sometime, but not today.'

"Mary rocked the baby and thought for a moment. 'It's not right that you have to take care of the baby all by yourself. If you can't see fit to let the baby stay here, how about letting the baby stay with the Langs?'

" 'Missus Lang's got enough work, and I don't think that she's . . . well . . . up to the job. She's gettin' kind of long in the tooth.'

"Mary let out a laugh, her eyes brightening. 'That's a perfectly awful thing to say about a woman, Hugh Buchman. We're not horses, you know.'

"Hugh looked down and felt his face flushing.

" 'Well, if that's the case,' said Mary, 'suppose I were to stay with the Langs to help with the baby? Despite everything that's happened, they are the child's grandparents. And if I were there. . . .'

" 'Fact is, Mary, I'm feelin' mighty sore at them right now.'

" 'And I'm certain that they are as heart-broken about Jessie as you are and are feeling mighty guilty about the way they suspected her of . . . well . . . you know. You ought to give them a chance to make it up to you . . . and to Jessie.'

"Hugh closed his eyes and rubbed them. He then watched Mary rock the baby and thought about it. He finally said . . . 'Thank you, Mary. I've been pretty much stuck in my own saddle here, haven't I?'

" 'And no one would blame you a bit, Hugh.'

" 'You're probably right about Mister and Missus Lang. Still, supposing they let you stay there with the baby, what about your husband?'

" 'You may have no high esteem for Ashton,' said Mary, 'but he's a good man. It will not be easy for him, but, given all and everything, he'll understand.'

" 'But you ought to be with him,' said Hugh. 'And have a baby of your own.'

" 'I wish we could,' said Mary wistfully. She looked down with adoration on the youngest Buchman, and then looked up at Hugh. 'You'd best go get some rest. Go on into town and stay at the Weidemeier store. I'll send Nathan or Claibourne along and let you know when the preacher's set the service for Jessie.'

"Blake entered the room and looked to Mary for instruction. She sat with the baby, rocking to and fro. Hugh and Blake went outside. Blake looked into Hugh's eyes directly.

" 'I am truly very sorry,' said Blake. 'You have never been partial to me, and I know it,' he added. 'But I have never been your enemy, Hugh Buchman. I hope you can understand that. I hope you can call me friend, one day.'

" 'Thank you,' said Hugh. He extended his hand. Blake gladly shook.

"Hugh avoided folks as much a possible and had an especially hard time being sociable at the funeral. The reverend gave a touching sermon, which was filled with his own jeremiad of guilt and grief. At times, the reverend's words were clouded out entirely by the weeping of Haddie Montbatten, Missus Campbell, Missus Lang, and even the Stumbo brothers.

"After the last shovel of dirt was piled on top of Jessie's grave, reluctantly Hugh took the crying baby over to the Langs'. While driving the wagon, he realized that he couldn't both drive and comfort a baby. He stopped the wagon and checked the diapers, only to find that they were unsoiled. There and then he knew that he would need help with this baby business, at least for a while.

"It didn't surprise him at all that Mary was already at the Langs' and that they were busy planning which room would be best for the baby. Hugh was still uncertain about leaving the baby with his grandparents, but as Mary had predicted, the Langs begged for a chance to make amends and welcomed Mary's offer to help. The final argument in favor of Mary's plan was that the baby quit crying the moment it was in Missus Lang's arms.

"Hugh did not stay at the Langs' that night. He started out for his own spread, but took a turn up the road toward the Stumbos'. They were already good and drunk and sitting on chairs outside their cabin. Leaning against the walls of their place was a very drunken Johnnie Campbell. They were all drinking strong whisky by starlight. They seemed to know that it was Hugh who rode up and brought out a chair for Hugh to sit on. Nobody said a word. Johnnie offered Hugh the jug, and Hugh took a long drink. The caustic mixture made Hugh choke. William slapped his back and softly said . . . 'Glory, Hugh Buchman, glory.'

"Hugh's little ranch was immensely profitable in the days to come as Mister Lang paid him twice the going rate for cattle and horses which were, in turn, sold with a healthy mark-up to the railroad. Most of Hugh's visits to the Lang place were not so much as they had been in happier times. He played with his growing son, whom he named Herman, after his own father. He also talked with Mary about his son and how to properly attend to babies. Beyond that, he kept his visits with the Langs and all their friends short and focused on business matters only.

"Hugh had posted a long letter to Herman Buchman at Weidemeiers', and Missus Weidemeier told everybody that it was about twenty-five pages long and was probably about everything that had happened. She never opened a single letter that passed through her hands on its way from or to the stage-coach, but she liked to divine the contents and had a knack at guessing the contents of each envelope. A letter addressed to Hugh and postmarked from Texas came into Bang a month letter. Missus Weidemeier accurately guessed, by thoroughly feeling it before putting it into Hugh's box, that there was a one page letter and about two hundred dollars in five dollars bills. Hugh opened the letter at Weidemeiers' fountain, and Missus Weidemeier quietly, but at a distance, counted the five dollar notes sticking out of the envelope while Hugh read the letter. For the first time in months, a smile passed over Hugh's lips and brow like a momentary burst of sun in storm.

"A month later, the town finally got a look at Hugh's father, old Mister Herman Buchman. He came through town with his wagon full of books and shouted out hellos to everyone like he'd known them for all their natural lives. After that grand entry, Hugh kept his father to himself, with the exception of one dinner at the Langs'.

"Hugh delighted in watching his father mercilessly take on the reverend, the senator, and Mister Lang point for point about the benefits or, depending upon your viewpoint, the evils of socialism. Old Herman Buchman, you see, had been one of the principals in the Knights of Labor and had distributed the writings of the British and German authors on the subject of socialism. He even had copies of a manifesto written by a burly old bearded German named Marx. Old Buchman first threw the burden of responsibility of evil back onto God for creating a sinful species like man in the first place, an argument the reverend couldn't verbally out-maneuver. Buchman outlined the history, great and noble kingdoms, of diverse races to Mister Lang and to Ashton Blake, by way of showing that the sons of northern Europe had no superior claim to civilization. He stumped them all when he asked, if we were all descendants of Adam and Eve, then why are there so many races and colors of skin? The reverend tried to say that Negroes were descendants of Cain to which old Buchman posed another question, that being if the Chinese and Polynesians were therefore descendants of the Negro. And, to the delight and confounding of all present, old Buchman's question to the reverend was why all the portraits of Adam and Eve display them with belly buttons? If everybody hadn't felt so guilty about what they'd done to Hugh and Jessie, there's no question that they'd all have found a way to get old Buchman out of Bang and as far from Paradise Valley as possible for not showing the reverend the proper amount of respect. When it came to social issues, there just wasn't any way to talk the old man down, no matter which side of the fence he wanted to be on. And that could change from one course in the dinner to the next.

"Old Buchman stayed with his son for a month and sold just about everybody in the valley a book or two. He even talked the reverend into buying a volume of Dante's Inferno, illustrated by Gustave Dore. Still, the city fathers of Bang were mighty glad when old Buchman announced that he was on his way to San Francisco to sell books for Herbert Howe Bancroft. In fact, he had in his possession a manuscript, a history of Utah, which Bancroft was considering for publication to help finish off his exhaustive history of the West. Only Hugh had the presumption to ask just what his father might know about Utah, having never lived there. Before leaving, Buchman gave his grandson an entire run of books published for children by the firm of the McLoughlin Brothers in New York City. The child, however, used these for teething, not reading.

"Hugh promised to join his father in the months to come, as soon as little Herman was big enough to travel. Herman, in turn, promised to have a place suitable enough to raise a child and had high hopes of being able to get Hugh work in San Francisco.

"In the meanwhile, Mary proved to be a fine mother to little Herman. Blake was visibly bothered to leave his wife at the Langs', but he was smart enough not to say so. He stayed busy with his job as marshal and as rancher.

"A new group of settlers had come to Bang in the spring, and for the first time that Hugh could remember there wasn't enough food at Weidemeiers' as the game animals had become scarce due to all the hunting. The Weidemeiers had to order foodstuffs to be sent by wagon down from Portland, Pendleton, and Spokane, and this resulted in higher prices. Nobody seemed to mind at first because of the need. Before too long, however, Hugh began to hear Blake and Mister Lang discuss the damnable profiteering Jews. Hugh pointed out that they attended the reverend's services and, therefore, weren't orthodox Jews by any stretch of the imagination. The reverend nodded to this but added that he knew that, if other Jews were to come to Bang, he feared that the next thing you'd know there'd be a synagogue and even more Jews. Hugh shook his head and hoped that the reverend's concerns wouldn't go any further than words.

"On little Herman's first birthday, Hugh decided that he would take him into town and buy him a flavored soda drink at Weidemeiers'. The Langs offered him dinner on their return, and Mary asked if she could come along for the ride. Hugh had kept his relationship to Mary very formal. To do otherwise would open a door that Hugh knew he would be tempted to go through.

" 'A fine day for a ride,' said Hugh, first helping Mary into the wagon, and then lifting up his son to her waiting arms.

" 'It is, indeed,' said Mary, taking in a deep breath.

" 'I think I'll take the long way into town,' said Hugh. 'Herman, would you like to play with the Lo children?'

"Herman seemed to understand but was not yet old enough to give an answer.

" 'The Chinese?' asked Mary.

" 'The only Lo family I know,' said Hugh. 'The Los have a lot of kids, some Herman's age. He ought to have some friends around here.'

" 'But they're Chinese,' said Mary.

" 'What's that got to do with anything?'

" 'Nothing, I guess,' said Mary. 'I've been meaning to pick up some eggs and such. Maybe I can get them at a better price direct.'

" 'Maybe so,' said Hugh.

"Mister Lo welcomed Hugh and Mary and showed them around his swamps, filled with older children harvesting rice. Every visit to the Los had its required tour of the place. The only thing that had changed was that there was now a little yellow and ochre gazebo that housed a plaster cast statue of a jolly, fat Buddha.

" 'What will the reverend say about that?' asked Mary.

" 'Reverend?' asked Mister Lo, 'He no like us anyway. Make us stand in back of church, or outside in rain. We no like his god anyway. Kill his own son. What kinda god is that?' Pointing proudly to his place of worship, Mister Lo beamed at Hugh. 'What you think?'

" 'It's pretty,' said Hugh.

" 'I think so, too,' said Lo.

"Little Herman was plainly the doll for the little Lo girls. They led him to the ducks, which he chased about. They carried him from there to their room, where they put a dress on him, and then they took him to Mama in the kitchen who shrieked with delight at the sight.

" 'Do you think that's proper for him?' asked Mary.

" 'They're playing with him,' said Hugh. Mary closed one eye and looked disapprovingly on the scene.

"Missus Lo summoned her family for a noontime meal. 'You come, too!' she ordered Hugh.

"Hugh and Mary sat down at the table, and Missus Lo became upset. 'No women at table!' she ordered Mary. 'Men here. Now. We eat in kitchen.'

" 'I'm not that hungry,' said Mary. 'Hugh, I think we should go now.'

" 'But they've invited us for a meal,' said Hugh. 'And I ain't never had Missus Lo's cookin'.'

" 'You've promised the Langs you'd be there for dinner,' objected Mary. 'And don't forget, you've promised Herman a soda.'

" 'I eat at the Langs most all the time,' said Hugh. 'And as for the soda, Missus Lo, after supper, what do you say, I take your kids into town and buy them a soda at Weidemeiers'.'

"The children's eyes were all focused on Missus Lo.

" 'You pay?'

" 'I'll pay,' said Hugh.

" 'You take me?'

" 'I'll take you.'

" 'We go!'

"The children squealed with delight. Hugh noticed that Mister Lo was concerned.

" 'You don't mind?' asked Hugh.

"Mister Lo said nothing and started to eat his supper.

"The streets were busy that afternoon. Hugh helped Mary and Herman off the wagon and then pulled the Lo kids off their wagon like a teamster hauling barrels.

" 'Mary!' shouted Blake, stepping out of his office.

" 'Ashton,' replied Mary loudly.

"Blake came over to Mary while Hugh offered to help Missus Lo from the wagon. 'Get you hand off me,' she said. Hugh pulled back his hands and held them up as though under arrest. Mister Lo chuckled.

" 'Wife no let me touch, too,' said Lo.

"Hugh looked around at the twelve Lo children and rubbed his chin. Mister Lo saw Hugh's point and let go a loud belly laugh.

" 'That different,' he said. 'She touch me first.'

"Missus Weidemeier saw the Lo family through her large, decorated window. Hugh went to the door and held it open for the Lo clan.

" 'Hello, Hugh,' said Missus Weidemeier.

" 'I hope you got enough soda water,' said Hugh.

" 'Sodas! For the whole family! Oy!' shouted Missus Weidemeier. 'Joseph!' she cried like one calls for a sow. 'Joseph!'

"The oldest Weidemeier boy came out, dusting off his apron.

" 'Joseph!' ordered Missus Weidemeier, 'you go tell the girls to bring up all the sodas and all the flavors. And get Papa. He makes them best!'

"Joseph smiled and went to the back room as the Lo family took seats all around the fountain area. Blake approached Hugh.

" 'What do you think you're doing?' he asked.

" 'I'm buyin' them sodas,' said Hugh.

" 'But they're Chinese.'

" 'I don't care if they're Zulus,' replied Hugh.

"Blake shook his head and left. Hugh saw a number of Bang's newer faces, most of whom he'd never formally met. They all eyed the large family and went out of their way to finish their shopping and get out of Weidemeiers'.

"The soda fountain was a circus of activity with Weidemeiers serving up sodas and the Los drinking up as quickly as they were provided. Hugh saw Blake outside with the reverend, Senator Campbell, and some other men he didn't recognize. They looked into Weidemeiers' with anger, disgust, and concern. Hugh felt a shiver of anger, but was distracted by his son spilling his soda on the hardwood floor.

"Hugh was late getting Mary and Herman back to the Langs'. Dinner had been long over.

" 'Sorry we're late,' said Hugh.

" 'It's not that which bothers me,' said Mister Lang.

" 'Well, what then?'

" 'I understand you took the Chinese into Weidemeiers'.'

" 'I did.'

" 'That ain't proper, Hugh.'

" 'What do you mean it ain't proper,' said Hugh.

" 'I tried to tell you,' said Mary.

" 'That's about the most stupid thing I ever heard,' said Hugh.

" 'I hope you don't do that again,' said Missus Lang.

" 'I'll take them, or anyone I please, in for a soda any time I like,' said Hugh. 'It's my money.'

" 'Of course, it's your money, son,' said Lang. 'But they just shouldn't be going into white establishments.'

" 'You've said more than once that the Weidemeiers ain't white,' said Hugh.

" 'I mean, they shouldn't be going into places for whites only,' said Lang.

"Not thinking in his anger, Hugh said . . . 'Well, there ain't no law against them going in there.'

"Much to Hugh's distress, Mister Lang thought about that and rubbed his chin.

" 'Let's get him into a nice hot bath,' said Missus Lang to Mary, taking Herman by the hand. 'Grammy will wash off all that Chinese.'

"Hugh looked to Mary and stomped outside. He didn't so much as say good night to the child for fear that his son would feel his father's rage and become fearful. He rode away and was back to his home just after dusk. He could see the glow of large fires burning over toward the Blake spread and shook his head.

"The week went by quickly, and Hugh started to calculate just how and when he and his boy were going to get to San Francisco. Surely, he thought, the boy was old enough to take to the road by now. Hugh was more than ready to go, that much was certain. He'd figured that he'd stop by the Langs' and take little Herman for a long day's ride, just to size up the boy's ability to travel. By the time he got to the Langs', he had planned just what he was going to tell Mary.

" 'I think I'll take Herman for a ride around the valley,' he said.

"Mary frowned. 'That's a pretty long ride for boy his age. And I bet you haven't got extra clothes or even a picnic lunch, do you?'

" 'Extra clothes?'

" 'What if you get caught in a rainstorm?'

"Hugh cocked his head. She was right, of course.

" 'Why don't you come inside while I fix some sand-wiches?'

" 'I got a better idea. Whenever we get hungry, we'll just stop by the nearest place and see what they got on the fire.'

203

" 'Hugh Buchman! You think the whole valley's some kind of New Orleans hotel and that you got standing dinner reservations!'

" 'Ain't no one ever not offered me something to eat. Except the Stumbos, and, as near as I can figure, they don't eat.'

" 'You're terrible.'

"At that moment little Herman toddled out of the Lang place and was scooped up by Hugh and placed on the wagon. 'Want to go for a ride?'

" 'Not so fast there, cowboy,' said Mary. 'You just wait a minute while I get his coat and a change. Just in case.'

"As promised, Mary returned momentarily with a coat and a change of clothes for the boy. She had also put on her riding coat and climbed up on the wagon.

" 'Where you going?' asked Hugh.

" 'For a ride around the valley,' said Mary.

"Hugh sighed. Still, for the purposes of this expedition, Mary could be plenty helpful if it turned out that little Herman wasn't ready for a long day's ride. He hadn't quite reconciled himself to her attitude towards the Lo family and how she had acted the week before. Since there wasn't much new to see on the road, he decided to talk it through with Mary.

" 'I don't know exactly how I want to talk about this, Mary,' said Hugh. 'But after what you and the others said about not mixing with the Lo family last week, I came that close to packing up and taking little Herman out of Paradise Valley.'

" 'You do have peculiar beliefs,' said Mary. 'I guess that's what comes from having a socialist for a father.'

" 'He's got nothing to do with my beliefs. What I want to know is what's so wrong with being different than us? I mean, being Chinese or black-skinned or even Jewish?'

204

" 'I don't know that there's anything wrong with it, Hugh,' said Mary. 'And only the Lord knows His own purposes. But the truth is, we are not all equals. And it isn't proper for everyone to be mixin' with everyone else.'

" 'And I suppose God's got different parts in heaven, so's to keep everyone apart?'

" 'I wouldn't know about that, Hugh. I only know what's right for me and mine. I want you and Herman to have the best in *this* world, Hugh. And in this world, it isn't good for white children to be playing with yellow children or for white men to have black friends.'

" 'Why not?'

" 'Because it isn't, that's all.'

" 'But why?'

" 'I don't know, Hugh. Maybe there isn't anything wrong with it. It's just not done.'

" 'Well, what if it was done? Would that make it right?'

" 'I suppose. If the right people did it.'

" 'The right people?'

" 'Of course, silly.'

"Hugh laughed, scratched his head, and pondered just how he was going to get Mary away from the circle of logic that seemed to guide her point of view. The air suddenly filled with the sound of gunfire, and it was coming from the Lo farm just up the road.

" 'What the . . . ?' said Hugh, shaking the reins. 'Hee-yah!'

"The carriage pulled into the trail going down to the swampland the Los called home. Six hooded men were riding around the Los, firing their pistols into the air. Hugh stopped the carriage. He got out and got into the toolbox, where he kept an old pistol. There were only three cartridges in the chambers.

" 'Mary, get to town and quick,' he said. 'Get your husband, and, if they're there, get the Stumbo brothers. They're on the way into town. Tell 'em to bring guns and to hurry it up.'

"Mary, pale with fear, sped the wagon down the road toward the Stumbos' place outside of Bang.

"Hugh walked up toward the house and raised his pistol into the air. He let go a round, and the riders all came to a halt.

" 'Get out of here!' demanded Hugh, summoning up his marshal's persona.

" 'Let's kill him,' said one of the riders. There was no mistaking the voice of Blake's hand, Nathan.

" 'Let me!' said another. Hugh got a good, daytime look at that rider, and from the size of the rider and the poor horse that carried him it had to be Heff.

The riders came together and cautiously approached Hugh.

" 'Go home, Hugh Buchman,' said a deep voice.

" 'Reverend?' asked Hugh. There was no mistaking the voice he'd often slept through on Sunday morning.

" 'This is none of your affair, sir,' said Ashton Blake's voice.

" 'It is now,' said Hugh. 'Now get out of here.'

" 'I said, let's kill him,' said Nathan.

" 'No need for that,' said the reverend. 'Go on home, Hugh.'

" 'I'm not going to let you kill the Los,' said Hugh, raising his pistol.

" 'That is not our intention, Hugh,' said the reverend. 'We are just giving them a message.'

" 'And that is?'

" 'To stay out of town.'

"Hugh stood silently. He could hear the woman and children crying behind the walls of the house. 'I ain't leavin',' said Hugh. He wished he'd had more rounds and, even more, wished he hadn't sent Mary off for her husband.

" 'Suit yourself,' said Blake. 'You might find this instructive.'

"Blake swung around and charged his horse around the Lo homestead. He was followed by his men. The reverend rode slowly about the spread and stopped at the sight of the little Buddhist shrine.

" 'Heathen idolatry!' cursed the tall, hooded reverend. He dismounted and began to gather up what combustible branches and bushes he could find. Two of the riders got off their mounts and helped the reverend gather up wood. When it became plain that there just wasn't enough to start a good fire, they began to tear up the duck house and throw the flowers planted along the bottom of the gazebo.

"Hugh ran over to the house to see if the Los were harmed. 'Mister Lo?' he shouted at the door.

" 'Go away!'

" 'It's me, Hugh Buchman.'

"The door had several gunshot holes, and Hugh could see an eye looking out at him. The door opened a crack.

" 'Go away . . . go away,' said Mister Lo. 'They kill you, too.'

" 'They aren't going to kill anyone,' said Hugh, hoping he was right.

" 'Tell them to go, leave alone,' said Mister Lo.

"Hugh pushed open the door and got into their home. They were all, except for Mister Lo, cowering in the corner. Mister Lo had the axe he used to remove the heads of ducks and chickens clutched tightly in his right hand.

" 'I know that this isn't easy, but stay calm,' said Hugh. 'They'll be gone soon enough.'

"He looked out through the bullet holes in the door and found all the riders, except for Heff who could not easily dismount, looking for wood. Hugh put his hand on Mister Lo's shoulder.

Mister Lo was shaking with fear, but had a determined look in his eyes. 'What doing?' he asked.

" 'Don't know,' said Hugh, lying. He knew darn well what the reverend had in mind, but didn't want Mister Lo to know.

"They stood and listened as the riders tore up the duck house and then went on to tear up the chicken coup. An hour passed, perhaps longer. It seemed much, much longer to Hugh. He then heard the reverend.

" 'Let us pray! God, Thy vengeance is cruel and swift. Let us be the instrument for Thy will here on Earth. Let us remove that which is unclean. Let us remove that which is unholy in Thy sight. Amen.'

"There was the sound of a crackling fire.

" 'What doing?' demanded Mister Lo.

"Hugh put his arm up to hold Mister Lo. 'Don't look,' said Hugh.

"But that is precisely what Mister Lo did. Seeing his family shrine ablaze, he rushed out the door, waving his axe. Hugh ran after him, and, before Hugh could shout out a warning to the riders, Lo had brought the axe down on the skull of one of the five men standing around the burning shrine. The rider collapsed, his skull split in two.

"Hugh shouted . . . 'No!' . . . in vain. The riders had their pistols in hand and emptied their chambers into Lo. Lo reeled back from every hit, collapsing to his knees and jerking back before falling on his side. The riders continued to blast the corpse until every round was gone. Hugh stood motionless. He knew that it was time for him to make a stand. He raised his pistol and fired into the nearest hood. The rider collapsed in a heap. The other riders stood in disbelief that a white man would fire on his own.

" 'Well, damn you anyway!' said Nathan's voice. He raised his pistol and fired, but it only clicked. He'd run out of rounds on the Chinaman. Hugh didn't wait and let his pistol finish off Nathan, whom he'd never liked anyway. The large man on the Percheron charged and jumped from his horse on top of Hugh. Hugh lost his breath and was in Heff's mighty clench.

" 'I'm a-gonna beat you to death!' boasted Heff, landing a large blow into Hugh's face. Hugh felt blood run down his throat and struggled to break the grip. Suddenly Heff dropped Hugh to the ground.

" 'What the hell?' said Heff.

"Mary had returned with the carriage. She looked at this portion of hell and cried . . . 'Oh, God!'

"Hugh looked up, his vision blurred. The Stumbo brothers leaped out of the wagon. Each had his pet rifle in hand.

" 'Form ranks!' shouted William.

" 'Take aim!' shouted John.

" 'Now wait a minute, boys!' shouted Blake.

" 'Ashton?' shouted Mary, recognizing her husband's voice.

" 'Fire at will!' shouted William.

"The Enfield and Springfield spewed a cloud of sulphurous gas. The reports echoed through the valley. Both balls pounded into Heff's large chest. He stood as though unaffected and opened his mouth to curse at the brothers. A jet of blood exploded from his mouth and nostrils. The Minié balls had torn through the fat and into his heart. He fell face forward, nearly on Hugh.

"Hugh watched as two of the remaining three riders raced to re-load against the Stumbos, who swiftly and carefully plunged the barrels with ramrods. But as good as they had become on the killing fields, their rifles required seventeen separate steps for preparation and were no match for the quick-loading, cartridge-fed Colts the riders sported. The two riders opened fire on the Stumbos.

" 'Thy will is hard, oh, Lord!' said the hooded reverend, looking skyward.

"The Stumbos withstood each shot, pushed back by the impact, but continued to ready the next volley. William was the first to fall, his rifle discharging into the sky. John got one shot off, hitting one of the rider's horses. The horse shrieked, ran a small ways, and fell to its knees and died. John collapsed. William pushed himself up and looked over to the riders. He whispered . . . 'Glory.' . . . and fell dead. John, mustering all of his strength, threw his arm around William and expired.

"The only sound was Mary's weeping, her face buried in her hands.

" 'You, sir, are a great deal of trouble,' said the voice of Ashton Blake.

"Hugh looked as the reverend stooped down and picked up one of the dead rider's pistols and stood over Hugh. He drew back the hammer. 'I'm sorry, Hugh,' said the reverend. 'I truly am. May God forgive you.'

" 'No!' shouted Mary.

"Hugh looked up, and the last thing he saw in this world was the flash from a pistol going off in his face.

"Johnnie Campbell rode up in his white robes, his head uncovered.

" 'You're late,' said Blake gravely.

"Johnnie Campbell looked down sadly at his friend's dead body and looked accusingly at the reverend. 'What d'ya do that for?' "

The old man stopped in his narrative, and by the moonlight Jack could barely see him close his eyes and rub his temples with his hand.

"So, that's why the Blakes adopted my father?" asked Jack.

"Old Blake kept waiting for the boy's grandfather to come and fetch him. But he never did."

"But what about . . . I mean, didn't anybody do anything about the murder of Hugh, or Mister Lo?"

"Nope," said the old cowboy.

"So what happened? And how come the railroad never came to town?"

There was a long pause.

Chapter Five

"Well," said the old cowboy finally, "after Hugh Buchman's funeral, things started to change, and not for the better. Some folks got scared and moved out of Paradise Valley altogether. Not all that long after all the trouble ended, old Ben Holladay himself came to Bang, representing the interests of all the railroad companies concerned. And he was put up at the Campbells'. In style. Mayor Blake . . . and, yep, he was made mayor . . . and Lang, and Catley and the senator all showed him around. And old Ben was pretty observant.

" 'That store there,' said Holladay. 'The one called Weidemeiers. It looks abandoned.'

" 'Yes,' said the senator. 'The owners have moved. But we'll have someone up and running it in no time. Especially if we have a railway through town.'

" 'Why they leave?' grunted old Holladay.

" 'Didn't say exactly,' said the senator. 'Said something about it being too much like the old country and were out of town the next day.'

" 'And I see the wheelwright's place is boarded up,' said Holladay. 'What happened to the two brothers who worked it?'

" 'We'll have plenty of carpenters move to Bang,' said Lang, avoiding the question posed by Holladay. 'Providin' we get a railroad, of course.'

" 'I haven't seen much evidence of all that big game you were telling me about, Reverend,' said old Holladay.

" 'The herds haven't come in large numbers lately,' said

the reverend. 'It must be the wolves.'

" 'The big two-legged kind that kill 'em all to extinction,' mumbled Holladay.

" 'There's still lots of waterfowl,' said Blake.

" 'That's dandy come time for goose dinner at Christmas time,' said Holladay. 'Now, about the ranching. When am I going to see a herd of cattle?'

" 'We've been buying them up and selling them to you for the workmen,' said Lang.

" 'You mean you ain't kept enough around to feed yourselves?'

" 'We've got lots of waterfowl,' said Blake, repeating himself and growing conscious of it.

" 'You folks must be awful fond of duck,' growled Holladay. 'Too greasy for me. And it don't go far with the hungry men who build railroads.'

"Old Holladay took a ride around town with the boys, getting grumpier with each inch of the way.

" 'So, what I see is plenty of speculators,' said Holladay. 'But where's the laboring class?'

" 'What do you mean, sir?' asked Blake.

" 'Oh, I see lots of pleasant folks around,' said Holladay, 'but where's the immigrants?'

" 'Why on earth would you want them around?' asked Lang. 'We like to think of ourselves as a wholesome and pure community.'

" 'Wholesome and pure don't get the work done,' said Holladay, pulling out a cigar and lighting it. 'It's the unwholesome and the impure that do the work that the captains of industry need. We can get speculators . . . boys like you are a dime a dozen back East. And they, at least, got money to spend. I've seen enough, and I'm going to tell you what I think. The railroad has several options for routes. We were hoping to find a thriving community for our midway point from Reno to Spokane. Gentlemen, I'm sorry to say that Bang is about the furthest thing from a thriving community I've seen in a long time. You must have worked hard at it, 'cause most every spot out West, exceptin' those come-and-go mining towns, has made a good show of it.'

" 'Surely, Mister Holladay,' said the reverend, 'if the railroad comes here, we'll be back on our feet in no time.'

" 'Railroads exist to get people or goods from one place to another place with people or goods,' said Holladay. 'Railroads do not exist solely to build up a town. The railroad has to have a reason to come here, and I just don't see one.'

" 'We are a good community,' said the reverend. 'There must be a million good, white families itching to come out West and find a home in a place like Paradise Valley.'

" 'Reverend,' said Holladay bluntly, 'let me be frank with you. I heard that the Klan is pretty much in charge here. It's been my experience that fear and ignorance are very bad for business. If you don't believe me, just look at the South.'

" 'The South, sir,' said Blake defensively, 'was ravaged by the federal Army.'

" 'Like I said,' said Holladay, 'fear and ignorance ain't good business. Just you remember who started that fight, Mister Blake.'

" 'If not here, then, where?' asked Lang, always on his toes when it came to investments.

" 'Well, I seen a lot of Indians and plenty of immigrants over by Klamath Falls,' said Holladay thoughtfully. 'And there's a whole lot of immigrants over in Boise. Granted, they're Mormons, but they work like the devil. You will receive my formal statement and report to the trustees in several weeks.'

The old man took a long drink from his cup and coughed.

"And that's why the railroad never came to Bang, Jack."

"Just one more thing," asked Jack. "Did Johnnie Campbell kill old Frenchy?"

"Old Frenchy's murder was never officially resolved, and probably never will be," said the cowboy sadly. "All that's left of Frenchy are the names on the land around here, like Napoléon's Creek, Belle Lake, Toussaint Road, and a few others. But I can tell you this. Johnnie Campbell did not kill Frenchy. He made some bad mistakes in his life, and one of them was ridin' with those Klan boys. He saw the reverend kill poor old Frenchy in cold blood, and it bothered him plenty, and it still does."

"Campbell's still alive?"

"And who do you suppose would know so much about his dear old friend Hugh Buchman, and them early days in Paradise Valley?"

The cowboy's old worn face curled in the moonlight. His eyes were wet and reflected the moon's ghostly white light. Silver streaks sped down old Campbell's cheeks.

Jack stood up and stood over old Johnnie Campbell. There was no way for him to sort out all the feelings going through his heart, and all that he could do was put a hand on Campbell's shoulder. Campbell slowly rose from his chair and went inside to pour himself more whisky. He returned to the porch feeling as ornery and crusty as he had at the outset of his story.

"Just one more thing. What happened to the reverend?" asked Jack.

"You're gonna keep me up all night with me tellin' you just one more thing, ain't ya? Well, I can't blame you, and you, more than anyone else, got the right to know. But to answer your question . . . within about two years after the railroad not coming here, the reverend's congregation dropped

down to about two or three people. The reverend held out
and died all alone, givin' a sermon to a bunch of empty pews.
Now would you look at that. There's just a bit of a silver glow
over there to the east. Now watch. It's gonna turn all kinds of
red and then, bang, right into day. You want to crawl into
your bedroll, son?"

"No, sir. I want to see the sunrise. And then I'd like to
borrow old Kaiser Bill and go over to my grandfather's place.
Take a look around. Maybe settle in for a bit."

Chapter Six

Lightning streaked through the clouds. The thunder shook the ground. Jack Buchman sat up in the bed. His body trembled, and there was sweat on his brow. Another flash lit up the room, and he flung his feet from under his blankets and onto the floor. For a moment he could see himself in the broken mirror on the wall. The upper right side of his face had a thin, paste-colored layer of wrinkled skin dried over the skull. The eye socket was black and hollow. He grabbed for the flap of black leather and tied it around his head. He gave the lamp more wick and looked again in the mirror. The storm was now over the mountains, past the valley. His hands trembled. He wondered if it was the storm that had spoiled his sleep, or was it that he had heard someone shout—"Incoming!"—in a troubled dream.

Jack looked around the cabin. Books were in piles about the room. A table with legs taken from a large buck sat in the middle of the room. An old Winchester rifle hung over the fireplace. He smiled, for it seemed like he could tell that there was even more dust about the place than the day before, despite all the cleaning he'd done. He heard a muffled, popping sound outside and went out. There was an automobile moving on the dirt road along Napoléon's Creek. He watched it turn and start up the trail to his cabin. Buchman quickly dressed and looked in the mirror to adjust the fit of the leather flap.

He stepped out on the porch as the automobile came to a stop in front of the place.

"You Jack Buchman?" asked a man with wire-rimmed glasses.

"I am."

A large man in a gray shirt and gray pants got out of the car and put on a wide-brimmed hat. "I'm Marshal Packer," he said. "And this is Mister Garvin. Of the First State Bank in Broken Pot."

"Pleased to meet you."

Marshal Packer was visibly uncomfortable. "Well, hope you can say so after I'm done tellin' you what I got to tell you."

"Yeah?"

"Mister Garvin tells me you're livin' here."

"I am."

"Well, son, I am sorry. I truly am. But it belongs to the bank, and they want you out."

"Immediately," added Garvin.

"I've been here nearly two weeks and haven't seen anybody using the place. And, besides, it belonged to my grandfather."

"I know it did," said the marshal. "Old man Campbell told me all about it. And you're right. Nobody's usin' it. But it don't belong to your family no more. Belongs to the bank. Mister Garvin showed me the papers. Nobody's paid the county taxes for the last twenty years, and I guess that the bank did, and, well, now they own it."

"Where am I gonna go?"

"That's none of our concern," said Garvin.

"What if I don't want to go?"

Marshal Packer walked slowly up to Buchman and spoke softly. "You don't understand, son. You have to go. Ain't my idea. Hell, had my way, you could stay as long as you like. But the bank's got the papers on the place, and they want you out."

"Well, what if I buy it?"

The marshal thought for a moment and looked over to Garvin. "What if he buys the place?"

"The price is one thousand dollars," said Garvin. "You got that kind of money?"

"No. But I got a horse old man Campbell gave me. And three maverick cows I found."

"One thousand dollars, Mister Buchman."

"Can't I at least get some breakfast and pack up some of my things?"

"Right away, Mister Buchman."

"Hell, Garvin," said Packer. "Cut him some slack. My boy went over there to France, too. They all had a pretty rough time."

"Life's no bowl of cherries, Marshal."

"Well, it sure won't look good when the *East Oregonian* goes off and says you and your bank evicted a veteran. One who won a Medal of Honor." Packer sadly looked back to Buchman.

"Veterans have to obey the law like everybody else, Marshal Packer. And the paper knows who lends the money to the companies that buy the advertising."

"Can I keep my granddaddy's books?"

"Books!" laughed Garvin. "You can keep all the trash you want. Bank might even pay you to clean up the place."

Packer slowly went back to the car and looked back at Jack. "You take your time, son. But be gone by sundown, you hear?"

Jack watched them drive away and decided that he'd best sell the cows and horse. He went out to the barn and found Kaiser Bill lazily munching on the corn he'd thrown down the night before.

"We got some ridin' to do, Bill."

Chapter Seven

"One thousand dollars! One thousand dollars! Ain't nothin' in this stink hole of a valley worth one thousand dollars!"

"Take 'er easy, Mister Campbell. You'll give yourself a stroke!"

Johnnie Campbell kicked the hitching post again. "That son-of-a- . . . ."

"It's OK, Mister Campbell. Really."

"Well, it ain't OK."

"I've just got to come up with the money is all."

Campbell kicked the hitching post again and yanked a pack of cigarettes out of his Pendleton shirt pocket. He lit up and frowned. "First of all," said the old man, "the place is rightfully yours. Second, it ain't worth no thousand dollars. And third . . . third . . . I wished I had one thousand bucks to give you."

"Well, you want to buy my cows?"

"Sure, I'll buy your cows. And I'll give you every penny I got. One hundred and fifteen dollars and thirty-four cents."

"That's too much, Mister Campbell."

"No it ain't, son. It really ain't." He looked off and away. "Your grandpappy was the best friend I ever had, and, if I could, I'd buy the place for you. I owe him that." Campbell looked away and brushed his eyes. After a moment he turned back to young Jack. "But I got an idea. They's havin' a big horse show outside Broken Pot next Saturday. Sure to be some ranchers from Redmond there, and maybe they need a hand or two. They'll be havin' to move the herds up to the Dalles 'fore winter."

"I don't know nothin' about movin' cows."

"Hell, you don't. It's in your blood, boy. You brung over your three mav'ricks, didn't you?"

"But that was just three of 'em. And the poor things were so hungry, they just followed me back to the house."

"Three or three hundred. Don't make no difference. That's what you do, son. You get your hide over to Broken Pot and get yourself hired on."

Jack rubbed the back of his neck while considering the plan.

"Oh, and another thing," added Campbell. "When you get that job, best you use another horse." He saw that young Jack was lost in thought.

Chapter Eight

Jack looked at the house and then back at Kaiser Bill. The saddle pack had slid off Kaiser Bill's rump and hung limply down around his belly. Jack pushed it back up and tightened the cinch. Kaiser Bill stepped back, and the saddle pack slid off his rump again. Jack walked around Bill and realized that he hadn't packed anything in the other half of the saddle pack. He ran back into the house to find something to weigh down the other side of the saddle pack.

When Jack arrived in Broken Pot, he tied Kaiser Bill to a rail and strolled into the store on the corner. He looked up and down the street and saw a hundred cars. It struck him funny that all the folks coming to buy horses didn't seem to need them.

"*Eeeuuuu,*" said one of the young girls sitting in a booth.

The red-headed girl next to her shoved an elbow into her ribs.

"*Oowww.*"

"That wasn't very nice," said the redhead.

"I can't look at him," said a girl sitting across from the red-head.

The boy at the fountain looked pale and avoided looking at Jack. "What can I do for you, mister?"

Buchman saw himself in the mirror. The flap had slipped a little. He quickly adjusted it. "I'd like a Coke," he said.

The boy at the fountain managed to make up the drink, hand it to Buchman, and take the money without looking him in the eyes. Buchman drank in a hurry and went back outside.

He walked up the street and saw that the town had put together a large, makeshift corral and had suspended a sign: **Horse Show and Dance**. It struck him funny, and he laughed a little to himself but stopped when he saw the sign: **Horse Race. One Hundred Dollars Prize**.

Jack studied the men talking by the gate of the corral. One wore fancy chaps with leather braids and sported pearl-handled six-guns. He had a wide-brimmed hat that looked like it'd just come out of the box. He smoked and talked like he ran the show. Another older man wore a plain shirt, jeans, and had no hat. He seemed disinterested in the fancy man but was too nice to say so. The man paying the most attention to the fancy man was large with kind eyes. Jack could tell by his hands that this man had worked hard for most of his life. His hat was caked with years of dirt hardened by the burning sun. Jack felt at his flap to make sure it was on correctly and went up to them.

"I understand there's a race?"

"Sure is," said the fancy man. "And my boys will be filming it. I'm gonna use it in my next picture . . . BILLY SIX-GUNS AND THE OUTLAWS."

"Picture? You an artist?"

"Heavens, no," laughed the fancy man. "Motion pictures."

"Oh," said Jack. He had heard about them but had never seen one.

"You must be the Buchman boy," said the plain man. He extended his hand. "I'm proud to meet you, son. Heard about you. Name's Whitaker. You can call me Paul."

The large man extended his hand. "George Curtis."

"About the race?" asked Jack.

"Tomorrow afternoon. After the swap meet," said George. "Entry fee of one dollar, proceeds going to Malheur County Four-H."

Jack noticed that the fancy man was trying to look at his face without being too obvious about it.

"You don't want to see what's under it. The flap, I mean," said Jack.

"Don't have to explain it, son," said Paul. "We know all about it, and what you done in the war."

"Must have been in the newspapers," said Jack.

"Not much, no," said George. "It's just you can't keep no secrets out in the country, son. You may not have been born and raised here, but most of us remember your grandfather and the good things he done around here. It's only natural we'd stick our snoots into your affairs, no matter where you've been."

"I remember when old Hunk Barkley took them **Whites Only** signs Marshal Blake was handin' out and crumbled them in his big old hands like they was soda crackers," said Paul. "Right in old Blake's face. And then he told Blake to clean it up."

George smiled at the memory.

"Well," said the fancy man, "best be gettin' back to the truck. Say, you got electricity here?"

"You can run a wire out of the bank," said Paul. "They got electricity."

"Or the hotel," added George.

"Nice visitin' with you boys. Sure is nice out here," said the fancy man, strolling away.

"Who's that?" asked Jack.

"Force Harper," said Paul doubtfully.

"Force? Harper?" repeated Jack.

"Not his real name," said George, shaking his head. "Simon Peterowski's his real name."

"Say, there's a dance tonight. You ought to go," said Paul. "Get around some of the folks your own age."

Jack avoided Paul's course of conversation. "Who do I pay to get in the race?"

"I'll take it," said George. "Printer ain't got the numbers done yet, so I'll give you one tomorrow."

"Numbers?"

"You got to wear a number," said Paul. "Gonna be a lot of riders, and our spotters won't know everybody."

"Oh." Jack reached into his pocket and pulled out the money old Campbell had given him. "Here you go."

Paul and George watched the way Jack carefully examined the money as he pulled out a dollar and looked at each of them.

"Where you stayin'?" George asked.

"Hotel, most likely."

"They're gonna be full up by now," said Paul.

"Sign said vacancy a few minutes ago. Besides, I won't be in town but long enough to find myself a job as a hand around here. At least, I'm hoping to. And I don't want to impose."

"Paul, here, is my foreman," said George. "Just 'fore that Force Harper fellah came along and started jabberin', we were discussing how the place might be needin' some more boys. For the summer drive."

"We was?" asked Paul. "Oh yeah, we was. Sure."

"Why don't you come on over and take a look around. See what you think?" asked George. "Hands are all in town, and there's sure to be an empty bunk."

"I couldn't. . . ."

"Sure. 'Sides, I got a tank of gasoline out by the barn. You could get 'er filled up."

"I don't have a car, Mister Curtis."

"How you get around?"

"My horse. Kaiser Bill."

"Old man Campbell's Kaiser Bill?"

"Yep."

"You're not tellin' me you're runnin' Kaiser Bill in that race?" said Paul.

"Sure."

"Give 'im back his dollar, George," said Paul.

Chapter Nine

Buchman had never seen anything like the Curtis place. There were two new John Deere tractors, hauling hay off on the hill. The house had a brand new roof with Millarky shingles, and men were adding on a new room and extending the porch. It wasn't easy to count the cattle, but there were more than he'd ever seen in one place.

"What d'ya think?" asked Paul.

"It's great!"

Paul pulled up the car to one of the brand new cabins.

"Go get yourself a bed and then go on into the house. Missus Curtis will get you something to eat."

"Business must be real good."

Paul smiled. "For now. But not that long ago things wasn't so good."

Jack went into the cabin and threw down the bedding on an empty bunk. He looked around the place. It was tightly caulked, had a woodstove, and an electric light suspended from the ceiling. There was even an electrical outlet by the door. He made tracks to the kitchen to look into the prospect of getting a meal.

The ranch house was an even greater marvel. He hadn't seen so many electrical outlets in one place since the city. The kitchen had a Westinghouse stove and Frigidaire icebox. Even more interesting to Jack were the women in the kitchen.

"You must be Jack," said a large, aproned woman standing in the middle of the kitchen. "I'm Molly. Molly Curtis."

"Howdy, Missus Curtis."

"Call me Molly. And that's Elizabeth," said Molly, glancing over to the side and then becoming perplexed because nobody was there.

"Don't call me that. It's Betty," said a young woman's voice from inside the pantry.

Molly frowned at the pantry and then looked over to Jack with a determined expression. "You're gonna have to be patient with Elizabeth. She's just come back for spring break from college." Molly then added loudly: "And without a man!"

"Mother!" said an exasperated voice. Betty came into the kitchen with a bowl of flour. It was the redhead Jack had seen at the fountain. She looked at him and smiled.

"Howdy!" Betty said pleasantly. She put down the bowl and looked around the counter. "What d'ya do with the eggs?" she asked her mother.

"I put 'em back in the icebox."

Betty rolled her eyes and got the eggs out of the icebox.

"What's the temperature?" asked Molly, squinting at the thermometer on the Westinghouse. "Feels like three hundred."

Betty looked at the thermometer, and then looked over to Jack. "Says two hundred and seventy-five. Jack, you mind goin' into the livin' room and gettin' Mother's readin' glasses, before she puts baking soda, instead of flour, in your biscuits."

"I only did that once."

"Yeah, and the hands all burped and passed gas for a week!"

"Elizabeth!"

"Well, they did!"

"Ain't proper talk around a gentleman."

Jack went off to the living room to avoid what appeared

to be the makings of a pretty good squabble. He took his time looking around, found the glasses, and returned to the kitchen to find the mother and daughter in perfect harmony.

"The pie's just right," said Betty.

"Hope one'll be enough," said Molly.

"The men are all in town, except for Paul and Mister Buchman here."

"And your father."

"Excuse me, Missus Curtis," said Jack.

"Molly."

"Mister Curtis said he'd be back late tonight, so not to hold supper. I guess Mister Whitaker forgot to tell you. Mister Curtis told him to tell you that he was staying in town to take care of some business and said he'd eat in town. He was going to be a chaperon at the big dance."

"No, Paul didn't tell me," said Molly. "Probably 'cause he wants me to fix up a big meal so he can eat up George's share, that old fox. He's pretty cagey, and you'd better keep an eye on him." She froze and looked at Jack. "Sorry. I didn't mean. . . ."

"It's OK," said Jack. "I kinda have to watch what I say once in a while. Things like . . . keep an eye out."

"Or . . . caught my eye," added Betty.

"Elizabeth!"

"Or the ayes have it," said Jack.

"Both of you. You're terrible!"

Betty smiled, winked at Jack, and said: "I knew a girl with a glass eye named Iris."

Jack laughed. "Must be a friend of that girl with the wooden leg. Peg."

"Shut up and eat!" said Molly, placing hot biscuits, gravy, and steak in front of Jack.

Jack shoveled the food into his mouth and mumbled with a full mouth. "This is great!"

Molly smiled and started to take peas out of their pods.

"You goin' to that dance tonight?" asked Betty.

"Don't think so. Don't want to scare folks off."

"That nice young Clarence Garvin is going," said Molly. "He's still sweet on you, you know."

"He any relation to Mister Garvin from the bank?" asked Jack, swallowing quickly.

"His son," said Betty. "And I ain't sweet on him. Poke Garvin's a big bully."

"I wished you wouldn't call him that," said Molly.

"I'd like to call him worse." She looked at Jack. " 'Cause his daddy owns the bank, thinks he runs the town. He just a big, fat bully."

"I met his dad," said Jack. "He ain't that big."

"Well," said Molly, "there's a lot of girls . . . girls with good sense . . . that'd like a man that's as high, wide, and handsome as Clarence Garvin. He's got a future."

"Why don't you take me to the dance, Jack?" asked Betty.

"I don't know."

"I think it'd be good for you," said Molly. "Meet some kids your age. Besides, if Elizabeth had to drive you in and back, she'd get home at a Christian hour. For a change."

Betty drove the Ford slowly up to the gate and looked over her shoulder. Molly waved and went back into the kitchen.

"Goody!" said Betty. She stepped on the accelerator, and the Ford shot down the road.

"Hey!" shouted Buchman. "You've goin' twenty-five miles an hour. Slow down!"

Betty grinned and continued to accelerate. Jack looked up

the road. He relaxed when he saw that there wasn't anything solid on or near the road for as far as he could see. The only thing bothering him now was that the wind might mess up the flap on his face. He felt at the leather cord around his head and adjusted the flap. Betty looked over at him and appeared frustrated when she saw that he was taking it all in stride. She relaxed her foot on the accelerator.

All things considered, Jack Buchman had it pretty good right now. He had a job lined up and was going to a dance with a cute red-haired girl. And unlike the women he'd met in France, she was about his own age! He leaned back against the leather seat and enjoyed the feeling of the wind on his face.

"Would you look at that!" said Betty, slowing down as they came onto Main Street. "Thing's got four doors on it."

A long black automobile was parking in front of the hotel.

"That's a Rolls Royce!" said Jack. "I saw one in Paris. One of the fellas in the hospital said it was President Clemenceau. Inside it, I mean."

"You saw Clemenceau?"

"Not that I could tell. But I guess I saw his Rolls Royce."

"I'm impressed."

Force Harper stepped out of the hotel's front door and opened the back door of the Rolls. A tall black man with silver hair stepped out, shook Harper's hand, and followed the actor into the hotel. Betty parked her father's car in the alley behind the hotel. A boy in a tee shirt was cranking up his car, trying to get it started. The car let out a backfire, and the boy jumped back. The crank spun around and around. He reached down to grab it and got a terrible smack on the hand. He jumped around, swearing up a storm before he realized that Betty was giggling at him.

Betty started into the hotel.

"The dance's this way!" said Jack. "Down at the school gymnasium."

Betty didn't seem to have heard him and was through the back door. Jack looked at his reflection in the glass door before following Betty inside.

Betty was standing with her father and some other men. Jack went over to them, but stood well outside their circle.

"Who's that?" asked Betty, pointing to the tall black man sitting with Force Harper in the foyer.

"Don't know," said George.

"From Texas," said one of the men with George. "One of them oil tycoons. Here to buy some of Davenport's Arabians."

"Some fellas have all the luck," said another of George's friends. "They say he was dirt poor till they found out that the family homestead was sittin' right on top of the biggest pool of oil in all of Texas."

"Hmm, Daddy . . . ?" said Betty, blinking her eyes sweetly at George.

"Oh, yeah," said George, smiling back at her. George's friends all laughed.

"Got me a daughter, too, George," said one of the men. "Think that's bad, wait till you see how much all them weddin' bills gonna add up to." The other men laughed, and George grinned sheepishly.

"Here's five dollars," said George. "You have yourself a good time." He looked up and noticed Jack. "Hey, Buchman. You get squared away back at the bunkhouse?" Jack dumbly shook his head up and down. "Good. Come here. Gentlemen, I want you to meet Oregon's greatest hero. Jack Buchman."

"You the Rock of the Argonne?" asked one of the men. "Well, it's my pleasure."

"You done a good job over there, son," said another.

Jack found himself shaking numerous hands.

"You know Alvin York?"

"Let's see that medal."

"How d'ya get it?"

"One at a time, boys, one at a time," said George.

Jack didn't know exactly what to say. "Well," he started, "I did meet Alvin York. When they gave us all the medals. He's a good egg. And, no, I can't show the medal to you 'cause it's back with my stuff in the bunkhouse. And the Rock of the Argonne is another fella from Oregon. Lives in Portland." Jack didn't really feel like answering the remaining question. The men stood with looks of expectation.

"It's all right, son," said George finally. "Didn't mean to put you on display like that. Some things about the war are best left unsaid, boys. You get yourself on down to that dance. Have a good time."

Betty took Jack's arm and wrapped hers around it. He wasn't expecting her to pull him, and he nearly fell. The men laughed.

"Dance doesn't start for another half an hour," said Betty. "Let get some cokes."

"Sure. Far as I'm concerned, we can skip the dance all together."

"Why'd we want to do that?" Betty stopped at the door leading in to the fountain. "Let's get out of here," she said quietly.

"What for?"

A fat young man pushed his chair back and rose from his seat. He bumped into the table, and his friends swiftly grabbed their soft drinks to steady them. Silverware and napkins fell to the floor.

"Hey, Betty!" called the fat man.

"Hello, Clarence."

"Let me buy you a soda."

"Can't stay. Just looking for a friend."

The fat man saw Betty's arm around Jack's and glared at Jack.

"It ain't Halloween, so you can take off the mask."

"Let's go," said Betty.

They got outside, and Jack could feel a little anger rushing through his veins. "That the Garvin boy?"

"The one and . . . thank God . . . only," said Betty. "Let's go on down to the gym, before Poke decides to come outside."

"Why you call him Poke?"

"Most of us call him that on account of what they say about him. What he got caught doin' with some farm animals."

"I don't get it."

"Well, it isn't a proper story for a woman to tell a man she's just met, so let's just leave it at that."

Jack walked with Betty down the street and suddenly started to laugh.

"What?" asked Betty.

"I just figured it out. And then I was thinkin' that, if people called me Poke, I wouldn't want to be showin' my face in town. Then I thought that I ain't one to talk about showin' my face in town."

"Well, why do you cover it up? Let me see," said Betty, suddenly reaching up and grabbing at the flap on Jack's face.

"Hey! Don't!"

Jack tried to stop her but was too late. He nervously looked around. Fortunately they were the only ones on the street at the moment. Betty's expression was not one of revulsion, but of curiosity. Jack pulled her hands away from the flap, and he quickly covered up the side of his face.

234

"Looks like a burn," she said.

"Yes, it's a burn."

"Don't be such a sourpuss. It'll look a lot better in a few years. After some more skin grows back."

"And how would you know?"

"I've helped my father castrate an old steer or two. And I've helped geld a few horses, too. I've seen my share of cauterized skin."

"And you think you know so much. Well, that kinda skin's on a different part of the body."

"And so you think that it's a different kind of skin. Well, it ain't. Skin's skin. You ought to let your face get some fresh air, and some sunlight."

"I can take care of myself."

"Don't be so touchy!"

"I don't want you, or anybody, foolin' around with me or my wound."

"I'm just trying. . . ."

"Well, don't."

"What's wrong with you?"

"Ain't nothing wrong with me. What's wrong with you! Goin' off and messin' around with me like that."

Jack stomped away from Betty and didn't look back. He didn't know where he was going, but he wasn't going to go to the dance with her. Jack walked up Main Street, down Washington, up Adams Avenue, down Jefferson, and found there were no more streets. He decided to look in on Kaiser Bill.

Chapter Ten

Kaiser Bill was lying in the stable. When he saw Jack come in, he lifted up his front legs and ever so slowly rose up on his backside.

"Hey, Bill," said Jack, feeling a little better.

Kaiser Bill started over to the gate of the stall, and Jack saw him favor his right front hoof.

"What's wrong, Bill?"

Jack opened the gate and went into the stall. He lifted up the right leg and rubbed his hand around Bill's fetlock and cannon. Kaiser Bill snorted and threw back his head. Jack gently put the hoof down and went out to find the stable boy.

The stable boy was the same boy who'd been trying to start up the car behind the hotel.

"Didn't I see you out back at the hotel? How's your hand?" Jack wondered.

"Hurts like hell. Think I got a bruised bone," said the stable boy, rubbing his hand. "I'm stickin' to pumpin' gasoline from now on. Let them get it started themselves."

"Either that, or charge for the service," said Jack.

"That's the ticket."

"Say, you know what happened to my horse . . . Kaiser Bill, in number six?"

"You was gonna run him in tomorrow's race. Well, now he's favorin' his right, ain't he?"

"So, you saw it, too."

"Sure. He's just trying to get out of the race tomorrow."

"How'd he know about the race tomorrow?"

"Hell, horses ain't stupid. And if he didn't hear from you, probably heard about it from Mister Davenport's Arabian in number five."

Jack laughed. "I don't think so."

"Goes to show you don't know much about horses. Most horses got better sense than we people do. And I don't know but that most of them can read and could write, if they had hands, 'stead of hoofs."

"You know what happened to Bill?"

"Like I said, he's trying to get out of the race. He's a sly old bird. Word is, he always acted sore when old man Campbell had work for him to do, too. Pretty nearly everyone knows 'bout Kaiser Bill."

Jack was getting impatient. "Is there something you can do to fix his leg?"

"Do I look like a veterinarian? 'Sides, ain't nothin' wrong with his leg. He's play actin'. Just you watch. After the race, he'll be just fine."

"Well, is there a vet around here?"

"Sure. Doc James. Takes care of all of us, don't matter how many legs you got. He's chaperoning' the dance."

Jack started back to Main Street and heard the sound of fiddles and guitars. The sun was going down, and the dance had commenced. He felt better, thinking that with dark setting in he could get around without having too many people take notice of him. He came to an historic marker sign that explained that the town was called Broken Pot because the first settlers were brought there by Frenchy Lematrie and found an old Indian pot in the middle of an old hunting trail. By the time he got back to Adams Avenue, the sound of fiddles and guitars filled the air, accompanied by the smell of burning barbecue sauce.

"Can you tell me where Doctor James is?" Jack asked one

of the cowboys out in front of the gym.

"Sure. He's standing just inside the front door. Or, at least, he was a minute ago."

"Thanks."

Jack started into the gym. A body slammed into him on its way outside. He stepped back and saw that it was Betty.

"Excuse . . . Jack?"

"Oh, hi, Betty. Say, I'm sorry about. . . ."

Poke Garvin filled the doorway. He grabbed Betty's arm. "I told you I wanted to dance!" he said.

"Get your hand off me!"

Jack grabbed Poke's hand. Poke took a swing and caught Jack right on the flap. Jack fell back onto the cowboy, got his balance, and lunged into Poke. Jack bounced off Poke and straightened up. His lunge had no effect, and Poke grinned. Poke slammed his fist into Jack's face, again hitting the flapped area. The flap dropped to the ground, and Poke pulled his head back.

"God damn! That's disgusting!" shouted Poke.

George Curtis and another older man stepped out of the door.

"Go home, Clarence!" said the man with George.

"But I ain't had my dance!"

"You know the rules. No fightin'."

"I weren't fightin'."

"You can't lie your way out of this one, Clarence. We saw it all. From right inside the door," said George.

Poke filled his chest with air. "My pappy ain't gonna be real happy with you."

"I don't give a damn who that little runt likes or don't like. Now, go!"

The man with George looked at Jack. "You better come down to my office, son."

"Oh, my God," said Betty, looking up at Jack.

"What?"

"Best go with Doc James," said George.

"Yeah, get that freak out of here!" shouted Poke.

Jack started to feel a little dizzy and followed Doc James away from the gymnasium. The doctor hurried across the street and opened the door to his office. Jack suddenly felt very weak, and every thought and feeling inside of him vanished in an instant. It felt like the ground came up to his knees.

Jack heard shouting and gunshots. He opened his good eye. There were diplomas on the walls around him and a padded table in the middle of the room. The hurt part of his face itched, and, when he tried to scratch at it, he felt bandages. He tried to sit up, but was too weak.

"Take 'er easy there, son," said a vaguely familiar voice.

Jack rolled over to look at the other side of the room. Paul sat on a chair, smoking a cigarette and watching him. The shouting outside got louder, and he heard sounds of galloping horses going down the street.

"Dang," said Jack. "The race."

"Maybe next year, son."

He forced himself to sit up and felt Paul's gentle hand on his shoulder.

"Don't try to get up, son. You got hurt pretty bad. Took the doc all night to fix it. Poke tore up that old wound pretty bad."

Jack laid back down and slowly fingered the bandages around his face.

"Let me go get you somethin' to eat," said Paul finally. He rose from his chair.

"All the same to you, Mister Whitaker, I'd rather head

back to the ranch and eat there. Don't like hospitals. Besides, I could meet the boys and start learnin' the chores."

Paul sadly looked down. "I wasn't going to say anything just yet. But you might as well know it now."

"Know what?"

"Mister Curtis and I . . . we didn't know how delicate your wound was till last night. Cowboyin's hard work. Hard on the body. And there ain't no part it ain't hard on. Mister Curtis, he couldn't bear it if somethin' more were to happen to you out on the trail. No, sir, out on a drive, hell, even out on the farthest stretch of fence, if you got cut up on the face, there'd be no Doc James with antiseptic wash and clean bandages. You could get an infection in no time. Next thing, you'd be sick as a dog. Or worse."

"You sayin' I don't have a job?"

"Oh, you got a job with Mister Curtis. But not this year, son. You got to give yourself time to heal."

"But I need that job, Mister Whitaker."

"I know you do, Jack. But it's for your own good. And I like you, but, bein' Mister Curtis's foreman, I got to be the practical one. Some fella gets hurt on the job, everybody else's got to work all that much harder, and you never do catch up when you lose a man. No, sir. It just ain't practical we hire on a hand who's in a delicate way."

"What am I going to do?" Jack could feel tears streaming from his good eye.

Paul looked away, and his voice cracked with sorrow. "Don't you worry, Jack Buchman. George Curtis will take care of you. Yes, sir. Why he's already got you a room at the hotel, and you can stay as long as you want. Now you just rest, and old Paul will fetch you a steak and gravy. Come next year, I'll be makin' you do all the fetchin', you'll see."

Jack stared at the ceiling and felt very beaten. Weariness

overcame him, and he closed his eye.

When Jack awoke some time later, he saw the plate of rock-like biscuits and gravy sitting on the padded table. The shouting and noise outside had gone and was replaced with the distant sounds of voices. He felt stronger and got to his feet without difficulty. The meal was cold but delicious.

Jack looked at himself in the mirror. He carefully undid the bandages and saw that Poke had torn the thin layer of skin around his eye. It seemed to be healing just fine, but he carefully placed the bandages back over the wound, just to make sure. The flap for his face was laying on the doctor's table. He shook the dust out of it and stuffed it into his back pocket before stepping outside.

Everybody was down at the other end of town at the show. He made his way through town without having to talk to anybody except the stable boy.

"You all right?" asked the stable boy.

Jack saw that the stable boy's hand had turned black and blue overnight. "Been better," said Jack. "I come for Kaiser Bill."

"You sure?"

"Sure, I'm sure."

"Well, I heard all about it, and all I can say is iffen I took two slams on the noggin' from Poke Garvin, I'd be on my back for two weeks. He hit me once, and he's got a wallop a fella don't forget. Sure am glad you stood your ground. That by itself cut him down to a proper size. Too bad you didn't get to rub his fat face around in the dirt."

"How much I owe you?"

"A buck'll do it. One thing's for certain, wherever you're goin', you ain't gonna be gettin' there fast."

"Kaiser Bill can't run, but he can walk."

"It ain't Kaiser Bill I'm talkin' about. Soon as the race started, he was gettin' around just fine. It's you I'm talkin' about."

"Don't you worry about me. I can take care of myself."

Jack handed the boy a dollar and went down the row of stalls. Kaiser Bill was standing at the back of the stall and strolled over to see who was opening the gate. His leg wasn't bothering him at all. Buchman growled and carefully set about to putting the saddle and saddle pack over Kaiser Bill's back.

When Jack and Bill got to Main Street, Jack had to stop and consider just exactly where it was he was going. The only thing east was Bang, and after the trouble with Garvin's son there'd be no chance of ever getting his hands on the family homestead. The road south was a good long ride to Carson City. Likewise, the north road wouldn't have anything to offer until Baker City. The west road led to numerous little towns and Klamath Falls. He could get on the Applegate Trail from there and go just about anywhere. Jack started to pull the reins to his left and realized that he'd have to go through town and past the horse show. He gently kicked at Kaiser Bill's sides and hoped that the horse would hurry, but Kaiser Bill was not to be rushed.

Cars were parked beside horses tied to a post. Between them were members of the camera crew working with Force Harper. They were taking apart their cameras and putting the pieces into crates. The tripods for holding the cameras stood like featherless herons next to the hitching posts. One of the crew members picked up a long cable in the road and started to wind it up.

"Hey!" shouted Harper to the man, "it ain't disconnected."

The crewman wasn't paying attention to the actor and tugged at the cord. It snapped out of a box, and its end touched on a tripod. The tripod flashed and sparked like it had been hit by lighting. The tied-up horses began to kick and scream, and the cable writhed and sparked at their feet. Crewmen shouted at one another, and some of them ran off to the hotel to shut down the power.

Kaiser Bill didn't seem affected by the commotion, so Jack kept riding until he saw the distinguished-looked man with silver hair trying to calm the Arabian. The horse was dangerously frightened and had already kicked in the headlamps and front end of the Rolls Royce. The oilman had a grip on the reins until the horse lunged forward and knocked him over. Jack slid off Bill's back and ran over to help. The Arabian reared up and brought down its front hoofs around the oilman. It reared up again and would have hurt him on the second try, if Jack hadn't grabbed the bit and pulled it down and to the side. The Arabian jockeyed left and right, and Jack held on tightly until it quit fighting. He tied the reins to the hitching post.

"You all right?" he asked the oilman, who was on his feet and dusting himself off.

"Thanks to you, I am."

Jack didn't want to hang around, and he started to walk back to Kaiser Bill. He stopped and shook his head. The saddle pack had slid off Kaiser Bill's back, spilling everything all over the road. Some folks were heading over from the show to see what all the noise was about.

He pulled Bill to the side of the road and began to stuff things back into the saddle pack. The oilman got down on one of his knees to help Jack pick up the mess.

"Thanks," said Jack.

"Least I could do." The oilman froze, and then slowly picked up a large book.

Jack let out a light laugh. "I had to balance the pack, so I used some of my grandfather's books."

"You know what this is?" asked the oilman.

"Yeah. It's a book."

"This is Buchman's HISTORY OF THE REBELLION," said the oilman.

"So?"

"There's only one known copy. In the Lincoln collection in the Library of Congress."

"That so?"

"Want to sell it?"

"I suppose."

The oilman then picked up the largest book and opened it. He began to laugh. "This old Bible says first edition on the copyright page. And no wonder. It's got the Buchman imprint."

"Buchman imprint?"

The oilman gathered up as many of the books as he could and took them over to his Rolls Royce. He spread the books over the hood and then returned for the others.

"What am I going to do? To balance the load?" asked Jack.

The oilman smiled. "You know, you could put a little of your other things in the other side of the bag." He went back over to the Rolls and continued to study the books.

Jack felt stupid for not having thought of that in the first place. He got the pack back on Kaiser Bill and tied it as tightly as he could.

"And where do you think you're going, Jack Buchman?"

Jack turned around and saw Betty standing with her girl friends.

"To Klamath Falls," said Jack.

"Over my dead body." She stepped up to Jack, took his arm, and pulled him out of the road. "Let me see." She quickly reached up his face and gently lifted up the bandage and quickly put it back. Jack could hear her friends gasp. Betty looked over at them and scowled. She then looked directly at Jack. "You ain't going anywhere, Jack Buchman."

"Why not?"

"In the first place, your cut ain't healed. In the second place, you ain't apologized to me for bein' such a proud greased pig last night and leavin' me to go into the dance by myself. And in the third place, I ain't thanked you for being my hero! Which you wouldn't had to've been if you hadn't gotten so mad and walked off on me in the first place." She stood on here tiptoes and planted a kiss on Jack's face. The girls behind her made noises, and she looked back at them. "You all hush. Jack may only have two thirds of a face, but it's a lot better than any of the whole faces you been kissin'."

The oilman was suddenly in front of Jack. "I heard her call you Buchman."

" 'Cause it's my name. That's why. Jack Buchman."

"And your father would be?"

"Herman Buchman the Second."

The oilman's eyes grew wet, and he put his arms on Jack's shoulders. "Would you mind coming over to the hotel? In half an hour. I want to buy you dinner and have a long talk with you."

"I couldn't do that," said Jack.

The oilman then looked sadly down, and then up at Jack. "Because I'm . . . ?"

"Oh, heavens, no," said Jack. "I mean . . . I couldn't accept a fancy hotel dinner. All I did was steady your horse. And you already helped me plenty. Now that I got the pack balanced, I don't need them books."

The oilman inhaled and relaxed. "You don't understand. My name is Jubal Franklin."

"Pleased to meet you, Mister Franklin," said Jack, extending his hand.

Franklin clasped both of his hands around Jack's one hand. "Now, please. Come over to the hotel. I have a great deal to tell you. And I want to pay you for those books."

"How much?" asked Betty.

"Betty!" said Jack.

Franklin thought for just a moment. "When I was at Sotheby's last year, I missed getting one of the Buchman imprints of Scott's works. I should have tried harder, but I quit bidding at two thousand dollars."

Jack felt his jaw drop. Betty's eyes were wide.

"What's so special about that set, Mister Franklin?" asked Force Harper, stepping up from what was now a large crowd.

"Well, for one thing," laughed Franklin, "the publisher changed the story when it didn't suit him. And he palmed them off as first editions. Funny thing when forgeries become worth as much as the real thing. But that isn't why I collect Buchman imprints. They mean a lot to me and my family."

"How much you gonna pay us?" asked Betty.

"Four thousand for the whole saddlebag, and more, if you got more! On the one condition that you and your young lady join me for dinner," said Franklin.

"You handled that scared horse just right," said a voice in the crowd.

Jack saw Paul coming out from behind Betty's friends with George Curtis.

"Maybe I best rethink what I said earlier," said Paul, smiling at Jack.

George looked at Betty. "I think we'd better have us a talk, young lady." He looked at the people standing around and shouted: "Ain't you all got somethin' to do?"

When George Curtis talked, people listened. The crowd

quietly and quickly dispersed, with the exceptions of Force Harper and Paul. George looked at Betty. "When I sent you off to college, you were my little girl. It's time I got to meet the woman." She went off with him.

"An' it's time I got back to the ranch," said Paul. He looked at Jack. "So, you was thinkin' about leavin', huh? Well, you can't get far if I got your poor excuse of a horse." He took Kaiser Bill's reins and led him down the street.

"Great stuff! Wished I had it on film," said Force Harper before going back to help his crew.

Jack was suddenly standing alone with Jubal Franklin.

"One thing I don't understand," said Jack. "You could have had the books for free."

"No, sir," said Jubal Franklin softly. "You don't understand." Franklin began to walk down the street. Jack walked alongside the older man. "Fact is, Jack Buchman, we're as good as family, you and me. I couldn't be taking advantage of my own, not like that."

"Family?"

"Yes, family," said Franklin. He stopped and pulled out a gold pocket watch. He closed one eye and looked at the small hands on the watch. Franklin popped open the other eye and snapped the watch shut in the same instant. "We got an hour before they start servin' dinner. Yes, son. We're family. But where to start? Hmm. Well, to begin with, there was a man that came out West, all the way from Germany, named Herman Buchman. He'd be your great-grandfather. And there was another man. A man named Solomon Freeman. He was from New York State, and he was my grandfather. And there was a printing press, a caravan with a horse named Hegel, and a fiddle. It all started in about the year Eighteen Forty-Nine. . . ."

About the Author

John Henley is a native of Portland, Oregon. He was lucky enough to see the very last vestiges of the Old West in Oregon as they passed forever into history. Henley is a well-known antiquarian bookseller, specializing in works of fiction and non-fiction about the American West, from its pre-history to the present and, in some cases, future. BILLY AND THE EMPEROR'S NEW CLOTHES is his next **Five Star Western**.